I0608102

THE
DESCARTES
EVOLUTION

THE
DESCARTES
EVOLUTION

N.J. CROFT

This book is a work of fiction. Names, characters, places, and incidents are the product of the author's imagination or are used fictitiously. Any resemblance to actual events, locales, or persons, living or dead, is coincidental.

Copyright © 2020 by N.J. Croft. All rights reserved, including the right to reproduce, distribute, or transmit in any form or by any means. For information regarding subsidiary rights, please contact the Publisher.

Entangled Publishing, LLC
2614 South Timberline Road
Suite 105, PMB 159
Fort Collins, CO 80525
rights@entangledpublishing.com

Edited by Liz Pelletier
Cover design by Bree Archer
Cover photography by Andy/Getty Images

Manufactured in the United States of America

First Edition June 2020

ALSO BY AUTHOR

Disease X

The Lost Spear

The Lost Tomb

To Robin – my inspiration for this one!

PROLOGUE

IVORY COAST

Dr. Smith patted the sweat from his forehead with a clean white handkerchief. It wasn't yet ten in the morning but already the sun was merciless. A fiery orange ball in a deep blue sky.

The village was in the middle of nowhere, though he supposed that was the point. The buildings nothing but a cluster of mud and thatch huts and the surrounding land arid, just miles and miles of scrubby bush and red soil. Chickens scratched in the dirt and a few mangy-looking cows stood listlessly in a corral, flies buzzing around their eyes. God knows how the people survived here. Or even why they would want to. The place was disgusting, crawling with insects and stinking of cow dung. He was doing these people a favor, really.

He smiled at the thought.

"Everything is ready, doctor."

The man in front of him was tall with dark brown skin and a shaved head. He was dressed in khaki pants and a long-sleeved shirt. Sergeant Yakouba Sekongo was in charge of the convoy that had brought them here. The trip had taken

four interminable hours. They'd set off from Diva
at two a.m. driving through the dark to arrive
early in the morning the time best calculated to
have all the subjects in place. They'd been
sleeping, and the village had been surrounded
before any of the occupants had even realized
they were here.

"How many?" he asked.

"Two hundred and seven in total. Fifty-two
men, sixty-three women, and ninety-two children."

It was a good spread and should give the
results required.

The residents had all congregated in the open
area in the center of the village. Most were seated
on the ground. Children played in the red dirt and
somewhere a baby cried. The adults seemed
almost jovial, but then they had each received
more money than they probably saw in a year in
return for taking part in the test.

"Have the subjects all been labeled?" he asked.

Irritation flashed across Sekongo's face, and he
slapped at a fly on his arm before answering. "Of
course. Your instructions have been carried out
precisely."

Dr. Smith had the idea that the man didn't like
him. He was used to it and unconcerned. As long
as he did his job. "Are your men in place?"

"We have a secure perimeter."

He glanced at his watch. "Okay. Then we're

good to go. Time to suit up."

This was going to be extremely unpleasant but unavoidable when you considered the alternative.

He waited until Sekongo disappeared and then headed over to where his protective gear lay on a stool under the awning he'd had the men set up at the edge of the village. He took off his shoes and peeled off his socks, then stripped off his slacks and shirt. Thin latex gloves came first, followed by latex boots on his feet. The actual Hazmat suit went on next; silver and waterproof, it crackled as he dragged it over his body. He pulled the zipper up to his neck. A surgical mask covered the lower half of his face. Next he picked up a roll of gray tape and sealed the cuffs and ankles. He checked the suit; the slightest leak could be a catastrophe. Once he was sure it was airtight, he pulled on rubber boots and then finally, he donned the full face mask. The world took on a distant feel as though he were in a bubble.

He shuffled over to where he had set up the recording equipment and glanced at his watch. It was two minutes to ten and he waited. At precisely 1000 hours he flipped the switch, his fingers clumsy in the thick gloves. A shiver of anticipation ran through him.

"Ivory Coast. Field Test Four. Day One. 1000 hours." His voice came out muffled through the mask.

The screen showed the villagers seated in a ragged circle, chatting and laughing. Smith adjusted the machine so the camera panned out to reveal the men in silver Hazmat suits, masks covering their heads and faces, moving in from the surrounding bush. The villagers went quiet then. Maybe they were thinking that this was overkill for testing a new insecticide. They'd be right. A man stepped forward—Smith recognized Sekongo behind the mask—into the center of the village, carrying a cylinder. He set it down inside the circle, flipped open the top, and a trail of white gas rose slowly into the air. As it gained height, the gas diffused until it vanished from sight.

The villagers stirred uneasily. One man rose and backed away. A guard approached him and spoke, and the man returned to the circle.

Smith sat down clumsily on the stool and settled down to watch.

By 1400 hours most of the subjects were down, lying prone in the dirt. A single figure stumbled to his feet and took a swaying step to the edge of the circle. A guard stepped forward and knocked him with the rifle butt so he collapsed to the ground. Smith focused the camera in on him, to reveal bloodshot eyes, blood seeping from open sores on his cheeks and arms. Good. The test was progressing as expected.

Smith ignored the sweat rolling down his face.

He hardly noticed it; his attention focused on recording what was happening.

By 1800 hours the temperature was cooling as the sun lowered in the sky. The majority of the subjects were inert, either dead or too sick to move. The guards shuffled among them, checking for signs of life, removing the labels from the deceased, noting the time of death, then dragging away the bodies for disposal.

Off to the left, smoke drifted into the sky.

Then the sun vanished with that peculiar suddenness of the African nightfall, and the work continued under flashlights and the flickering light from the bonfires.

By 2200 hours they had achieved 100 percent mortality rate, exactly as anticipated. Beautiful.

The gas was like nothing he had ever seen before. Where had it come from? He knew better than to ask.

Inside his mask, Smith smiled with satisfaction tinged with relief. He could report back that everything had worked as planned.

Which was good. His employers did not appreciate failure.

CHAPTER ONE

The cloying stench of blood hung in the air, incongruous in the opulent surroundings of the up-market apartment. The muffled screams had died to almost nothing, but the whimpers grated on Luke's already raw nerves. Crossing the room, he dragged aside the brocade curtains to stare down at the view of Manhattan spread out below him.

Finally, he forced himself to turn around. He dropped onto the sofa opposite, rested his head against the back, and studied Fischer. The man was strapped into one of the delicate antique chairs, naked from the waist up, a makeshift bandage across his right shoulder. Blood had already soaked through, a perfect match with the crimson velvet upholstery.

They'd been watching Fischer for two days and had taken him that morning, when he'd shown signs of leaving town. Now, Luke needed to find out if he knew anything useful, or if this was yet another futile exercise in time-wasting.

So far, the man wasn't talking.

Callum stood beside the chair, his face impassive. In his right hand, he held a syringe filled with a pale yellow liquid. Luke nodded, and

Callum tapped the syringe, then pushed the needle into the prominent vein showing blue against the inside of Fischer's arm. The result was instantaneous. Fischer's spine arched out from the chair, and a low sound of agony vibrated in his throat.

Luke ignored the shiver of disgust that rippled across his skin. He'd taken this path ten years ago. He wouldn't back down when things got messy; not when, for the first time, they had a real connection. But the interrogation was taking too long, and impatience and self-loathing gnawed at his guts.

He tried to live his life by a code of rules, but he'd redefined those rules so many times; always pushing the boundaries that little bit further, until now they'd lost any real value. But he believed there had to be some people willing to cross their own lines, otherwise, the bad guys, the people unhampered by rules, would win.

Still, at times like these, he couldn't help but wonder what Leah would think of him now. Though that hardly mattered—Leah had been dead a long time.

The sound died away. Callum leaned forward and released the gag from Fischer's mouth.

"Tell me why you are in New York." Callum's tone was icy cold.

Fischer's head rolled up to look at him. A

sheen of sweat glistened on gray-tinged skin. "I don't know any more than I've told you already." His voice was weak and shaky.

Callum's eyes narrowed, and his finger tightened against the plunger.

"I don't know anything, I swear."

Callum glanced up at Luke and gave a slight shake of his head.

"Damn." Luke rose to his feet and slammed his fist into the wall behind him.

Was this all for nothing? Another dead end?

He rubbed at the skin on the back of his neck — the site of an old burn — the scar always itched when he was stressed. He turned back to Fischer. His head rested against the back of the chair, face slack, but his eyelids fluttered open, and Luke caught a flicker of awareness, a brief flash of cunning.

He strode across the room and snatched the syringe from Callum. Callum raised an eyebrow but said nothing as Luke grabbed Fischer's hair and forced him to look up. He held the man's gaze as he plunged the needle into the hard muscle of Fischer's thigh. Releasing his hold, he stood impassively as Fischer convulsed against his restraints. When his body went limp, Luke leaned over. "Talk to me."

When there was no answer, he removed the syringe, refilled it, and returned. He held it poised.

"Wait."

Luke placed the syringe down on the table. "Talk."

"Descartes."

The voice was thready, and Luke had to strain to hear the word. "What?"

"The Descartes Project. Some sort of terrorist attack—I think. That's all I know."

"When?"

"Soon."

"How soon?"

"I don't know. Days…weeks."

"Who do you report to? Who runs the Conclave?"

Luke searched for some reaction to the name, but nothing showed on Fischer's face. Still, he held his breath as he waited for an answer.

"I don't know anything about the Conclave." Panic flared in his face as Luke picked up the syringe. "I'm telling you the truth. It doesn't work like that. After they recruited me, I was given a contact. He's the only one I know, the only one. I swear."

"Give me a name."

The man swallowed, hesitated, but Luke knew he was broken.

"Lee Carson."

"Is he here in New York?"

"I don't think so. He's based in London."

The name meant nothing, and Luke ground his

teeth. A dull pain throbbed in his temple, and he rubbed his eyes, gritty from lack of sleep.

He'd thought this was a breakthrough. Instead, it was just one more layer in the complex web that made up the Conclave. He should have known it wouldn't be that easy. They hid themselves too well, each level protected by a series of intrigue and illusion. He was beginning to think he would never get to the true leaders behind the monster.

"We're not going to get any more out of him," Callum said.

"I know." He tossed the syringe onto the floor. "Shit."

"Look, it's something. I'll get working on the name. See if I can locate this Lee Carson."

Luke ran a hand through his hair and nodded. "I'll get on a flight to London. Call me when you have the details."

"You should sleep first. You're running on nothing."

"I can sleep on the plane. We're close. I know we are. For the first time, I've got their scent. And you heard him—this thing is going down soon."

Callum waved a hand toward Fischer. "What do you want to do with Fischer?"

"Get rid of him."

Callum nodded. "I'll see to it and follow you to London. So, Descartes? Does it mean anything to you?"

"It's a place."

"You plan on paying a visit?"

Luke's lips curved up in the semblance of a smile. The sensation felt strange. "I hardly think so. Descartes is on the moon."

CHAPTER TWO

Jenna slammed her fist into the punching bag, then whirled around and kicked out, following the move with a rapid series of punches, trying to rid herself of the frustration that gnawed at her insides.

Weak. Fragile. Sick.

The words hammered through her mind in time with the blows. Finally, she stood, hugging the punching bag, her forehead resting on the warm leather.

"Wow." A voice spoke from behind her. "Someone's upset you tonight."

She turned to see Steve, the owner of the gym, standing in the doorway and forced her face into blankness. "Hi there, and no, not really. No more than normal, anyway."

Though that wasn't completely true. Tomorrow was her monthly medical checkup with her father. No doubt, she'd have to listen to the usual long list of admonitions.

You have to be careful. You have to look after yourself. You're weak—not like other people.

All her life, she'd heard the same thing, until her father's words were ingrained in her mind, a part of her. He wanted only to protect her. He loved her, had given up so much for her. She knew all that. But she didn't feel weak.

"You know," Steve said, interrupting her black thoughts. "You ever want to go into the ring for real—MMA or kickboxing—I can get you some fights. You're ready, and you've got that killer instinct needed for the professional circuit."

"I have?" That was a surprise.

"Yeah. You like to win, and with your looks, you'd be a real draw."

Jenna almost smiled at the idea. Her father would go ape. He would go ape if he even knew she trained. So she didn't tell him. But she needed some way to get rid of the excess energy, the restlessness, and this worked the best of anything she'd tried.

"Well?" Steve asked. "I know you don't need the money, but I can get you a fee."

She shook her head. "I don't think so, but thank you."

"If you change your mind, let me know."

"I will." She glanced around; the place had emptied while she took out her frustrations on the punching bag. "Are you wanting to lock up? I didn't realize it was so late."

"I can wait until you've showered."

"No need, I'm going to run home. I'll shower there."

He raised a brow. "Across the Heath? Is it

safe?"

Jenna shrugged. "I'll be okay."

He nodded slowly. "In the mood you're in tonight, I pity any poor mugger who tries to attack you."

"Yeah."

She crossed the room to pick up her things, just a sweatshirt and a small bag that fastened around her waist. Her cell phone rang as she picked it up. She punched the off button without looking at the caller ID. She knew it would be her father checking up that she hadn't forgotten the appointment tomorrow. As if she could.

Steve was tidying the place, straightening the equipment, but he glanced across as she reached the door.

"You sure you don't want me to see you home?"

She shook her head. "I'll be fine."

The night was clear. Jenna breathed in the cool air, heavy with the scent of fumes and too many people living too close together. Maybe she should move out of the city, but she couldn't bear the idea of crowded commuter trains every morning. Living next to Hampstead Heath was a compromise. She could almost pretend that she was out in the open country, and the Museum of Anthropology where she worked as a curator was only a couple of miles away.

The gym backed onto the Heath, and she headed out to the open grass, feeling better once she left the orange glow of the streetlights behind.

She ran until her legs ached and her breath came hard and fast. Twice her cell phone rang, but she ignored it, her pace never faltering. She saw no one else and acknowledged the pang of disappointment that fluttered deep inside her. Some part of her craved confrontation, as though by proving she was stronger, she could deny the knowledge of her own frailness.

Her apartment was on the first floor of a converted Victorian town house that stood on the edge of the Heath. Jenna let herself in through the front door as her phone rang again.

She gritted her teeth but pulled out the phone and stared at the screen. She frowned. The number wasn't her father's after all. She didn't recognize it, and unease stirred inside her. She checked the log; it was the same caller all evening. Not her father for any of them. Which was odd.

She raised the phone and punched in the number.

CHAPTER THREE

Jenna lingered at the edge of the grave as the handful of mourners wandered away. She listened to the thud of the damp soil as it landed on the wooden casket. Her father had been dead for one week now, and it still seemed unreal. She'd moved through a haze of shock and anguish.

He was the only family she had. Or at least the only family she had ever known. It occurred to her that now he was gone, she was free to look up her mother. She could almost hear her father rolling in his grave at the idea. He'd told her that her mother had abandoned them both when they had found out about Jenna's illness. He'd remained bitter about it right up to the end, refusing to talk about his ex-wife. But he'd stuck by his daughter, never considered having her put into care. She knew he had spent long years researching her disease, coming up with the best treatment, given up his life for her, returning only recently to work in his own medical practice.

Which was why Jenna had always abided by his wishes.

She owed him her life. Without him she would have ended up institutionalized and probably dead or wishing she were dead by now.

Dead like her father. Her nostrils filled with
the heavy scent of lilies, and nausea roiled in her
stomach. She swayed, reaching out a hand for
balance, almost jumping when someone caught
hold of her arm and steadied her.

She glanced up to see David beside her. He'd
been her father's business partner and had hardly
left her side over the past week, helping her
organize everything.

"Are you okay?"

Jenna thought about the question then forced
her lips into a smile. "I don't know."

"Well, that's honest." He studied her, his head
tilted to one side. "You look pale. At a guess you
haven't eaten today, and you look like you haven't
slept since…" He broke off.

"Since my father died," Jenna finished for him.
"You know I still can't believe it."

There had been a head-on collision. Her
father's Porsche had slammed into a foreign lorry
driving on the wrong side of the road, and he'd
died instantly. She hadn't even gotten a chance to
say goodbye.

She'd insisted on seeing his body in the
morgue, but he had been unrecognizable, and
she'd wished she had heeded the doctor's advice.
That piece of bloodied meat hadn't been her
father. A wave of blackness washed over her at
the memory. She stumbled, and the hand on her

arm tightened.

"Jenna?" David's voice came from a distance. She tried to focus, but the blackness rose up and engulfed her.

When she came to, she was half sitting, half lying on one of the pews in the small chapel. David sat beside her, a look of concern on his face.

"Are you okay?" he asked.

She nodded. "You were right about the lack of food. I think breakfast yesterday was the last thing I ate."

David pulled a chocolate bar out of his pocket. "Emergency rations."

She took the chocolate and nibbled at a corner as she studied him. She needed help and advice, and David was the obvious man to ask. But she also knew he cared for her, and that complicated matters. He had tried to become more than a friend at one time, but she had put him off as she always did when anyone showed an interest. He was a nice man, way too nice and normal for her, even without the time bomb ticking away inside her.

Sometimes she would go out, pick up some man in a bar or club, go back to his place and spend a night. Always sex. Never making love, and always with a certain kind of man. One who hinted at danger. It filled some need inside her but left her lonely, and she never saw the same man twice. Something else she had never shared with her father; he wouldn't have understood.

Now she was going to have to talk to David. She'd taken her medication that morning, but it had been almost the last. Her father always gave her more after the monthly checkups, varying the dose depending on the results. And she'd been due a checkup the morning after he died. David didn't know about her illness; it wasn't something she talked about except with her father, but she was going to have to now.

"Can I come to see you, David? At the surgery, I mean?"

He frowned but nodded. "Do you need something? Sleeping pills? I can write you a prescription now."

"No, it's something else. I'd rather not talk about it here, but it is quite urgent."

"I have an evening surgery tonight. You could drop by after that."

Relief washed through her, and she realized how worried she had been. She could relax once she had this sorted out. "That would be perfect."

"Okay, I'm going to go make sure everyone has gone, but I'll be back."

She nodded. "Thank you. You've been a great help. I wouldn't have coped without you."

"Yes you would. You're amazingly resilient. Now, sit for a while longer, and then I'll drive you home."

She finished the chocolate, screwed up the wrapper, and looked around for a bin. When she didn't find one she reached for her bag. Opening it, she caught sight of the letter that had arrived in the post that morning. From the envelope, she knew it was from her father's lawyers, but she hadn't had the time or the inclination to open it before the funeral.

Now she pulled it out and tore open the seal. She scanned the letter quickly,

> *Dear Ms. Young,*
>
> *Please accept our condolences on the death of your father.*
>
> *We are enclosing an envelope entrusted to us by him and to be forwarded to you in the event of his death.*

She emptied out the envelope, and a smaller one fell onto her knee. She stared at it for long moments, heart pounding. Her hand trembled as she picked it up and turned it over. Her name was scrawled across the front in her father's handwriting.

Jenna,

If you are reading this, then I am dead. I'm sorry for leaving you. I would never voluntarily, but we are not always in command of our own destinies.

It is vitally important that you seek help for your illness. I cannot stress strongly enough—you must not stop taking the medicine.

I'm giving you the name of an old colleague of mine who will assist you. Professor Merrick is head of Biochemistry at Cambridge University, and you can find him through the faculty. Do not speak to anyone else regarding this.

Go and see him without delay.

Your loving father

P.S. In the event he will not see you, tell him "Descartes."

CHAPTER FOUR

Jenna sat in her car until the last patient had left the surgery.

She needed to think this through. She had found a number for Professor Merrick with ease. All afternoon she had sat with her phone on her lap, not quite able to make herself punch in the number.

Finally, she'd made the call, only to be told the professor was away at a conference and wouldn't be back for another two days. She'd been relieved; she didn't want to go to some stranger.

In the end, she had decided to talk it over with David first. He was a doctor, and even if her medication was still in the experimental stage, surely he would be able to help her. Or get her on some sort of program—there must be other people like her.

She got out and locked the car. The surgery was in an old converted house on the edge of the village. It was the last sort of practice she would have expected her father to work for, but he had seemed happy here.

The receptionist, Susan, looked up as Jenna walked through the door, recognition flickering in her eyes. "Jenna, I'm sorry about your father. He was a good man."

"Thank you," she murmured. "Is Dr. Griffith in?"

"Yes, he's expecting you. Go right through."

David stood up as she entered and gestured to the chair opposite him. Jenna sank into it and fiddled with the strap of her bag. She didn't know how to begin, and at the last moment, she wasn't even sure she should be here. Her father's warning echoed in her mind. Don't speak to anyone else.

But why?

What possible harm could it do to get a second opinion?

"Jenna, what is it?"

She glanced up at the softly spoken question. From his seat across the desk, David watched her, concern clear in his face.

She lifted one shoulder. "I don't know how to begin, or even whether I should begin at all."

His brows drew together. "Perhaps just tell me what this is about."

Jenna took a deep breath. "I have an illness. It's genetic—I've had it all my life."

"You've never spoken of this. Neither did your father."

"I know. I didn't like to, and my father…" She paused then forced herself to go on. "I think it was all tied in with my mother leaving. He didn't like to talk about it. But he was treating me, and now I need to sort something out."

"So what is this disease?"

"Some sort of mutation of Huntington's. I was hoping my records were here at the surgery. I haven't been able to find anything at Dad's house."

David leaned across and switched on the monitor. He typed in her name and stared at the screen, his frown deepening. "You're not listed as a patient."

Her heart sank. It looked like this was not going to be easy.

"Are you on any sort of medication?" he asked.

She nodded. "I had a checkup each month, and Dad adjusted my pills based on the results. He did tell me that the drug was experimental, though, and I've nearly run out."

Opening her bag, she pulled out the pill bottle and handed it across the desk. David read the label and his frown deepened. "I don't recognize the drug." He typed it into the computer and shook his head. "Nothing."

He unscrewed the lid and shook one of the small white pills onto his hand. "There are no markings. I have no clue what this is." He stared up at the ceiling, his eyes narrowed in thought. Finally, he looked back at Jenna and smiled, even if the smile did look a little forced. "How about I send this out to the lab? I can label it as priority, and we should get the results back quickly. In the meantime, I'm going to give a friend of mine a call. He specializes in genetic neurological diseases; he can get you tested, find out exactly what this thing is that you have. And we need to keep looking for your records. There must be some." He shook his head again. "I can't believe your father was so secretive about it."

"I was worried that maybe he was doing something illegal. He never talked about the past, but I know he used to work in research, and I wondered whether he was giving me medication that wasn't approved." She rubbed her finger across her forehead, trying to ease the ache.

David got to his feet and came around to crouch in front of her. "I'm not going to give you any platitudes here. If you have Huntington's, then it's a serious disease, but you obviously know that." He straightened, running a hand through his short, light brown hair. "I wish you'd told me."

"I didn't want people to treat me differently."

"And you think I would have?" He paced the room for a minute before coming to stand in front of her, hands jammed in his pants' pockets. "Is that why you wouldn't go out with me?"

Jenna bit her lip. She so did not want to have this conversation right now. But she didn't want to hurt David, either, and she chose her words carefully. "You're a serious sort of guy, and in the circumstances, I'm not looking for commitment."

He released his breath on a sigh. "No, I can see why, but I still wish you'd confided in me."

"Well, now you know." She tried to keep the irritation form her voice but knew she'd failed when he moved away and went back to sit behind the desk.

"I need some time to take all this in. In the meantime, I'll get onto the lab and get you an appointment with the specialist as soon as possible."

"There's something else. I don't know if it's any help, but perhaps you'd better see it." Taking her father's letter from her bag, she handed it to David. "This arrived today from my dad's solicitors. To be forwarded on the event of his death."

David took out the single sheet of paper and scanned it quickly. "So have you contacted this Professor Merrick?"

Jenna shook her head. "I looked him up on the internet this afternoon and found a telephone number. But apparently, he's away at the moment, at a conference. I'll try again in a few days."

"I can track him down if you want me to." David raised an eyebrow in query, and Jenna struggled to make sense of her thoughts.

"I sat there by the phone today," she said, "and I realized I just want everything out in the open.

So I'm ill—I've lived with that knowledge all my life, but I don't want it to be some dirty little secret anymore." Her speech picked up speed as her thoughts became clearer. "And who is this Professor Merrick guy? How did he know my father, and why have I never heard of him? Why should I go to a biochemist and not a doctor? Why shouldn't I tell anyone? And what the hell is Descartes?"

Her voice had risen as she spoke, and David now regarded her with a dazed expression on his face. "Wow," he said. "Well, I can answer the last one."

Shock ran through her. And hope. "You can?"

"Descartes is a place."

"I've never heard of it."

"Well, it's not likely to be one you've ever visited—it's on the moon. It was actually the site of the Apollo 16 landing. The Descartes Highlands." At her blank look, he smiled. "I'm a bit of a space enthusiast."

Thoughts whirled in her head. "I just don't understand. What could a site on the moon possibly have to do with me or my father?"

"It's probably something else entirely, a name perhaps. Why don't I have a look for you, see if I can get some connection. Maybe this Merrick guy has done research on Huntington's. Perhaps he worked with your father. It's possible."

He moved back around the desk and sank into his chair, scribbling some notes on a yellow pad. "There. I'm sure there's a sensible explanation for all this." He sat back in the huge leather seat and regarded her. "You know, your father was a brilliant man. I always felt honored to have the chance to work with him. But…"

"But?"

"I never understood why he was working here. He never talked about the past, but it was obvious that he was meant for something other than small-town surgery."

"I was surprised, as well. But he was a secretive man, even with me, and I was his only family. I always presumed my mother had broken his heart."

"You're a romantic."

She looked at him sharply. "No, I'm not. But he would never talk about her. You know, maybe this is my chance to look up my mother's family. Even if she didn't want me, it might be an interesting exercise."

"It might at that. Perhaps I could help you."

"Perhaps." She rose to her feet and picked up her bag. "Thank you for listening."

"You know I'm always here for you."

She nodded and turned to go.

David followed her out of his office and into the reception area. The receptionist had left for the night and the room was in darkness except for a small lamp on the counter that cast a pool of light.

"You know, all this wouldn't have stopped me wanting to see you."

Jenna reached up and stroked the palm of her hand down over his cheek. "That's the main reason I didn't tell you."

CHAPTER FIVE

Outside, the sun was rising, coloring the sky crimson and tangerine. Lauren stood at the floor-to-ceiling windows that made up two entire walls of her corner office and gazed down at the city of London spread out below her.

What would the view be like one week from now?

Not for the first time, the enormity of what they were about to set in motion struck her. Perhaps she was getting old or developing a conscience—*God forbid*—but there was no point in getting squeamish at this point; she couldn't stop this even if she wanted to.

Which she didn't. Not really.

In many ways, she believed in what they were doing, that this was their only way forward in a society determined to self-implode. She wondered if people would understand that this was actually for their own good. The ones left alive, at least.

Lauren had never seen herself as a savior of the world. Now, she found herself smiling at the notion.

A quiet tap sounded on the door, and she turned as her assistant entered. "What is it, Mark?"

"We've been monitoring chatter on the web and picked up something we believed needed investigating."

A flicker of annoyance pricked her skin. "And that was?"

"A flag set by you."

Lauren frowned. "Descartes?" The project was on schedule; nothing could be allowed to go wrong.

"Yes. But more than that—a Professor Merrick?"

A thread of unease shivered across her skin. How long had it been since she'd heard that name? She crossed the office and sat behind her desk as she tried to see a possible connection.

"You set the flag over twenty years ago," Mark continued. "But I can't make out any link to the current project."

"No, you wouldn't," Lauren said. Though neither could she. The old connection was a dead end—literally. Why would Merrick's name come up now in connection with Descartes? She didn't believe in coincidences.

"Tell me," she ordered.

"A Dr. David Griffith. He's a small town GP. Last night, he did an internet search for Merrick and Descartes. We probably wouldn't have picked it up if it had been just one or the other, but both together set off the alarms."

"Yes, they would."

"We're sending Carson to check it out as he was available."

She frowned. "Hasn't Carson been compromised?"

"His contact in New York went missing a week ago, turned up dead in a car accident. Carson has been sidelined since. But he's been given the all clear, and we're a little short-staffed right now."

They were all busy. "Okay, let me know what he finds out from this doctor." She got up and paced the room. "And put an immediate tail on Merrick. I don't want anyone going near him that I don't know about."

"Yes, ma'am."

As the door clicked shut behind him, she returned to her desk. Something about all this was making her uneasy. Memories from the past. A past she'd believed she'd closed.

But with Project Descartes about to go live, it was unsurprising those thoughts should be at the forefront of her mind.

She switched her scrambled link on. "We may have a problem."

CHAPTER SIX

The buzz of his cell phone woke Luke from a light sleep. The heavy blinds cut out most of the sun, but outside it was still bright daylight. He glanced at his watch. Four o'clock in the afternoon. He'd told Talbot, the man currently keeping tabs on Carson, not to call unless something was going down.

So far, Carson had been a big disappointment, and Luke was starting to believe that if he was linked to the Conclave, then he'd been inactivated. That wasn't totally surprising if his contact in New York was believed compromised. Callum had faked a car accident with Fischer's body, but it was hardly likely to fool the Conclave.

Luke sat up and grabbed the phone, glancing at the caller ID. It was Talbot. "What's happening?"

"Carson is tailing someone, but I've got to say it doesn't make a lot of sense."

"Who is it?"

"A Dr. David Griffith."

Luke thought for a moment. "He's a doctor? Could he be a scientist? Maybe they need him for something."

"Unlikely. He's a medical doctor—a GP. I've had Stefan do a quick background check, and there's nothing that would suggest any involvement. The guy's a nobody."

Irritation flicked at Luke's nerve endings. "He can't be a nobody. There has to be a connection, we're just not seeing it."

"What do you want me to do?"

Frustration clawed at his guts. Every instinct told him he was on to something, but things weren't adding up. He'd devoted most of his adult life to unraveling the secrets behind the Conclave, yet the more he learned, the less he understood.

The Conclave had infiltrated just about every major organization on the planet, but as far as he could tell, at least at the higher levels, each man they recruited knew only one or two others. The person who had recruited them and eventually the one they recruited themselves. Any mistakes were ruthlessly eradicated.

Luke's father had been one such. No doubt, he'd appeared an ideal potential member, with his wealth and connections to the arms industry. But he'd also been a deeply honorable man. He'd attempted to expose the Conclave and had died as a result.

"Luke?"

He shook his head to dispel the memories. "Stay with Carson until Callum gets there to relieve you. Do not lose him, but don't show yourself, either, and don't approach him. We need him to believe he's in the clear. Keep me advised of your position. I'll get there as soon as I can."

He shut off the phone and got out of bed. He'd caught up on his sleep over the past week while he'd waited for Carson to make a move. Now he itched with impatience for something to happen.

He showered, made coffee, then switched his laptop on and opened up the secure server. He typed in "Dr. David Griffith" and read the report with increasing confusion. Talbot was right. There was nothing. Not even a speeding ticket. The man was perfect. No one could be that perfect. Was that a sign that he was more than he seemed? Luke couldn't see it. He had an instinct for people, and that instinct told him that the doctor was everything he appeared.

He thought for a few minutes then typed in "Dr. David Griffith" followed by "Descartes." He hit search and scanned the results, but there was no connection he could discern, and in the end, he slammed the lid down.

He'd go see for himself, maybe something would occur to him. And he had a feeling that time was running out.

Maybe they'd be better off picking up Carson. Though they were likely to get only the same useless information.

Just the next low-level soldier in line.

No, he had to let this play out.

CHAPTER SEVEN

Darkness had fallen by the time Luke arrived at the outskirts of the village, fifty miles north of London. He drove slowly through the quiet streets until he spotted the black SUV parked in the shadows between streetlights on the edge of the road.

Pulling up behind, he got out of his own vehicle and slipped into the passenger seat of the car ahead.

Callum tapped his earpiece to show he was listening to someone and glanced up. "You look like shit."

"Thanks." Truth was he felt like shit. "Where are they now?"

"In there. It's the doctor's surgery." Callum nodded toward a building opposite. It stood back from the road with a parking area in front containing a single vehicle. Lights shone from the front windows. "Carson's questioning him. So far it's been *just* questions, but I have an idea Carson's about to up the game."

"What's he asking?"

"Apparently, the doctor has been doing some searches on things he shouldn't be."

"Such as?"

Callum turned to him with a grin. "Descartes? Does that cheer you up?"

Oh yeah. The muscles in his belly clenched tightly. Maybe they were on to something, after all. "Do you have a comm unit for me?"

Callum handed him one, and Luke placed it in his ear.

"Sit down."

A man's voice.

"Look, I don't know who you are, but I suggest you leave before I call the police."

The sounds of a scuffle came down the earpiece.

"Now, tell me about Descartes."

"I told you—I don't know anything about any Descartes."

A dull *thud* and the doctor's next words were panicked.

"It's a place...on the moon...I don't know what else it means."

There was a moment's silence followed by a shrill scream.

"Shit." Luke reached for the door handle, but Callum halted him with a hand on his arm.

"Where are you going?"

"To stop this."

"Luke, think. This doctor is one man. We're trying to stop an attack that could kill thousands, maybe more, and he's our only lead."

"We'll take them both in. Find out what they know."

"And you reckon they'll talk if we ask them nicely?" Callum's tone held disbelief.

"There are some lines we don't cross." While he had few qualms about questioning anyone connected to the Conclave, as far as he could tell, this doctor was an innocent.

Callum's expression hardened, his mouth tightening into a narrow line. "Maybe we need to start."

A low moan echoed in the earpiece. Luke gritted his teeth. "And if we do, what's next? We might as well just give up and join the bad guys."

He stared into Callum's cold eyes until the other man looked away. Then he shrugged off Callum's hand and climbed out of the vehicle. Another scream from his comm urged him on, and he raced across the road. From the conversation in his ear, time was running out.

Luke drew his pistol and edged around the building until he reached a window where light spilled from the interior. As he peered inside, the breath left him. The light clicked out.

"You're too late." Callum's voice came over the comm.

"No fucking kidding."

"What do you want me to do?"

He rubbed at the scar on the back of his neck.

A dull pain throbbed in his temple. He pressed a finger to his forehead and tried to force his brain beyond the heavy weight of defeat.

"Luke?"

"Stay with Carson."

He stood motionless in the shadows. A minute later, Carson strode out of the building just as a car pulled into the parking area, catching him in the fierce glare of the headlights. He turned, shoved his hands in his pockets, and strolled away, disappearing around the back of the building.

"Carson's on the move—don't lose him," Luke commanded, keeping his gaze on the approaching car.

"I'm on it."

The car parked in front of the surgery entrance. The headlights died, and the driver sat for a while. Hopefully, they would take the lack of lights as a sign the place was closed and drive off. Instead, a woman climbed out and slammed the door. The locks beeped, and her gaze shifted back and forth between the other car and the darkened building.

She appeared young, somewhere in her mid-twenties, tall and slender, dressed in a red skirt and black top, her long blond hair a vivid contrast against the darkness. As she turned slightly, her face was lit by the dim glow from the streetlights behind him. She was flawless. High cheekbones, wide mouth, pale skin, and eyes slanting under arched brows.

She walked toward the surgery, her movements graceful but tentative, then paused at the door and glanced around.

Luke took one last look at the woman, the urge to warn her flashing through his mind. He shook his head. Soon the place would be crawling with cops.

Time to get out of here.

CHAPTER EIGHT

Jenna paused in front of the main door into the surgery. Something wasn't right. The place was too dark, though across the car park, David's blue four-wheel drive stood in its usual parking space.

After pulling her cell phone from her bag, she punched in his number. It rang until voicemail kicked in, and she ended the call without leaving a message.

She gnawed on her lower lip. Should she just turn around and go home? Perhaps talking to him had been a huge mistake, and this was her chance to back out before she involved him any further.

But with enough medicine for only one more day, her father's warnings niggled at the back of her mind.

In the past she'd hated his constant nagging, but now she would do anything to have him back. How could he be dead? Over a week, and the pain was still raw.

Jenna turned the knob, half hoping the door would be locked, but it swung open easily. Groping inside, she found the light switch and pressed it on. Unease roiled in her stomach, as though something bad and unknown hovered on the edge of her consciousness.

"David?" she called out, wondering again why he'd not left the front lights on.

As she stepped into the reception area, the door clicked shut behind her, the noise loud in the silence. The scent of a doctor's surgery filled her nostrils, a mingling of people and antiseptic— familiar and unwelcome. The room appeared normal, nothing out of place, and she glanced across at David's office.

The door was closed. That wasn't unusual, yet a shiver prickled across her skin. She crossed the room, each step heavier than the last, until she stood in front of the door.

The wood was cool against her fingertips. She pushed gently.

The door opened at her touch. The office was in darkness, but the light from the reception area seeped into the room, revealing the shadow of a seated figure.

For an endless moment, she stood frozen in the doorway. She swallowed, licking her dry lips, forcing the word out of her locked throat.

"David?"

The figure remained motionless, and Jenna took a slow step forward. As she entered the room, her nostrils filled with a sweet, sickly stench, and she swallowed again. Her hand flew to her face, pressed over her mouth and nose.

When she knew she wouldn't be sick, she drew

in a deep breath and switched on the light.

The phone fell from her hand, hitting the tiled floor with a crack.

Jenna swayed as shock clamped her body in a viselike grip. The room blurred, and she reached out for the wall to steady herself. She forced herself to look, to make sense of the scene in front of her.

David was dead.

There was no doubt. He was tied to one of the solid wooden chairs, held upright by the rope around his chest. His head had fallen back, exposing the line of his throat, but the white wall behind him was splattered with a grisly medley of black and crimson.

She edged closer, needing to see his face, to confirm what she already knew. His eyes were wide open, and a neat black hole pierced the center of his forehead. Reaching out with a shaking finger, she touched his cheek. The skin was warm, and she jumped back.

Could the killer still be here? A man had been leaving the car park as she'd driven in.

Crouching on the floor, she fumbled for her phone without taking her eyes from the body. Her fingers trembled too much to press the numbers, but finally she managed, and after endless minutes, the police emergency line picked up.

"There's been a murder."

She gave the address and listened while they told her an officer would be with her within minutes.

Why? Why would anyone kill David?

Glancing around the room, she saw nothing was out of place. Only David.

She made herself look at the body again, take in the details. His wrists had been fastened to the arms of the chair with steel cuffs. The fingers of his right hand were splayed open and turned into a bloody, swollen mass. Dizziness washed through her, and nausea rose up in her throat.

He'd been tortured.

Swallowing, she turned away, unable to look any longer.

She stumbled from the office, back into the reception area, and sank into one of the hard chairs lining the room. The door stood open, and she wished she'd closed it as her gaze was drawn to the slumped figure. But she couldn't make herself get up and go anywhere near David's body again.

Her eyes burned, and she rubbed the tears away.

What could anyone possibly want worth torturing a man like David for?

His last moments must have been horrific. Had he known he was about to die? Tears welled up again. This time she allowed them to slide down her cheek.

The police would be here soon.

While she hated to be caught up in the middle of this, she had to do whatever she could to help. Her mind went again to the man she had seen leaving the car park as she'd driven in. Had he been David's killer? Her eyes closed; she visualized him, but he'd looked so ordinary.

Her thoughts were broken as a car pulled into the lot. She forced herself to her feet, crossed to the door, opened it, and watched two uniformed officers approach the surgery.

"Ma'am, are you the woman who called in the emergency?"

"Yes. Jenna Young."

"You said there'd been a murder."

She turned and gestured to David's office without allowing herself to look inside.

"Jesus."

One of them pulled out a radio and turned away as he made a murmured call. He came back to Jenna. "I've called in homicide. They'll be here in an hour. In a case like this, we bring in the specialists from London."

Jenna sat on one of the chairs as far away as she could get and tried not to think, but by the time she heard the sound of tires scrunching over gravel outside, she was going crazy.

Thank God. At least there might be an end to

the night.

"Ms. Young?"

A man stood before her, tall, in black jeans and a black V-necked sweater under a leather jacket. His hair was dark and messy, his face lean and handsome. He smiled, showing slightly crooked teeth.

"I'm Detective Inspector Mitchell." He nodded toward the woman beside him. "And this is Detective Jameson."

Jenna offered a small smile in reply but couldn't bring herself to speak.

"How are you doing?" he asked, taking the seat beside her.

She gave him a blank expression and a shrug. What was there to say?

"I'm sorry. It must have been a shock for you to find him. Did you know him?"

"His name was Dr. David Griffith. I'd arranged to meet him here tonight."

"A doctor? Were you a patient?"

"No. My father was his business partner."

"Was?"

"My father died just over a week ago."

"I'm sorry."

She didn't answer; the comment didn't seem to require one. "Detective Mitchell, there was a man leaving as I arrived here."

"Was he someone you knew?"

"No. That's why I noticed him. This is a small place, and strangers are rare. He came out of the surgery as I was parking the car. It had to be him."

"Sarah." Mitchell called the other officer over. "Go see if there's a CCTV camera in the car park, and if there is, get hold of the tapes."

He pulled a small handheld recorder out of his pocket and turned back to Jenna. "Can you describe him?"

Jenna attempted to picture the man, but his face remained vague, shadowy. "My mind was on other things. I noticed him, but he didn't really register."

"Try."

"He was average. I think that's why he's so hard to remember. Average height, probably about the same as me."

"And that is?"

"Five eight, five nine maybe."

"Go on."

"His hair looked medium brown, but it was dark. He was dressed in jeans and a black jacket of some sort." She shrugged. "I'm sorry I'm not being much help."

"You're doing fine."

Detective Jameson came back at that moment, stopping in front of them, hands on her hips. "You're not going to like this. There are CCTV cameras."

"Good so far. So what aren't I going to like?"

"They've both been taken out. Smashed."

"Damn."

A white van pulled up outside. Mitchell stood and stretched. "That will be the crime scene team," he said to Jenna. "I need to speak to them, but I'll be back in a little while, and we can finish up."

"Will I be able to go?" she asked.

"I think so, though we'll need you to come in to Scotland Yard first thing tomorrow."

"Fine. I'm staying at my father's house tonight, but I work in London. I'll come in on my way."

"Okay." He frowned as the door opened, then gave her a brief nod. "I'll be right back. Don't go anywhere."

He left her, and she watched as he spoke to the new arrivals. Everyone seemed to know what they were doing; soon flashes were going off and people wandered around with clipboards, taking notes, measuring things.

Someone handed her a coffee, and she sipped it, craving the heat. Her insides felt frozen despite the warmth of the night. Her life had never been normal, always overshadowed by her illness, but now everything seemed to be falling apart.

She dug into her bag and pulled out the letter. She smoothed the paper open with trembling fingers and reread her father's words. He'd told her not to speak to anyone about her illness.

But she had spoken to someone.
She'd spoken to David, shown him the letter.
And now he was dead.

CHAPTER NINE

Luke had a premonition of bad news when his cell phone rang as he entered his apartment.

"Carson's dead," Callum said.

Luke rubbed his temples and forced down the anger that burned to life inside him. He smashed his fist into the table. "Goddammit. How did that happen?"

"He knew I was tailing him and set an ambush. I had no choice."

"He must have spotted you."

"No way," Callum said. "I'd bet he already knew we were on to him."

"What about the body?" Luke asked.

"Not going to be a problem. I've set it up so it looks like a hit-and-run."

Another cover-up. But there was no reason for the authorities to connect a car crash in New York with a hit-and-run in the UK. Of course the Conclave would know they were connected. "Okay," he told Callum. "Come back here. There's nothing more we can do about Carson."

After the call, he headed into the bathroom, splashing his face with cold water. He needed to work out their next move, and right now, he had no clue.

Taking a seat at his desk, Luke switched on the computer and stared at the screen for a long while, finally pulling up the recording of Carson's interrogation of the doctor.

"Tell me about Professor Merrick. What's your connection?"

"I don't know him. I never heard of him until yesterday."

"How did you hear?"

Screams that died to whimpers.

"A patient. It was a patient. I wanted to consult with Merrick on a case."

"Give me a name."

For a moment, Luke thought the man wouldn't answer.

He whimpered again and finally spoke, his voice a hoarse whisper. "Jenna Young. Her name's Jenna Young, but she doesn't know anything, nothing. I heard Merrick might have information on her illness—it was a consult, nothing more."

There was a small silence before Carson spoke again, this time presumably on his cell phone.

"He knows nothing. I'll follow up on a lead, a Jenna Young, but as far as Descartes goes, he's clean."

A few moments of silence as he apparently listened to the other side of the telephone conversation.

"It's done."

Then the quiet thud of a silenced revolver.

So what did Luke have? Project Descartes, a dead general practitioner, Griffith, his patient, Jenna Young, and finally, a Professor Merrick. With the exception of Descartes, Luke had never come across any of those names before.

What could the connection be?

He typed in Jenna Young, added the name of the village where the doctor had lived, and came up with one candidate immediately.

The picture flashed up on the screen. The beautiful blond from the car park. Jenna Young.

He read the brief bio. Twenty-six years old. Mother and father both dead. She had a doctorate in anthropology and worked in the Museum of Anthropology in the center of London.

He'd get the analysts working on her. At first sight, she appeared clean, but from experience, he knew that meant nothing. In the meantime, he was going to discover exactly what Ms. Young knew about Descartes.

He could set someone tailing her, but perhaps there was a better way. Picking up his phone, he tapped in a number.

"I need a cover."

CHAPTER TEN

In the end, Jenna hadn't mentioned Descartes or Professor Merrick to the police. And through the long night, she'd convinced herself she was being paranoid even thinking they might be connected to David's death.

Unable to sleep, she'd spent the night going through her father's papers, searching for her nonexistent medical records. She'd found a few old documents that might shed some light on the past but nothing about her or her medication.

Without the medicine, the disease would cause progressive damage to the cells in her brain. Areas involved in control of movement, planning, motivation, and personality. If it ever caught hold, she could lose her mind, her very self, and eventually turn into a living vegetable. The image had haunted her adolescence ever since her father had told her the consequences, shown her pictures of people with advanced cases of the disease.

The night had been interminable, and she'd been glad when morning had come and she could get out of her father's house and head to the city.

Now, straight ahead of her loomed a huge building of glass and steel, the words METROPOLITAN POLICE in large letters on the wall and a rotating sign that read NEW SCOTLAND YARD outside the entrance. She entered the building into a large reception area and approached a uniformed police officer behind a counter at one end.

"I'm here to see Detective Inspector Mitchell," she said. "My name is Jenna Young."

Taking a seat, she tried to relax her tense muscles. But even after rubbing her forehead, the dull, throbbing ache refused to shift. She wanted desperately to get to her lab and immerse herself in her work, to try to forget this for a little while.

Minutes later, a set of swinging doors opened, and the detective's tall figure emerged. He was in the same clothes he'd worn last night, and there were shadows under his eyes, darker shadows on his cheeks. She rose to her feet as he came to a halt in front of her. He studied her for a moment, head cocked to one side, then reached out a hand. His felt warm and strong, the handshake firm.

"How are you feeling?" he asked.

"Not brilliant." She glanced away and bit her lip. "I can't get the image of David out of my head. What they did to him."

"That's not unusual. You might need to see someone, talk it out. I can get you a list of therapists who deal with this sort of thing."

"I'd rather get through it myself, but thank you."

"Okay, your choice." He searched her face, but then nodded. "Come on, I have one of our artists waiting to work with you."

Jenna followed him through the double doors and up one flight of stairs. He paused in front of a door and entered without knocking. They were in a small, cluttered room. A man sat at a desk, facing a computer monitor.

"This is Jeff Mailer," Detective Mitchell said.

Jeff was young, more like some college kid than a policeman. He examined Jenna in return and grinned. "I wondered why Mitchell was giving you the personal treatment; now I can see why."

"Piss off, Mailer."

The other man ignored the comment. "Call me Jeff."

"Jenna."

"Okay, Jenna. Come and tell me everything you know."

She sat down beside him and watched, curious, as he switched on the program. Mitchell leaned against the wall opposite, arms folded across his chest. Jeff glanced up at him, one eyebrow raised. "If you're not going to go out and catch the bad guys, you might as well do something useful like get us some coffee."

"Hey, I'm off duty."

"You could go home, then. It's what normal people do."

Mitchell stared at him broodingly as he pushed away from the wall. "Jenna, how do you like your coffee?"

"Black, please."

She waited until he'd left the room before turning back to the other man.

"I think our rough, tough DI Mitchell is in lurve," Jeff said with another grin. "But I'm guessing you're used to that reaction."

She was, but she also knew it meant nothing, so she just gave a small meaningless smile.

"Okay, back to work." He typed in a few words, and the figure of a man flashed up on the screen. "I've put in some data from your interview last night. Now we have to fine-tune it."

Finally, she sat back, satisfied she had remembered all she could. "That's him. Or pretty close." A shiver ran through her as she studied the face. "He seems so ordinary."

"They often do," Mitchell said from behind her. "This was no off the cuff murder—the guy is a professional. They do their best to blend into their surroundings and be as unobtrusive as possible."

"Yes, I wouldn't have noticed him except he was leaving as I drove up. He was caught in the headlights, so I saw him clearly." She shivered again and rubbed her arms. "So is that it? Can I go?"

"Yes. We'll be in touch if we need you for anything else."

CHAPTER ELEVEN

Jenna picked up the fragment of bone and lowered it gently into place. The skeleton was nearly complete and one of the finest she'd reconstructed. The sounds of the museum faded into the background as she worked methodically.

Her lab smelled of dust and ancient decay. She loved this place. It filled her with a sense of peace and continuity.

She'd always presumed the lack of knowledge of her own past had resulted in her passion for discovering the history of the human race. This particular skeleton dated back to the beginning of the Neolithic period, probably around 9500 BC.

She stroked a finger over the smooth curve of the yellowed skull. So much history.

Losing herself in piecing together the puzzle of her skeleton, she looked up only when one of the assistants entered the lab.

"Jenna, there's someone to see you."

Her first thought was the police, and the memory of David flooded over her again, followed swiftly by a dull ache in her chest.

But for some reason, the stranger who stood in the doorway didn't make her think "police." He was tall, at least six three, with a lean body beneath black pants and a black shirt open at the throat. His face was pale, his hair short and black.

When he saw she'd noticed him, he stepped into the room and came toward her, each step controlled, giving the impression of leashed power.

Halting in front of her, he held out his hand. His eyes were a hazel, green-brown flecked with gold, and he had a scar down the right side of his face. His smile was polite, and she shook his hand briefly then pulled free and edged back.

"How can I help you?" she asked.

He studied her, head tilted to one side. "My name is Luke Grafton. I'm David's cousin."

Shock locked her muscles. "I don't understand. Have you heard—" She broke off as he nodded, his expression somber. "I'm sorry. I didn't even know David had a cousin."

"We were close when we were younger, but we'd lost touch over the last few years." He glanced around the lab, his eyebrows rising as he took in the half-formed skeleton on the table beside her. "Is there somewhere we can talk?"

"Of course." Visitors were often uncomfortable around her work, though she had the impression very little would bother this man. "We can go to my office."

She led him out of the lab and along the corridor to her tiny cubicle, leaving the door open behind them. With this man beside her, she realized how minute the space really was. He was big, not only tall, but also broad at the shoulders, and she couldn't help but be conscious of his closeness.

She shook off the feeling as she cleared a box of bones from one of the two chairs. Skirting the desk, she sank into her own seat and indicated the one she had cleared. He sat on the too-small chair, his long legs stretched out in front of him, arms folded across his chest, studying her intently, as though he could pierce her mind. Find her secrets.

Almost squirming under the concentrated stare, she picked up a pencil from the desk, twiddled it between her finger and thumb, then put it down again and focused somewhere over his left shoulder. "I'm sorry about David. He was a good friend, but I'm not sure how I can help you."

"David called me last night."

Her gaze flashed to his face. "He did?"

"I hadn't heard from him in a while—I was surprised. He told me he thought he was being followed. He was frightened."

"Oh." A tremor of unease skittered down her spine. She frowned as she thought about his words. "Why did he go to you and not the police?"

"I run a security firm, and he asked me to investigate something for him. I also provide protection for prominent people."

"You mean like bodyguards?"

He nodded.

"David wanted you to provide him with a bodyguard?"

"Not exactly. He wanted me to provide *you* with a bodyguard."

"I don't understand." Nor did she want to. She didn't like where this conversation was going.

"I don't want to alarm you, Ms. Young, but David believed whoever was following him was a result of something he was looking into for you."

Jenna rubbed a finger over the spot between her brows. Her headache had returned with a vengeance along with her — supposedly paranoid — fears of the night before. "I don't understand. Why would he think that?"

"He told me he'd received a phone call asking him about something related to you."

"Asking what?"

"Does the word 'Descartes' mean anything to you?"

He was still watching her intently, as though searching for some sort of reaction.

She stood up and smoothed her skirt down over her thighs. "Are you telling me David was killed because of me? That's crazy."

"Descartes?" he persisted.

Her fists clenched at her side. "It's a place on the moon, or so David told me."

"Why were you discussing it?"

It occurred to her that she had absolutely no proof this man was who he said he was. An image of David's tortured body flashed before her, and she edged sideways so that she was between him and the door, every muscle ready to run.

His lips quirked, but the smile vanished quickly. As though he knew what she was thinking, he reached into his pocket, pulled out a wallet, and handed her a business card.

Luke Grafton, Security Services.

He also handed her his driving license and finally, a photograph of a much younger David with his arms around the shoulders of Luke Grafton. The knot in her stomach eased slightly, and she handed back the photo and license.

"I want to find out who killed David," he said, putting the wallet in his pocket.

"Can't you leave it to the police?"

"No." His answer was vehement. "David came to me." He shrugged and some emotion—guilt, maybe—flickered across his face. "He was worried, but I thought there was no urgency. I told him to stay calm, and I'd be with him today. If I'd listened to him, he'd still be alive."

That was understandable; she would do anything to find David's killers. But until she had looked into this man's background, she wasn't telling him anything more. Jenna glanced down at the card in her hand. Once he'd left, she would do a search on him and decide how much she could safely tell him. Besides, she didn't believe there could be a connection to David's research for her and his death. It was a coincidence.

"I'm also here because David thought you might be in some sort of trouble," he said gently. "He would have wanted me to protect you."

"I'm in no trouble, and I can protect myself."

A resigned expression crossed his face. "You found the body, didn't you? Can you at least tell me what you were doing there last night?"

"Have you spoken with the police?"

"Briefly, but I wanted to speak with you first."

She shrugged. "We'd arranged to meet after his evening surgery. David had been looking into some medication—"

"Medication?" He jumped on the word. "He wasn't your doctor, was he? I got the impression you were a couple."

"No, we were just friends."

"But David would have liked you to be more?"

"Maybe. It doesn't matter now. I have a medical condition. Up until recently, my father was treating me, but he died suddenly, and I had to sort something else out. David was arranging for me to see a specialist, a friend of his."

"How did he die?"

"My father?" Her gaze flashed to his face.

"Well, I assure you he wasn't murdered, if that's what you're thinking." She didn't try to keep the irritation from her voice. "He was in a car accident, but there was absolutely nothing suspicious."

"And your illness?"

"Is none of your business."

His eyes widened slightly at her angry tone, and another brief smile flashed across his face. He held up his hands. "Okay. So David was setting you up with a specialist. Anything else?"

She had no reason to lie, but something cautioned her to be circumspect with what she revealed. Maybe she was her father's daughter after all, and secrecy was ingrained in her personality.

"David had sent my medicine off to the lab for analysis, and he was expecting the results yesterday. He wanted to discuss them."

"And Descartes? Why were you talking about it?"

Jenna decided it was the time to take the offensive. This man was interrogating her. What did he really want? Revenge for his cousin's death? Or something else?

"I appreciate your concern, Mr. Grafton—"

"Please, call me Luke."

"But while I appreciate your concern, *Luke*, I don't see how David's death could be connected to me. I don't know anything about this Descartes, but if I think of anything, I'll let you know. Now I have work to do, so…"

She glanced meaningfully at the door. For a moment, she thought he was going to ignore her unsubtle hint. The silence stretched out but finally, he shrugged and rose to his feet.

Jenna almost took an instinctive step back but forced herself to hold her ground.

"My cell number is on the card," he said. "If you think of anything, call me."

He reached out his hand, and Jenna clasped it reluctantly.

"Jenna." He used her name for the first time, and it sounded odd coming from a stranger. "Whoever killed David is still out there. The police told me he'd been tortured. I don't want to see that happen to you."

Swallowing the lump that rose in her throat, she tugged her hand free. "It won't."

A small smile flashed across his face. "Call me."

He turned and walked from the room, and Jenna stumbled around her desk and sank into the chair, clutching the card.

Her fingers twitched as she recalled David's poor hand from the night before, and it occurred to her that Luke Grafton's words had sounded strangely like a threat.

• • •

Well, that had gone well.

Luke had learned little from the meeting, but strangely, he didn't feel bad about the situation. He and Jenna Young were far from finished. She might not know it, but she was somehow involved in this. He just had to find out how.

On his way out, he glanced through the open doorway to the lab where she'd been working earlier, his gaze flicking to the half-completed skeleton on the table.

What had drawn her to work with a load of old bones?

The interview had awoken a sense of anticipation he hadn't experienced in years. She was hiding something from him, but that was unsurprising—she was bright and obviously didn't trust him.

By the way she'd clutched his business card, she was probably on the internet now, finding out what she could about him. The cover would hold, but he wasn't convinced she would call him. Her face had been pale, her eyes red from lack of sleep and no doubt crying. Though she'd denied any connection to the GP's death, she was scared.

She didn't want to believe she was involved.

Luke needed to find some way to convince her she was.

• • •

Lauren was seated at her desk, going over the latest projections when a tap sounded on the door. She checked the monitor and swiped her hand over the lock control. The door opened and Mark entered. "What is it?" she asked.

"Lee Carson is dead."

Lauren's jaw tightened as she glanced up to where he loitered in the doorway. "What the hell happened?" She got up and paced the room.

"We're not sure. But he turned up in the morgue. A hit-and-run. Last night."

"When did you last hear from him?"

"He called after he'd...finished with the doctor."

"Finished? I take it the man's dead. What happened there?"

"Carson reckoned he knew nothing of interest. He was going after a lead the doctor had mentioned, but he was pretty sure it would turn out to be nothing, as well."

"Do we know who the lead was?"

"A woman—a patient."

Lauren took a deep breath and forced down the anger threatening to overwhelm her. She was surrounded by incompetents. Taking a seat at her desk, she tapped her fingers on the wood as she considered possible complications. Everything was in place. If they postponed now… She didn't want to contemplate the repercussions. The financial implications were the least of her worries. This had been her baby. And the blame would land squarely on her.

However hard she thought about it, she could not see how Merrick could be a threat. At the same time she also couldn't see any reason for a general practitioner to consult with Merrick on a patient. He'd never dealt with patients; he was a biochemist. Likely it was a coincidence. Except she didn't believe in coincidences. Even so, should they remove him now or leave him in place? For now, the latter.

"Have we heard back from the tail on Merrick?" she asked.

"Nothing out of the ordinary so far. He's been at a conference in Berlin, but it was scheduled six months ago, so unlikely to be anything we need to concern ourselves about. And according to the tail, he had no unscheduled meetings. He's due back today."

"I don't want anyone going near him that I don't know about. And send someone to find out about this patient. And for God's sake, send them with backup this time."

"Yes, ma'am."

Just a few more days and it would be done.

And the world would be changed forever.

CHAPTER TWELVE

Jenna forced herself to return to her father's house after work. She could have gone back to her apartment, but it felt like cowardice. Like an admission that she was somehow connected to David's death, and she wouldn't believe that. Then it would be her fault, and that was unbearable.

The house was set in the countryside, the nearest neighbors over half a mile away, and surrounded by oak woodlands on one side and open fields on the other. They had moved here when she was four years old, and she knew the area well.

She couldn't remember much of her life before the move. Her father had told her they lived in London, but she had no memories of a house or her mother. Just a white room with white walls and a door—maybe a hospital and she'd been ill even back then. Occasionally people watched her from behind a small window, eyes peering through the glass.

She poured a tumbler of water and pulled her medication out of her pocket. One lone pill lay at the bottom of the bottle. She placed it on her tongue, tasted the sweetness as she washed it down with the water.

Tomorrow would be the first day she hadn't taken one for as long as she could remember. With David gone, she needed to get something else sorted out, and she'd made an appointment for the morning at a private clinic around the corner from the museum. Hopefully they could help her.

After Luke Grafton had left, she'd tried to get back into her work, but his intent stare kept intruding. She'd never had any trouble dismissing men from her mind or her life, but now she couldn't get him out of her head.

Sinking onto the sofa, she pushed aside her father's cryptic lab notes she'd discovered yesterday and grabbed her laptop. She typed in Luke's company website and scanned the information. It appeared genuine and very successful, with branches in all the major cities of Europe and a few scattered across the States.

Luke Grafton was listed as the company CEO, and there was a small photograph of him. She studied it closely. In the picture, he wore a sleek gray suit and appeared every inch the successful businessman. There was only the bare bones of a biography with the picture—where he'd been to school, when he had started the company—it told her nothing of interest.

Next, she entered his name and found nothing to ring any alarm bells. It appeared he was exactly what he claimed to be, but she could remember

clearly the edge of danger that accompanied him,
and she knew instinctively he hadn't always been a
businessman.

By the time she finished reading, darkness had
fallen. She was almost sure Luke Grafton was who
he said he was, but that didn't mean she would call
him. She didn't know why David would have told
him she was in danger. Maybe he'd misunderstood.

On an impulse, she punched in "Descartes"
and found the reference halfway down the first
page.

*"The Descartes Highlands is an area of
highlands located on the near side of the moon that
served as the landing site of the American Apollo
16 mission in early 1972. The Descartes Highlands
is located in the area surrounding Descartes crater,
after which the feature received its name."*

How could a lunar landing site possibly be tied
in with her? She flicked back to the search. There
were other Descartes, including a French
philosopher, but that seemed as unlikely as a place
on the moon.

It was probably nothing. Maybe just the
random name of some project her father had
worked on with this Professor Merrick. Which
reminded her, the professor should be back from
his conference. Tomorrow she would call him

again and clear this up.

She rose from the sofa and stretched. The room was dark and full of shadows, the only light from the open laptop. She went to switch the overhead light on but hesitated. Instead, she crossed the room to stand beside the big bay window and stare out into the garden.

Tonight, the moon was covered by cloud. At first, the darkness appeared complete, but as she watched, faint forms emerged, black on black. She made to turn away but caught a movement out of the corner of her eye, something shifting in the darker shadows close to the wall. Jenna stepped back then froze.

She stayed still for what seemed an age, her muscles locked in place, her gaze fixed on the spot. Nothing else moved. A car drove past, briefly illuminating the garden. In the beam of the headlights, she saw a hunched figure pressed closely against the wall.

She whirled around, ran out of the room and into the hallway, keeping to the edge so she wouldn't be seen from outside. She stopped at the front door and slammed the bolts at the bottom and top.

Her breath came quick and shallow. Leaning back against the wall beside the door, she forced herself to breathe slowly. She had to think this through. David's murder was getting to her. The shadow could have been anything. Though it was too big for a fox. Maybe a large dog? But she knew it was no animal, and a vision of David flashed across her mind.

She picked up the hall phone and lifted it to her ear.

Silence.

Staring at the receiver clutched in her hand, her mind refused to process the implications. She shook it and pressed it tight against her ear.

Nothing.

No comforting purr of the dial tone.

Panic flared, and she threw the handset down. There was still her cell phone.

Her bag was on the sofa in the sitting room. She didn't want to go back in there, but she crept in and grabbed the bag. At the last moment, she picked up her laptop as well.

When she reached the door, she paused and glanced back over her shoulder, staring out through the windows. Nothing moved. She hurried into the hallway, feeling safer where there were no windows.

She put the laptop and bag on the hall table and pulled out her cell phone. Her hands trembled as she pressed the numbers, so it took three attempts to hit 999. As she lifted the phone to her ear, she swallowed the lump of fear in her throat.

There was nothing. No connection. She held

the phone in front of her face and stared at the screen—no signal. It wasn't possible. She always had a signal here.

She lifted the lid on the laptop.

We are unable to connect to the internet right now.

Fear slammed into her, and she swallowed a whimper.

Think.

A small gate in the wall at the back of the garden led directly into the woods. If she could get there without being seen, she would be safe; she would be able to elude any followers.

She crept down the hallway and into the kitchen, edged toward the window, and peered out into the night. A dark figure detached from the cover of an oak tree and glided toward the house.

Jenna jumped, and a small scream escaped her lips. Her pulse pounded and adrenaline surged in her veins. She tiptoed to the back door and slid the bolts shut, the scrape of metal on metal sounding thunderous in her ears.

Leaning back against the door, she focused her mind.

Closing her eyes, she slowed her breathing and ran one of the calming pre-fight mantras through her brain. Gradually, the mind-numbing fear receded, and a strange sense of calmness overtook her.

She opened her eyes.

One thing was clear—she needed to get out of the house. She didn't want to be trapped inside.

The room was almost in darkness, but if she concentrated hard, she could make out the pieces of furniture. She inched across the floor, her hands groping for the counter. She ran her fingers along the smooth marble until she came to the knife stand, feeling the handles until she found the one she wanted—a large meat carver her father kept razor-sharp for cutting the traditional Sunday joint.

Her palms were slippery with sweat. After wiping them down her skirt, she wrapped her fingers tightly around the knife handle.

She forced herself to return to the window and stood slightly to the side, peering out.

In the dim light, she could just make him out, a tall figure dressed all in black, a black balaclava pulled over his face so only a pale band of skin and the gleam of his eyes showed. He was close now, moving cautiously but with purpose toward the house.

One chance was all she would get. She edged away from the window to take up position behind the door, ready to use the element of surprise. If she messed it up, she was dead. But she would rather die trying than give in.

Each breath slow and controlled, she stood

perfectly still.

The latch lifted, and her stomach muscles clenched. The door didn't open, the bolts holding it locked. A few seconds later, a face appeared at the window. Jenna knew she couldn't be seen, but her body pressed against the coolness of the tiled wall anyway.

The man stepped back, and seconds later, something heavy crashed into the door. It held for the first blow, but at the second, the wood around the bolts cracked, and on the third it gave and the door burst open.

Jenna held her breath, waiting until the man was entirely in the room. As the door swung shut behind him, she whirled and kicked out, her foot catching him in the center of his chest. He staggered but came back immediately.

Holding the knife close by her side, she gave way before him. Her back came up against the counter, and she stopped, nowhere left to go. For the first time, she noticed the gun in his hand.

"We're not going to hurt you." His voice was muffled by the balaclava. "We just want some information."

Jenna clamped her lips shut. Biding her time. The memory of David made her strong.

When the intruder took another step forward, she lashed out with her left foot and caught him in the groin. He hunched slightly, but he was obviously well trained, because he straightened immediately and raised the gun as Jenna lunged forward and drove the knife into his belly. For a moment, they stood close together, almost embracing, until he slumped forward.

She forced her clenched fingers to release their grip on the knife handle, and the man collapsed to the floor. Her hand was sticky with blood, and nausea stung the back of her throat; her insides felt icy cold, and her whole body shook. Crouching down, she wiped her palm on his jacket. A low groan emanated from his throat. Jenna leaped back, falling onto her behind as a loud crash sounded at the front door.

She had to get out of there.

She scrambled to her feet, stepped over the man, and grasped the door handle, but his body was in the way, and she swore softly. Stepping around him, she grabbed his feet and yanked. He was heavy, but someone was moving down the hallway, and the sound gave her strength. With one last heave, he shifted, groaning again, and she wanted to scream at him to shut up.

Finally, she dragged him far enough away to open the door.

She slipped out through the gap and into the night, a whimper of relief trembling on her lips. It occurred to her that she should have taken his gun. Too late now. Her whole body screamed at her to go. Instead, she hovered in the shelter of the doorway, her gaze fixed on the gate. Only a hundred feet away.

She wanted to run so badly it was a pain in her chest. At the same time, the fear of leaving the cover of the doorway held her muscles frozen.

Whoever was searching the house was coming closer, so in the end, she tiptoed out and crossed to the cover of the first oak tree. Then the next. Finally, an open space of fifty feet was all that remained between her and her freedom. Taking a deep breath, she left the cover and sprinted.

"Stop!"

Jenna ignored the command and kept running. She would make it. But something crashed into her from the side, and she went down.

A heavy body landed on top of her, and she hit the ground hard, knocking the breath from her lungs.

She gulped in air and pushed at the weight.

"Keep still," a masculine voice said, and in the dim light, something silver glinted in his hand. At first she thought it was a knife, and her body clenched with anticipated pain. Then she saw it wasn't a knife but a pair of cuffs. Silver cuffs like they had used to tie David to the chair before they had smashed his fingers to a bloody pulp.

She fought and kicked, frantic with fear.

"Goddammit, I said keep still."

She threw back her head and screamed. Even as she did, she realized there was no one to hear her. It was a fight she couldn't win. The pressure on her chest increased, pushing her into the soft ground, holding her immobile.

Eyes stared down at her, cold, inhuman. He raised a fist, brought it down toward her, and everything went black.

CHAPTER THIRTEEN

Jenna opened her eyes then closed them again against the bright light. Her head ached viciously, and the skin of her cheek burned as though on fire.

Close by she could hear the low murmur of voices, and she forced her lids open. She was back inside the house, in the sitting room. Across from her, two men stood beside the sofa where a third one lay. He was naked from the waist up, a white bandage around his middle. At first, he appeared unconscious, but then his eyelids fluttered open.

"How's it look?" he asked.

"Not good, but you'll live."

"No thanks to that bitch." His head rolled to the side, and he caught her watching him. "The bitch is awake."

All three men turned to stare at her. Their faces were no longer covered, and the realization sent fear ripping through her. They didn't care if she saw them. In that moment, Jenna knew she was going to die.

She was tied to an upright wooden chair, one of the kitchen ones, and her wrists were cuffed to the arms. A rope fastened around her chest was all that stopped her from falling. A whimper of fear trickled from her throat.

"Good," a second man spoke. "We can finish this and get the hell out of here."

He stepped toward her, tall, whipcord lean, with dark blond hair and a long face. It was the man who had caught her out in the garden; she recognized the coldness in his eyes.

He considered her, his gaze wandering over her face. "Tell me what you know about Descartes."

For a moment, she considered telling him about the letter from her father, but some stubborn streak kept her lips clamped tightly closed. Besides, she suspected it wouldn't keep him from using whatever methods he needed to ensure she knew nothing else.

She licked her dry lips. "I don't know anything. I don't know what you're talking about."

He placed his hands on top of her forearms and leaned in close. His breath feathered across her cheek, and she flinched and pressed herself against the back of the seat.

"I don't believe you." He whispered the words into her ear, and a shiver ran through her.

His hands tightened on her wrists, hard enough to hurt, and the pain focused her thoughts. Could she make up some story, something that would persuade them to free her? Her mind raced. Maybe she could tell them she had some information, but it was at her office. Something only she could access. If they untied her, she might have a chance.

The man straightened and took a step backward.

"The thing is," he said, his tone conversational, as though he were discussing nothing more important than the weather, "you've pissed off Paul. He's the one lying on the sofa, with a hole in his belly." He gestured behind him to where the man she'd stabbed lay staring at her, hatred clear in his eyes.

"So he's quite happy to watch me do whatever I need to make you talk. You found your doctor friend, didn't you? That was hardly creative—no time. But I reckon with you we have all night."

He shoved his hands in his pockets and studied her for a minute. The silence stretched out until she thought she would scream.

"Denny, over there"—he nodded toward the third man—"thinks it would be a shame to finish off such a beautiful woman without at least showing her how much he appreciates that beauty." A small smile curved his lips, not reaching his cool gray eyes as he turned back to Jenna. "Would you like half an hour alone with Denny? See if you can persuade him not to kill you?"

Nausea roiled in her gut, and she swallowed it down. She shook her head, and he chuckled.

"Okay, so we'll try again. What do you know about Descartes?"

"Nothing. I don't know anything."

The force of his slap slammed her against the back of the chair. Pain exploded in her head, and the lights dimmed. She thought she would black out again, but the world righted itself. The blow had split her lip, and the warm wetness of blood trickled down her chin.

She stared at the patterns on the carpet while her head spun. When the pain faded, she looked up. He was watching her, the small smile playing across his lips. Hatred rose up inside her, swamping the fear.

"Well?" he asked.

"It's a place on the moon."

"What?"

"The Descartes Highlands. It's the site of one of the moon landings."

His jaw clenched. "Is this some fucking joke?"

She twisted her head to wipe the blood from her chin. Then glared back at him. "I don't know anything else."

He crouched next to her chair, reached down, and stroked the back of her left hand. A shiver of revulsion mixed with fear prickled across her skin. She wanted to pull away but couldn't move her arm. Her muscles tensed in the expectation of pain as beads of sweat broke out across her forehead. She wanted to beg him, plead with him to stop, tell him anything, everything, but it wouldn't be enough, and some perversity of her nature kept the words locked in her throat.

He grasped her little finger between his finger and thumb and bent it slowly backward.

The crack as the bone snapped sounded impossibly loud. Excruciating agony swamped her, and for a moment, she blacked out again. The sound of whimpering, like an animal in pain, brought her around, and she realized it was coming from her lips.

Her hand throbbed, and she had to force herself to look down. Her little finger bent backward at an impossible angle, and hot, acid sickness flooded the back of her throat.

"Jenna?" The voice was soft, almost gentle, and she tore her gaze from the mutilated finger to the man who stood over her. "That's just the start. We have all night. How long do you think you can hold out?" He glanced down toward her hand. "This is nothing—you wouldn't believe the amount of pain the human body can endure."

Again, hatred swept over her, filling her mind, dulling the pain. Something alien, something she hadn't known was inside her, slowly uncurled. Her jaw clenched as she glared at him. "One day, I will kill you for this."

His expression tightened, and he stepped

closer. Jenna braced herself. She wanted to screw her eyes shut, block him out, but they refused to obey, stayed locked on his smiling face.

He touched the broken finger, pressing lightly, and agony shot through her. Then he moved on to the next finger and nausea churned her stomach. Her body locked—

"Step away from her."

The voice broke through the fog of pain. Jenna blinked and twisted her head to look across the room. Luke Grafton stood in the open doorway, a gun in his hand. He lifted it to point directly at the man standing in front of her.

A wave of relief washed over her. He'd come to save her. The tears she hadn't allowed to fall welled up in her eyes and trickled down her cheeks.

• • •

Luke bit back the fury that threatened to overwhelm him.

Nobody moved, and his finger tightened on the trigger. He would so like an excuse to pull it right now. For a moment, he thought he was going to get the chance. The man standing in front of Jenna tensed, readying himself to make a move.

Luke allowed a small smile to curl his lip. "I said, step the fuck away."

The man's shoulders relaxed, and he took a

single step back from the chair. Luke kept the gun trained on him as he surveyed the rest of the room.

He heard Callum enter behind him. "Cover them," he said. A third man was laid out on the sofa, a bandage wrapped tight around his belly, crimson staining the cloth. Not much of a threat.

What the hell had happened here?

"You." He gestured to the man in front of Jenna. "Get over with the others."

The man shrugged and strolled over to stand by the sofa.

"Search them," Luke said to Callum.

Callum crossed the room. "Hands behind your heads," he snapped.

"See if you can find the key for the cuffs."

Luke pushed down his impatience as Callum frisked them efficiently, removed the pistols, emptied the bullets onto the floor, and tossed the guns onto the chair. He found the small silver key in the blond man's pants pocket and threw it to Luke.

Once Callum had them all covered Luke turned to Jenna, his fury rising again. Shoving his pistol into the shoulder holster, he crouched down next to her. Her cheek was already swelling, and a trail of blood dribbled down her chin from a cut in her lip, but she was alive and conscious. Her hair hung loose around her shoulders, and he reached out to stroke it from her face.

When she flinched, he drew back his hand.

"Are you okay?"

Her eyes widened in obvious disbelief. "No." She took a deep breath. "But I am alive and in one piece. Thank you." Her voice was shaky but strengthened as she spoke. He was surprised; he'd have expected her to be a gibbering wreck after what she'd been through.

"I should have been here sooner. In fact, I shouldn't have left you alone this morning."

"I told you to go."

"And after what happened to David, I shouldn't have listened. Now, I think we need to get out of here in case these guys have backup."

"Do you know who they are? What they want?"

He shook his head. "I'll leave Callum to question them, but I think we should get you away." The little finger on her left hand stuck up at an awkward angle, clearly broken, and his fury rose a notch higher.

The plan had been for his men to come in, scare her a little, and he would do the rescue before things got too unpleasant. But someone else had beaten them to it.

Conclave?

Probably. But low-level soldiers, hired thugs from the look of them. Callum would question them later, but they'd know nothing of any use.

Still, this whole thing had worked perfectly in his favor, better than his original plan. Jenna Young would trust him now, would go with him, would hopefully spill everything she knew. And if nothing else, the Conclave would no doubt be coming after her at some point, and he could use her as bait.

So why was he pissed off?

Because maybe he should have expected this and protected her, kept her safe. But Jenna Young's safety wasn't the priority here. Or shouldn't be.

In the past, he'd never balked at doing what was needed. His one goal for the last ten years was to find the identity of the shadowy figures who controlled the Conclave. He'd done things in the pursuit of that goal, things he wasn't proud of but had deemed necessary, and he'd always considered the end worth the sacrifices. So why was he having these doubts now?

A fine tremor ran through her limbs, revealing she wasn't as in control as she appeared. Her face beneath the blood and tears was chalky white. He needed to get her out of here.

He uncuffed her right arm first before carefully unlocking the cuff from her left wrist. He could sense the tension in her, her muscles rigid, but she didn't make a sound.

Finally, when her arms were free, she lifted her

injured hand and held it cradled to her chest.

"I'll give you something for the pain once we get out of here."

She nodded, and Luke straightened and stepped behind her to untie the knots holding her in place. He must have jolted her arm, because a small whimper of pain escaped her. Pulling a flick-knife from his pocket, he sliced through the rope instead, grabbing her shoulders as she slumped forward.

He glanced toward Callum. "Secure them."

Callum frowned at the blond man. "Stand up and turn around." He cuffed his wrists behind his back and pushed him back down onto the sofa, repeating the process with the second man. "What about him?" He waved toward the hardly conscious man who lay on the other sofa.

"I don't think he's going to be a problem. What happened to him?"

"The bitch cut him," the blond man replied. "Fucking carving knife in the belly."

Luke glanced down at Jenna, her injured hand still cradled against her chest, her long lashes shadowing her cheeks. She didn't appear capable of knifing anyone, and she went up in his estimations.

He tightened his hand on her upper arm. "Jenna."

She blinked a couple of times as though she

was having trouble focusing. "Yes?"

"You need to stay awake. Just a little while longer. I want to get that finger looked at and make sure you don't have any other injuries or any sign of concussion."

Headlights flashed through the window, and she glanced up, her eyes widening.

"It's just some of my people," he said. "I need to have a word with Callum before we leave, but I'll be right back." He crossed to stand close to Callum and gestured to the three men. "Find out what they know and hand them over to the authorities."

"That one is going to need a hospital." Callum nodded toward the man on the sofa. "She very nearly gutted him."

Luke bit back a smile. "Take him to the clinic."

"You're not taking the woman there?"

"No. I'll look after her."

Callum raised an eyebrow.

"She's not badly hurt." He realized he was actually defending himself and decided it was time to shut up. Callum knew him too well, and he didn't want him leaping to any conclusions.

The woman was a means to an end. Nothing more.

"And what will you do if she doesn't talk?"

Luke looked at him sharply, but his expression was bland. "I don't know." Without waiting for

Callum to respond, he returned to Jenna. "Let's go."

Her right hand gripped the chair back for balance as she rose to her feet. Luke reached out and scooped her up, held her close. For a brief moment, her body stiffened then she relaxed against him, her head resting on his chest, her hair trailing over his arms.

Surprise crossed Callum's face, which he immediately blanked when he saw Luke watching him.

Luke ignored the look and carried Jenna down the hall and into the open air. For such a tall woman she was light, and he carried her with ease. Halting in front of the two men who stood by the black car, he spoke, "Go help Callum, then you're finished for the night."

He set Jenna down, and this time she stood upright without any help. She seemed to be fine until she wheeled away, bent over, and vomited onto the gravel of the drive. She retched until nothing more came out and wiped her hand across her mouth and straightened.

"Sorry," she muttered.

"Don't be." He smiled. "I'm impressed you managed to hold off until you got outside. I'll go get you some water."

He opened the passenger door, and she staggered across and sank down onto the seat as he headed back into the house.

CHAPTER FOURTEEN

Jenna held up her good hand in front of her face. In the dim light spilling out of the front door, her fingers trembled visibly. Her stomach churned, though there was nothing left in it, and her mouth tasted of acid. She lowered the hand into her lap, careful not to bang her injured finger, which throbbed as though repeatedly slammed in a car door. The pain was almost unbearable. But it was amazing what the human body could bear, and better a little discomfort than the alternative.

It was settling in that she wasn't going to die, and a surge of euphoria overcame the pain.

Leaning her head back against the seat, she relived the moment when she'd seen Luke standing in the doorway. Truthfully, she'd never been more ecstatic to see anyone in her whole life.

She wanted him back, and as though the thought conjured him up, he strode out of the house. Brows drawn together, he appeared preoccupied, but as he walked toward the car, the expression was smoothed away until his face reflected nothing of his thoughts.

He climbed in beside her, unscrewed the lid from a bottle of water, and handed it to her. After gulping huge mouthfuls, she clamped the half-empty bottle between her knees.

"Do you want me to have a look at your hand now or wait until we get somewhere safe?"

She glanced at the house and shuddered. Those men were still in there. "Later. I want to get away from here."

"I can give you an injection for the pain."

Her father had always warned her about mixing her medications. "No. I'll be okay."

He nodded briefly and started the engine. She glanced back as they pulled away. Callum stood in the open doorway, watching them.

"Will your friends be all right?"

Luke glanced at her, a startled expression on his face. "They'll be fine."

"Are we going to the police?"

"Not yet. Callum will contact them and hand the men over, but I want you away from here. They can take your statement tomorrow."

That sounded like an excellent plan. She supposed she should contact Detective Mitchell, but she had no wish to spend the night at the police station or to relive the evening. Tomorrow would be soon enough.

She cast Luke a sideways glance. He had saved her life tonight. Those men would have tortured and killed her. She remembered the fury on his face, the casual ease with which he held the gun as though it was an extension of his arm. That he appeared so at home in this shocking new world should have terrified her. Instead, it made her feel safe.

"Why did you come tonight?" she asked.

"David had given me your home and cell numbers when he'd called. I couldn't get through to you on the phone and got suspicious. Luckily Callum was already with me—we were checking out David's place—and we came straight over here."

"When I first saw them outside, I tried to call the police. I couldn't connect. The landline, my cell, even the internet wasn't working."

"They must have put some sort of signal block around the house."

"I didn't know that was possible."

"It's possible, but it requires specialized equipment. Which means they came well prepared. I think we can presume they're not your average thugs hunting for easy pickings."

She wasn't ready to pursue that line of thought just yet. "So why did you call? Not that I'm not grateful, but I wasn't very helpful this morning."

"I found a report when I was going through David's paperwork. I thought it might relate to you."

She latched on to that. "A lab report? David was getting my medication analyzed."

"Why would he need to do that?"

"We couldn't find my records. I told you this morning—I have this illness, it's genetic. My father managed my treatment, and when he died, I asked David to look into it for me."

"Go on."

"I had these pills, but they were blank, no markings, nothing. David didn't know what they were, so he sent them off to the lab for analysis. It was one of the things we were going to talk about last night."

Except David was dead.

"Your father was a doctor?"

"Yes. He worked in research when he was younger, but the last few years he's been happy working with patients and treating me. It used to annoy me; he'd go on and on about how careful I needed to be. How I had to look after myself. How I wasn't like 'normal' people. He would drive me insane." She bit her lip, tasting blood as she reopened the cut. She was rambling; she never spoke about her illness. Not to anyone but her father. "Now I'd give anything to have him back. Since he died everything seems to be falling apart." She turned her head and peered out at the passing landscape. "I can't believe everything that has happened over the last couple of weeks. My father dying...David...tonight."

"You still don't believe they're related?"

She hated to admit it, but there had to be a

connection. "I don't see how any of this can be related to my father, but those men tonight knew about David. I still have no idea why or what they wanted with me."

Except Descartes.

She knew she should bring it up but needed to think things through first.

"Well, we'll go over it later. We'll find something. It could be a mistake, something else David was working on and you just ended up in the middle."

"I can't believe David could have been doing anything illegal or even bad. He was such an honorable man."

"I agree. Now why don't you rest? We can talk later."

Jenna closed her eyes and laid her head back against the seat, but she couldn't sleep. The pain was excruciating, and her mind was racing, so she stared straight ahead. They were on the motorway, heading toward London. The road was quiet, and Luke drove fast, his hands relaxed on the wheel.

Though she'd told him she'd be okay, now she wasn't so sure. Nausea washed through her, and she burned hot until a shiver shook her body. She peeked at her hand where it lay curled on her lap, and winced.

Luke must have sensed the movement, because he glanced toward her, and in the dim glow from the road lights, she saw him frown. A minute later, he signaled and pulled onto the hard shoulder.

Without speaking, he stopped the car and climbed out. She twisted her head to watch him as he walked around to the back of the vehicle and rummaged in the trunk. When he resumed his seat, he held a small brown bottle of pills. He shook two out onto his hand and held them out to her.

"They're only painkillers," he said when she hesitated.

"I'm on medication."

"These shouldn't affect you adversely. Take them—you'll feel better." His voice was rough with impatience. Jenna looked a moment longer then picked up the pills and swallowed them with the last of the water.

They set off again. Within a few minutes, the pain started to dull until soon it was no more than a low throbbing ache, still present but bearable, and she dozed.

As they drove down a ramp into an underground parking area, she awoke. Luke pulled up in front of a set of solid steel doors. He hit the button to open the driver's window, leaned out, and pressed his thumb to a panel. The doors slid open, and he drove through and pulled into a parking space.

He climbed out, came around to the passenger

side, and opened her door. "Come on. We'll get your hand seen to, and afterward, you can sleep."

The warmth of the car was soothing, and she knew if she moved she would start to think all over again. She didn't want to move, didn't want to think.

"Jenna?"

She sighed and looked up. "I'm coming."

She swung her legs around and climbed out. Her head swam with the movement, and she steadied herself against the car, but she realized she could hardly feel her finger, merely a faint throb at the end of her arm.

"Where are we?" The parking area was large with only a few vehicles, mainly black SUVs.

"My company headquarters in London. You should be safe here until we work out who those men were and what they wanted with you."

Jenna found her legs were shaky, but she could walk. With his hand on her upper arm, he led her toward an elevator. Inside, Luke pressed the button for the top floor.

The doors opened directly into an apartment. She followed Luke down a hallway that led into a large modern kitchen, where he gestured to one of the steel chairs around the table. "Sit."

Jenna sat and watched him move around the room, obviously familiar with his surroundings. He fetched a large ceramic bowl from the cabinet beside the sink and ran the tap, feeling the temperature of the water. After filling the bowl, he brought it across and placed it on the table in front of her. "Soak your hand in here while I go get the medical kit."

"Don't I need a doctor?"

"I'm a trained paramedic. I can set a finger."

No doubt he could; he was so competent. She placed her hand in the bowl, careful not to knock the injured finger. The warm water was soothing, and she leaned forward, resting her forehead on the cool metal surface of the table.

Something touched her arm, and she jumped, biting back a small scream. Her eyes flew open, and she sat bolt upright as fear shot through her.

"Sorry," Luke murmured.

"I must have dozed off. I was dreaming—"

Her mind came back from the bad place, and she shook her head to get rid of the lingering shadows.

"That's the drugs." Luke sank into the seat next to her and placed an impressive array of medical supplies on the table beside him. He picked up her injured hand from the bowl and patted the skin dry with a paper towel. His touch gentle and sure, he turned her hand palm up and studied her finger.

It looked horrible to Jenna, twisted up at an odd angle, the skin dark and shiny, the knuckle swollen.

"The break is clean," Luke said. "But I'm going to have to straighten the finger, and it's going to hurt. Do you want that injection now?"

Jenna swallowed the lump forming in her throat. "No. Thank you, but I can hardly feel it."

"Okay."

Focusing over his left shoulder, every muscle in her body rigid with tension, still she wasn't ready for the agony that shot from her finger directly to her brain and then to every other part of her body. She managed to bite back the scream, but beads of sweat broke out on her forehead, and black dots danced before her eyes.

"Here, bend forward." Luke placed a hand between her shoulder blades and pressed her down gently. Her breath was coming short and fast, and she sucked air into her lungs, holding it in until the darkness receded and she could force her muscles to relax. After a minute, she was able to sit up.

Luke was watching her. "That's the worst bit over with."

"Finish it."

He tore open a packet, emptied a small wooden stick onto his palm, and measured it against the length of her finger before snapping off the excess.

"I'm going to splint it and attach it to the next

finger. The splint will hold it in place, which should stop the pain."

As he placed the splint on the broken finger, she bit down on her lip. He squeezed it against the next finger, then wrapped white tape tight around both, fastened it off, and sat back. "Done. How does it feel?"

With an enormous sigh, she released the air from her lungs. "Like I've been hit with a hammer." But in fact, her hand felt much better. She lifted it up and held it in front of her face. "Very neat."

"It will take a while to heal, probably six to eight weeks."

She forced a smile, the first in a long time. "I'm just glad I'm going to have six weeks. I was sure I was going to die tonight. Thank you."

He pushed himself up and crossed to the fridge, rummaging for a moment. "Here's an ice pack. Hold it against your hand. It will help with the swelling."

Taking it from him, she did as she was told, pressing the ice to her knuckle. The pain receded to be replaced by blissful numbness, and she leaned back in her chair. "That feels wonderful."

"Good. Come on, I'll show you to your room. You can clean up and get some sleep."

Jenna glanced down at herself and grimaced. Her shirt was stained dark with blood. Some of it was hers from her split lip, but more of it was from the man she had stabbed.

When she pulled herself up the room whirled around her. Somehow, she managed to follow Luke out of the kitchen and down the hallway. Pushing open a door, he gestured for her to enter. "Try to sleep, and we'll talk in the morning."

Jenna swayed as she passed him. Putting her hand out for balance, she encountered the hard heat of his chest. Swearing softly, he closed his eyes for a second. Then he picked her up, carried her into the bedroom, and placed her down on the bed.

"Come on, Jenna, just a few more minutes and you can sleep."

"I'm fine, really I am. Just everything keeps spinning."

He straightened. Was he leaving? She didn't want to be alone, and she had to swallow the urge to ask him to stay. Instead, he disappeared through another door and came back seconds later, carrying a black terry cloth robe and a washcloth. He crouched in front of her and wiped her face with the damp cloth.

Jenna closed her eyes and gave herself up to his touch. She was floating, suspended in time, aware only of his closeness, his hands gentle as he stripped her clothes.

When she was naked, he wrapped the robe

around her shoulders. "Sleep."

Exhaustion rolled over her and she lay down on top of the blanket. She would rest a little while, then get up and shower. Curling herself into a ball, her hand held against her chest, she was vaguely aware of Luke moving around the room, picking up her clothes. His presence reassured her, and she closed her eyes.

But behind her lids, she saw the blond man who had snapped her finger. He came toward her, his eyes mocking, and the same sense of helplessness washed over her.

That had been the worst thing, even worse than the pain. The feeling that she had been powerless, that they could do what they liked to her, and she could do nothing to stop them.

Tears rolled down her cheeks, soaking the pillow, but she couldn't seem to stop. The mattress depressed as Luke sat down beside her. He didn't speak, just leaned back against the wall and pulled her into his arms. Sighing, she burrowed her face against his chest, and finally drifted into sleep to the throb of his heart.

• • •

Luke stifled his unease, aware of the woman in his arms. Shit, he shouldn't be here; he should be keeping his distance from her. Not lying in bed, holding her.

He tried to live his life by a set of rules, but he'd redefined those rules so many times, always pushing the boundaries a little bit further.

One of those rules was never to sleep with someone he might need to sacrifice later on. So far, he'd never been tempted. But something about Jenna tugged at emotions he'd thought long dead.

He didn't know what her role was in this, but he knew she was involved up to her gorgeous neck. Strangely, he also believed her—whatever tied her to Descartes, she was unaware of it.

He needed to work out what her connection was. In fact, what he should be doing was getting up off this bed and digging up any information he could find. The doctor was a false lead. His only link to the case was Jenna.

It all came back to Jenna.

Tomorrow he would talk to her. Go over every detail of the last few weeks until something jumped out at him.

She whimpered, and he tightened his arms around her, promising himself he would get up soon. Instead, he closed his eyes and slept.

CHAPTER FIFTEEN

Jenna felt like shit.

Her head throbbed, and there was something burning hot and pulsating at the end of her arm. The light in the room was dim, but she could see daylight seeping through the heavy blinds.

She had a memory of Luke holding her through the long night, comforting her when she half woke, soothing her back into a troubled sleep. She'd never spent the whole night with a man before. And she'd never been in bed with a man and not had sex.

He was gone now but had left a glass of water and two pills—identical to the painkillers she'd taken yesterday—on the table by the bed. After swallowing them down with a gulp of water, she leaned against the wall behind her and waited for something to happen.

Relief came quickly. Her head cleared, and the throbbing eased until she could get up and face the day.

She slipped out of bed and crossed the room to stand in front of a full-length mirror. Holding up her bandaged hand, she touched the swollen skin of her cheek and the split lip. Apart from the bruises, she looked like herself, and it surprised her, because she felt changed. Last night she'd been more terrified than she'd ever been in her entire life, but she'd also sensed an inner strength she'd never realized she possessed.

In the bathroom, she ran the shower until it steamed. Even standing awkwardly with her bandaged hand held out of the spray, the hot water felt wonderful, and she stayed under the jet for a long time, washing away the stench of pain and fear.

Finally, she stepped out and blotted her skin dry. She had no clothes to put on—no way was she wearing her blood-stained clothing from yesterday. Instead, she pulled the robe back on and wandered out into the hallway in search of Luke.

She'd decided to tell him everything—which was actually very little—and hope he could make some sense out of it. Though she suspected there was more to his story than he was telling, she had to trust someone, and right now, he appeared to be her only option.

As long as she didn't fool herself that Luke was doing this for her. He wanted revenge for David's death, and logic told her she was a means of getting to the people responsible.

The sound of voices drifted out from the kitchen, and she paused before pushing the door open.

Luke sat at the table, and her eyes were drawn to him. He cast her an almost wary glance, then his lips curved into a slow smile.

Someone coughed and she dragged her gaze away. The second man from last night, Callum, leaned against the counter sipping a mug of coffee. She'd barely noticed him yesterday; now she studied him curiously. He was around her height, with a wiry frame that vibrated with energy. She'd met men like him before at the gym. They were deceptively strong and almost always ex-military. His blond hair was cut close to his skull, his face hard, with pale eyes that stared back at her coldly. For a moment, he reminded her of the men who had broken into her father's house last night, and she pressed her injured hand to her stomach as a shiver ran through her.

"How are you?" Luke asked.

Shrugging, she stepped into the room. "Okay, I guess. Thanks for the pills."

He pushed out his chair and rose to his feet. "Coffee?"

"Please."

He poured a cup from the machine on the counter and placed it on the table next to his. As she sat down, her stomach rumbled, and she glanced up in embarrassment. "I don't suppose there's anything to eat."

"What would you like?"

"Anything. I just realized I haven't eaten since this time yesterday."

Luke placed croissants and butter on the table in front of her, and Jenna dove in, only slowing down on the third croissant. She glanced up to find them watching her, Luke with that small smile on his lips.

"This is Callum." He waved a hand toward the man who stood silent. His face was blank as he nodded to Jenna.

"Thank you for last night," she said.

He shrugged, and she got the impression he didn't like her. Though possibly "like" was the wrong word. Didn't trust her, maybe.

"Callum brought some things from the house. I thought you might need clothes and your bag."

Jenna glanced down to see her black overnight bag on the floor at Callum's feet. On top of it was her handbag. She gave a sigh; this would make things easier. The letter from her father was in there.

"Good. There's something I wanted to show you."

Picking up her bag, she opened it one-handed and found the letter. After reading her father's words one last time, she gave it to Luke.

"My father left this with a solicitor, to be sent to me in case of his death." She watched as Luke scanned the letter. "That's the first time I'd ever heard of Descartes or Professor Merrick."

"And the names mean nothing to you?"

"Nothing, but my father was a very private person. I tried to contact Professor Merrick, but he was away at a conference. He should be back now."

"Did you tell anyone about this?"

Guilt flooded her. Biting her lip, she glanced away. She didn't want to talk about it, as though speaking the words aloud would lay the blame squarely at her feet.

"Jenna?"

"I told David. You think that's why they came after him? Something to do with this?" She gestured toward the paper. "That makes no sense at all. How would they have found out?"

"David probably did an internet search. These days, it's easy to flag certain words. If somebody were monitoring Descartes or this professor, they would have picked up his search. After that, it's simple to trace to an IP address."

Could that be what had happened? But it didn't explain why. What was Descartes that it would make them come after an innocent man? Torture him? Murder him?

Her appetite vanished. She pushed her plate away but picked up her coffee to give herself time to think. Luke and Callum watched her intently, their faces equally expressionless.

It occurred to Jenna that Luke could have also made the same connection to David. Until she remembered the photo of Luke with his "cousin." But wouldn't that be easy to fake? Thinking like this would make her crazy.

The truth was, last night Luke had saved her, and while she didn't entirely trust his motivations, she trusted *him*. "Is your only interest in this to find David's killers and bring them to justice?"

"Basically. And I want to understand why he died."

"What about the men who attacked me last night? Weren't they responsible for David?"

"They were minions. Just carrying out orders, and none of them is talking."

"What happened to them?"

"Callum handed them over to the security forces last night."

"Not the police?"

"No," he said. "My company has connections with some of the intelligence agencies. We do a lot of government contracts. They'll coordinate with the police."

"So, do you know what Descartes is?"

For a moment, she thought he wouldn't answer. He glanced at Callum and shrugged. "No."

"But you have your suspicions?" There were things he wasn't telling her, and she pressed for a response.

He looked again at Callum before he replied. "We think it might be some sort of code for an imminent terrorist attack."

Her mouth fell open. "Terrorist attack? What sort of attack?"

"We suspect biological. We're not sure, but that would give us a tie-in with Merrick, who's a biochemist."

She slammed her cup down on the table. "That doesn't make sense. What would my father have to do with an imminent terrorist attack? He was a GP. Besides, have you seen the date on the letter? Seven years ago. Hardly 'imminent,' and the seven years coincides with Professor Merrick taking up the post at Cambridge University. I think my father must have updated the letter, so chances are this goes back much further."

Luke shrugged. "Maybe it is a coincidence, and your Descartes is something completely unrelated."

She wanted to believe that so badly. "You don't think that's the case, do you?"

"I don't believe in coincidences." His tone was gentle but firm.

"Will these people come after me again?"

"I think we have to assume that."

A shiver prickled across her skin when she glanced down at her bandaged hand. "How can I stop them?"

"The only way you'll be safe is if we find out who's behind this, who ordered David's murder. For now, you stay close, and we'll protect you."

"Maybe I should go to the police."

"It's your choice, but you'll be safer with us. We suspect this organization has contacts everywhere."

This whole thing was crazy and getting crazier by the minute. She needed a dose of reality. "I have to go in to work."

"I've already called you in sick. They're not expecting you anytime soon."

She opened her mouth to argue but clamped it shut as she saw the sense of it. There was also her clinic appointment; she'd have to phone and rearrange it. That reminded her of something. "Last night, you told me you'd found a lab report about my medication. Do you have it?"

"Yes, it's in the paperwork we brought from David's place."

Luke got up and left the room. He came back a few minutes later with a file and handed her a piece of paper.

Someone—David perhaps—had highlighted a paragraph:

Analysis incomplete, unidentified substance presumed due to contamination. Please send new sample for reanalysis.

Her shoulders slumping, she sat back and closed her eyes. There were no more samples to send.

"Bad news?" Luke asked.

"Disappointing. I'd hoped…" Her illness would have to wait until she solved the much more pressing problem of who wanted her dead. "What do we do next?"

"The first thing is to set up a meeting with the professor. In the meantime, I think we should go back to your father's house, see if we can't find anything that might lead us to Descartes."

He turned to Callum. "You know what you have to do?"

Callum grunted. "I'll get on it." After one last long look at Jenna, he left the room.

Jenna waited until the door shut behind him. "I don't think he trusts me."

"Callum doesn't trust anybody, but he's a good man." Luke smiled. "Actually, he's impressed by the way you took out one of those guys last night. He thinks you're tough, and that's a quality he admires."

A shiver coursed through her. "I don't feel tough." She fiddled with her mug, staring at the table while she studied him through lowered lashes. "Thank you for staying with me last night."

A brief flicker of discomfort flashed across his

features, and she looked at him with interest. She guessed he wasn't a man who offered comfort often.

Finally, he shrugged, and his face returned to its normal impassive facade. "You'd been through a terrible experience. You shouldn't have been alone."

"Well, whatever the reason—thank you."

CHAPTER SIXTEEN

"You sure you want to go in there alone?" Luke asked.

They'd come to a halt in the corridor, outside Merrick's suite of offices.

"I think I have to," she said. "If I give him my father's letter and he knows I've already shown it to someone else, he's not going to trust me."

Luke pushed open the door. "I'll wait for you out here. And I'll be listening. You don't like anything he says or does, then just speak my name and I'll be in there."

She nodded. He'd already fitted her with an earpiece and microphone so he could listen in on the conversation. She'd felt a little silly at the time, but now she was glad.

The door led into a reception room, which was empty. Beyond that was a second door, which presumably led to the professor's office. Luke had arranged the meeting, telling the secretary that she represented a security company with a government contract to carry out research into possible biological threats and Merrick had been recommended as a specialist. The incentive of a large fee had ensured the meeting.

She tapped lightly on the door and pushed it

open without waiting for a reply. The office was huge, with a large oak desk across one corner and windows overlooking a courtyard below.

The professor rose to his feet as she crossed the room. A short man, probably around her father's age, somewhere in his mid-fifties, with faded blond hair and pale gray eyes that didn't reflect the professional smile pasted on his thin lips. He held out a hand as she came to a halt in front of the desk. Jenna stared but forced herself to take it, though she made the contact as brief as possible. Something about him repelled her.

She sat and wondered briefly where to begin.

Merrick started to fidget. "Would you like coffee? Tea?"

"No."

He picked up a pen from the desk then put it down. "I believe you're exploring research possibilities for potential biological warfare products?"

Jenna ignored the question. "Professor, I think you knew my father, Dr. Jonathon Young?"

The man pursed his lips as he thought. "No, I'm afraid I know no one of that name."

"He suggested I come to see you and said I was to mention the word 'Descartes.'"

The result was instantaneous. His jaw dropped open, his eyes widened, and he made a small choking sound. The damage was done, although he pulled himself together quickly and cleared his throat. "Descartes? I have no clue to what you're referring."

Jenna pulled the letter out of her bag and laid it on the desk in front of her. "Professor Merrick, my father died recently. He left me this."

His brow furrowed. To Jenna, he appeared genuinely confused. "I don't know any Jonathon Young. I've never heard the name before. Could I read the letter?"

She nodded and Merrick unfolded the paper she slid across the desk. As he read the words, his frown deepened. "I'm sorry. I have no idea what this is about." He glanced up at Jenna. "Your father mentions you're ill. Could I ask the nature of your illness?"

"It's a genetic condition, related to Huntington's disease."

"I'm sorry, but I don't see how I could be of help. I've never worked in that field."

Jenna slumped in her seat and stared at her hands clenched in her lap. She'd expected so many answers from this meeting, and defeat left a sour taste in her mouth. He *had* to know something. She raised her head and held his gaze. "And you don't know anything about Descartes?"

He appeared to think for a few moments. "You know, it might ring a vague bell. I think I was involved in a project by that name over twenty-five years ago. But I can't remember the details."

"Please…think. It's important."

Something flickered in his eyes as he studied her. Jenna couldn't define the emotion; curiosity, disbelief, a dawning dismay? Finally, he shook his head as though to dismiss whatever unpleasant thought had crossed his mind. Frustration welled up inside her, and she wanted to scream at him to tell her what he knew, how he had known her father, but she clamped her lips closed to keep the words in.

"Please, professor. Anything you can tell me…"

Merrick licked his lips. "I may have some old files at home. If you leave a contact number, I'll see if I can find some information."

As she took out a business card and placed it on the desk in front of him, the professor regained some of his composure. "Now, I don't know why you saw fit to lie your way into this interview, but I really must ask you to leave."

Forcing down her frustration, Jenna picked up the letter from the desk, shoved it back in her bag, and rose to her feet. "I'm aware you know more than you're telling me."

"I assure you—"

A wave of her hand cut him off. "I'm ill. I've lived with the knowledge all my life. But without my medication, I'll die. I don't understand any of this, why my father sent me to you rather than a doctor, but he must have had his reasons. Until I find out what they are, I can't move on."

At the door, she glanced back. The man appeared in shock, his face gray.

"Please," she said. "Just call me if you remember anything, anything at all."

His head shook in denial. "You don't understand—I can't help you."

CHAPTER SEVENTEEN

Jenna trembled slightly as she handed the earpiece back to Luke. There was a tightness in her chest, and she rubbed the back of her neck to ease the tension. "What a total waste of time."

"Not necessarily. Come on, we'll get some lunch and maybe, given time, the professor will decide he remembers something."

Luke tucked the earpiece in his pocket and led her off the university grounds and along the river. It was a glorious day, the sky clear and the trees along the riverbank were just changing color.

They found a small restaurant with views over the river and chose a table by the window. Luke ordered drinks while Jenna studied the menu. She glanced up to find him watching her.

"How do you feel?" he asked.

"Actually, fine." It was true. The pain in her hand had faded to a dull ache. Her head was clear.

Sitting here, sipping a glass of cold mineral water, everything seemed so normal. It was hard to remember the horror of the night before.

There was an unspoken decision between them that they wouldn't discuss Merrick until after they'd finished eating. Luke seemed to take on another persona—a suave, witty companion—and she allowed him to do so. They ordered salmon and strawberries and talked of nothing important while they ate.

He was very good at not giving anything away. And afterward, she sat back, filled with an urge to find out more about him, how his mind worked. "Tell me how you got involved in all this. I mean, I know you're after David's killers, but how did you get into the security business?"

"Perhaps one day I'll tell you. But not right now—it's not suitable conversation over lunch. Tell me about you and David instead."

"We were friends, that's all."

"But he wanted to be more?"

"David was a nice guy, too nice, and he was looking for something more serious than I'm willing to give."

"Why? You're a beautiful woman."

Jenna glanced at Luke before she answered. She hated to talk about her illness, but maybe he needed to know the situation. "I have a genetic illness."

"So?"

"I don't do relationships."

"Neither do I."

They were both loners, it seemed. While she knew and understood her reasons, she couldn't help but wonder what had made Luke the man he was. She studied him as the waiter cleared their plates and brought coffee, but his face gave nothing away. Jenna stirred her coffee and gazed out the window. They had to plan their next move, though she was reluctant to bring up the professor again.

"So, what did you make of Merrick?"

"He was lying."

His words confirmed what she had thought as well. "But why?"

Luke raised an eyebrow. "Maybe he's aware that anyone who mentions Descartes ends up dead."

It was a stupid question, when you considered what had happened in the last few days, but she couldn't believe her father would have deliberately put her in danger. She swallowed the last of her coffee and slammed the cup down. The action jolted her finger, and she winced as pain shot up her arm. "Perhaps we should go back and torture him. Break a few fingers."

"I was considering it."

Even studying his face, she couldn't tell whether he was joking or not.

"You don't mean that?" She hated the fact that it was a question, but what did she really know about this man?

"No, we won't go back and torture him. We'll give him a little time to come to his senses." A flicker of amusement flashed across his face as he

finished the last of his coffee. "And if he doesn't—
then we'll torture him."

"So how will we know if he comes to his
senses?"

"He'll call and tell you he's remembered
something. Or there's always the bug I had
someone place in his office. Chances are he's
sitting in his big leather chair right now burning
up with the need to talk to someone about
Descartes."

"What if he emails instead of phones?"

"I have someone tapping into his IP address.
And I called Callum. We'll have a tail on the
professor the moment he leaves."

Jenna stared at him in disbelief. Somehow she'd
wandered into a world that had previously existed
only in movies and TV. How often had she wished
for a little more excitement in her life? Now she
wasn't so sure.

"And if we don't hear from him," Luke
continued, "we'll pay him a visit together. See if
we can't persuade him to see the error of his
ways."

Either way, it appeared she hadn't seen the last
of Merrick. Stretching her legs beneath the table,
Jenna tried to ease the ache of restlessness, the
twitching of her nerves. The feeling was a familiar
one; she needed to run or work out at the gym but
had no idea when she would get the chance.

Luke's cell phone rang, interrupting her thoughts. He listened for a minute without speaking, his brows drawing together in a frown, and then he disconnected and put the cell on the table between them.

"Merrick's on the move, and he's made a stop. He's using a public phone. Either he's calling you, or calling someone else, and he doesn't want to be overheard. He's cleverer than we thought."

"Well, he is a professor at the best university in the country, so we should have thought he was pretty clever."

Luke drummed his fingers on the table and a minute later, Jenna's cell phone rang, and he grinned.

"Hello?" she said.

"It's Merrick. Meet me at my house at seven p.m. tonight. I may have something for you."

Luke slowed the car to a crawl. "We should be nearly there."

They were driving along a narrow road a few miles outside the city of Cambridge. The sun was close to setting, tinting the sky with crimson. The road was overhung with trees, but between the occasional breaks, flat fields spread out for miles.

Merrick had refused to say anything further over the phone except that he'd remembered something about a former project, and he might have information of use to her.

Jenna turned from studying the road to look at Luke's profile in the fading light. As usual, his expression gave away nothing. He appeared as fresh as when she had first seen him that morning, while she felt wrecked. She knew it was likely a combination of delayed shock and the painkillers, but she was an hour past the time she normally took her medication, and worry niggled at the back of her mind.

She had no medication left to take.

Yesterday's had been the last, and tonight would be the first night in her memory when she didn't take the pill. Unless Merrick miraculously had something for her, although she doubted that was going to happen.

Today she'd missed her appointment at the clinic, but tomorrow, she would spend some time researching her illness. She would find a specialist and get things moving. She lifted her hand in front of her face. One of the first symptoms was a fine tremor in the limbs, but her hand held steady.

Luke glanced from the road to her. "Is your finger bothering you?"

"No. I was just —" She dropped her hand onto her lap. "It's fine. I can't even feel it, but I've always been a fast healer."

She pushed the worries to the back of her mind

and focused on the coming meeting. Her illness was trivial compared to everything else that was going on. Callum had called in earlier, saying Merrick had arrived home, and his tail was watching the house to make sure he stayed there.

"Why do you think Merrick wanted to meet me here, rather than back at his office?" she asked.

"I don't know for sure, but if he was cautious enough to leave his office and use a public phone, he obviously suspects someone might be watching him."

"Wouldn't they be watching his house, as well?"

"Probably, but if he keeps his records here, maybe he had no choice."

Jenna shivered and pulled her jacket tighter around her.

"That's the address," she said, pointing to a set of double iron gates that stood open, leading into a long gravel drive. A dark SUV was parked just down the road. Luke raised a hand as they passed but otherwise ignored the vehicle and turned the car into the drive.

"Well, he's obviously not too concerned about security if he leaves his gate open."

Through the trees, she caught sight of the house, a large, graceful, Georgian building. Luke pulled up in front of the steps and sat for a moment, his hands resting on the wheel.

Lights blazed from the downstairs windows. It looked like the professor was home—or at least someone was.

"Is he married?" she asked.

"No. He's homosexual but not in a relationship right now."

"How do you know all this stuff?"

"It's easy to get information on people these days. Easier than it's ever been. I had a report run on him yesterday."

Something occurred to her. "Did you have a report run on me, as well?"

"Would it bother you?"

"Yes." The thought of someone delving into her secrets made her twitch uncomfortably; she'd always kept to herself.

"We did a preliminary report as soon as your name came up." A frown formed between his brows as he studied her in the dim light. "It didn't tell us much—age, profession. There was a photo, but for someone today it was strangely deficient. For instance, it never mentioned your illness."

"David told me I had no medical records at the surgery, so Dad must have kept them to himself."

Luke's frown deepened. He picked up his cell phone and punched in the speed dial. "Callum, run a report on Dr. Jonathon Young. The last known address is the house where we picked up Jenna last night."

He listened for a moment.

"Go back as far as you can. Merrick mentioned twenty-five years this morning."

"You're going to investigate my father?" Jenna asked as he ended the call.

"I can't believe I didn't do it sooner. It's obvious he was involved with Descartes a long time ago."

She scowled. "Investigate him if you want to. I'm sure he had nothing to hide."

But as she spoke, doubt nudged at her mind. Her father had always been so secretive about the past, but the puzzling laboratory notes she'd found while going through his papers were a clue there was more to him than he'd ever told her.

He had no family, or none he had ever owned up to. She knew nothing about her mother other than the name on her birth certificate — Sandra Leavsey. Jenna had presumed he'd been bitter about her abandoning them, but could there be something more sinister?

"Then there will be nothing to find," Luke said. "Come on, let's go see what Merrick has to say."

He climbed out of the car and Jenna followed. A dark, expensive-looking sports car was parked at the side of the house, otherwise the gravel drive was empty. The place appeared prosperous and well cared for. Merrick was obviously conscious of his image. She walked beside Luke up the stone staircase at the front of the house. They came to a halt in front of the impressive double doors and Luke pressed the bell.

Nothing happened.

Though he pressed the bell again, Jenna knew there would be no response.

Dread unfurled inside her. A lump formed in her stomach, and she edged closer to Luke.

He glanced down at her. "Do you want to wait in the car?"

"No." She inched even closer to him. She wasn't letting him out of her sight.

He nodded and pushed the door. It didn't open, and he turned the handle. It didn't budge. "Come on."

• • •

Luke glanced over at Jenna as he made his way down the stone steps. In the light from the house he could see her face was pale, her features set. He had a bad feeling about this, and it was obvious Jenna was picking up the same vibes.

That was definitely the professor's car parked at the side of the house, so he was home. But not answering his door.

Luke made his way around the side of the house with Jenna close behind him. Halting beside a French window, he peered inside. The room was in darkness. He rattled the handle but wasn't surprised to find it locked.

He raised his foot and kicked the center of the door. The glass shattered, and the door sprang open.

Beside him, Jenna jumped at the noise. "What—"

He shook his head. Pushing the door fully open, he stepped through and into the room.

The faint light from the open door allowed him to see the furnishings, two large sofas facing each other. He crossed the room and opened the door opposite that led into a hallway. Stepping through, he paused as his nostrils picked up the faint, unpleasant smell that permeated the air.

"Fuck."

He thought about telling Jenna to wait for him, but he doubted she would listen.

Her strength impressed him. Many people would have collapsed under the strain of what she had gone through over the last few days. Instead, she'd remained determined to continue, but he suspected this might send her over the edge. He was pretty sure he knew what they were going to find and cursed himself for not taking Merrick in—for his own safety and to protect their source of information. The truth was he hadn't taken the professor seriously, had believed a connection twenty-five years in the past too distant, and Merrick a harmless, aging man.

Down the hall, a light shone from an open doorway. He stepped toward it and peered into the room. It was a study, a large oak desk and bookcases along each wall, empty of people, no sign of the professor.

Behind him, Jenna screamed, the sound quickly cut off. Luke whirled around to find her standing with her hand slapped across her mouth, her wide eyes fixed on something above her head.

CHAPTER EIGHTEEN

Professor Merrick hung suspended by a thick rope around his neck from the banister high above. His head tilted at an odd angle; his neck must have snapped as he fell.

Luke took a step closer. Merrick's bowels had voided, and this close, the stench hung in the air.

"Are you okay?" he asked Jenna.

She forced her gaze from the swinging body and nodded, but her movements were jerky. "Is he dead?"

"I think so."

"Sorry. Stupid question. I just—"

He reached across and pulled her into his arms, holding her trembling body close and stroking his hand down her hair. They stood for a minute, and he could sense her gathering her strength, pulling the pieces of herself together. Finally, she raised her head from his chest.

"I'm okay."

He steered her back toward the sitting room, his hand groping for the switch, and the room flooded with light. He pushed her down on the sofa.

"Stay there," he murmured.

After searching the room, he found the liquor

cabinet and poured her a large brandy. She stared at the glass for a moment before taking it from him.

"I don't drink."

"Tonight might be a good time to start. I can't deal with a hysterical female right now."

The deliberate harshness of his tone got through to her. Though she cast him a hurt glance, she sipped the brandy and pulled a face. She took a deep breath and swallowed the rest in one gulp before placing the glass carefully on the small table beside her and visibly squaring her shoulders.

"I'm fine, really. It was just the shock. I looked up, and he was hanging there. Did he kill himself?"

"I doubt it."

"Oh. I thought maybe it was my fault. That something we said this morning triggered him to…"

"It's been set up to look like a suicide, but I think it's likely he was pushed rather than jumped." He studied her face; a little color was creeping back. "Are you okay here for a few minutes? I want to go have a look. See if I can find something that might tell us what happened."

She glanced at the broken French window but nodded.

Maybe he should take her away from here. He could leave the men to keep an eye on the place until Callum turned up. But Callum would say he was going soft. And he'd be right.

He couldn't remember the last time he'd felt protective about anybody. Actually that was a lie—it had been Leah, and look how well that had turned out. Besides, Jenna was somehow involved with Descartes, and the last thing he needed was feelings for her clouding any decisions he might have to make. He'd spent ten years building up to this. He wouldn't be distracted by inconvenient emotion now he was close.

He stood gazing down at her a moment longer, then turned away. He headed back to the study first. The note was on the center of the desk.

I can't live with myself any longer.

Short and to the point.

The writing was shaky, but that could have been a man about to commit suicide or a man with a gun held to his head. As far as Luke was concerned, the latter scenario was far more likely.

He pulled out his cell phone and called Callum. "Merrick's dead. Get a team over to my location. I want a full search of this place with no sign we've been here."

When he ended the call, he headed back into the hall and studied Merrick's body. It appeared a clear case of suicide. There was no sign of a fight, no sign he had resisted at all. Maybe they'd drugged him before they'd tied the noose around his neck and tossed him over the balcony. Luke would get the team to check for that.

The staircase was broad and curved around the hallway. Wide landings wrapped around the first and second floor with doors leading off. The rope holding Merrick had been tied to one of the upright banisters on the second floor landing.

Luke ran up the stairs. Crouching down, he studied the knots, but there was nothing to give away whether Merrick had tied them himself.

He rubbed his forehead, pressing his fingers hard against his skull.

There was a terrorist attack going down any day now, and he was no nearer finding anything that would help him stop it. All he knew was the who. Not where, or what, or even why. And that bothered him the most. What did they hope to gain? A terrorist attack made no sense—overt aggressive actions didn't tie in with the Conclave's normal pattern of behavior.

What had changed, and how could Jenna be involved?

Could it really be due to her father and a twenty-five-year-old secret between two men? Both now dead.

He returned to the study and started a systematic search. There were no locked drawers or cabinets, and he found nothing of any interest.

It was over an hour before Callum turned up. "Another lead dead?" he asked, staring up at the professor's body. "It's getting contagious."

"Yeah. I want you to keep looking here. Tear the place apart if you have to."

"And where will you be?"

"I'm taking Jenna back to London."

"One of the others could do that," Callum said.

"I don't think she needs to be with a stranger right now."

"Really? And does she need to be with you?"

Luke sighed. Callum had never known when to stop pushing. "Say what you're thinking."

"Just that I've never seen you like this. It's not like you to be taken in by a pretty face."

Luke shoved his hands in his pockets. "I'm not taken in, and I know what I'm doing. We need her on our side and this is the best way."

"You think?" Callum raised an eyebrow in disbelief. "I have a feeling you're about to rejoin the human race, and I've got to tell you—your timing stinks."

Luke didn't bother with an answer, and he and Jenna left shortly afterward. His cell phone rang when they were half an hour out. Callum.

"There's been an explosion."

"At Merrick's? What happened?"

"We'd just started searching the place when

some sort of incendiary device was detonated."

Luke swore under his breath. He should have checked the house before he left, but he'd been so concerned about getting Jenna out of there and to safety that his mind had been clouded. Shit. He'd thought Merrick wasn't going anywhere.

Nowhere, but up in smoke.

Callum was right. He couldn't allow himself to lose focus.

CHAPTER NINETEEN

The drive back to London seemed to go on forever. Luke had said something about an explosion but Jenna was beyond taking any more in.

"Jenna."

The car had stopped. She forced her eyes open and turned to him. "What?"

"I'll see you upstairs then I'm going to work. See if I can find a link to Merrick." He guided her across the garage.

Jenna leaned against the wall of the elevator and wondered whether the alcohol was affecting her. It felt like a buzz in her brain.

Luke frowned. "Are you okay?"

Was he crazy? She was as far from okay as it was possible to be. "I just want to go to bed."

For once, there was an expression on his face she understood—worry. It almost made her smile.

He led her through the apartment and stopped in front of her door. "Get some sleep."

Yeah, right. That wasn't going to happen. "Can I have another drink?"

"I'll get you something. Do you need more painkillers?"

Shaking her head, she pushed open the door to

her room. She could feel Luke's gaze following her as she walked through, but she ignored him. Once inside, she stood in the center of the floor, unsure what to do. A minute later, Luke stepped in behind her. He placed a half-full glass of amber liquid on the table by the bed and walked away.

At the door, he paused. For the first time, he appeared unsure. "I have to go."

Irritation flicked at her nerves. Why didn't he leave? "I'll be fine. Just go."

His eyes widened a little at her abrupt tone, but he turned and left the room. Sinking onto the bed, she picked up the glass. There was a fine tremor in her fingers, but she didn't know whether it was the onset of her illness or merely reaction. Right now, she didn't care. She swallowed the drink down in one gulp, almost choking as the burning liquid flowed down her throat. Leaning back against the headboard, she closed her eyes, but images of David, of Merrick, of her father on a slab in the morgue, played across her mind.

Her nostrils clogged with the stench of death, and a wave of dizziness washed over her. Her stomach recoiled, and she lurched to her feet, ran to the bathroom, and threw up in the toilet.

Collapsing to her knees, she laid her cheek against the cool porcelain, waiting for her head to stop spinning. Her mouth tasted foul, and she pulled herself up and drank straight from the tap, then brushed her teeth until her gums bled.

She tore off her clothes and stood under the steaming shower, trying to wash the stink from her body. She felt as though she were the only real thing in an unreal world.

• • •

Luke stopped off in the control room on the ground floor.

At this time of night, the room was quiet, just a couple of guys monitoring the chatter, and a third in charge of internal security, reviewing the CCTV cameras around the building.

He nodded to the man sitting at the bank of monitors. "Gary. Anything happening?"

"No, sir. It's all quiet."

Luke made to move away, but on an impulse, he sank into the seat next to Gary instead. He leaned across, punched in his security code, and switched the monitor to the bedroom in the apartment.

An image of Jenna curled up on the bed filled the screen. She must have showered; she was wrapped in a white towel, her hair damp about her shoulders. At first, he thought she was asleep, she was so still. But her eyes were open and staring.

He switched off the connection and turned to Gary. "I want you to have someone watch the penthouse apartment."

"Yes, sir."

"Make sure no one goes in or out. Except me."

"Yes, sir."

Luke rose to his feet and hurried from the room, punching in Callum's number while he waited for the elevator. "What's happening?"

"It was definitely murder, not suicide. I'll get a report to you by morning."

Luke felt no shock at the words. In fact, he'd been expecting them. "Did they get the body out?"

"Yes." Callum replied. "I'll make sure we get a copy of the autopsy report, but I'm betting it won't come up with anything other than suicide."

"Did you pick up any prints?"

"Nothing suspicious. These guys were professional. We did get the hard drives off Merrick's computer and his laptop and phone, so we'll get the lab analyzing them to see if we can't find something. But I'm guessing the place had already been gone through."

"That's what I came up with." The elevator arrived and he stepped inside.

"But the fact they set the place to blow suggests they thought there might be something still there. If there is, we'll find it. How's the woman?"

He was pretty sure the question didn't arise from any concern about Jenna's well-being.

"Sleeping," he snapped. Then he sighed. "Look, Callum, I've not gone soft on you — I'll do whatever's needed. But I don't think force would work with her. Did you see the report from the man who tortured her?" It had made interesting reading.

"Yeah. He reckoned she wouldn't have broken. But everyone talks in the end."

"Not everyone. There's a small proportion of people who respond differently. They reach a point where they're physically unable to talk. A sort of stubbornness."

"You think she's one of those?" Callum asked, his tone skeptical.

"The report said she became angry rather than scared as the interrogation went on."

"I still think you should keep it as an option."

Maybe as a last resort, but he didn't actually believe she *could* tell them anything. "We'll dig into Merrick's background first. I have a feeling if we can find a link between Merrick and Jenna it will give us something to work on. At the moment, everything points to the link being her father."

"Stefan's already investigating him. We should have the information by morning."

As the call ended, Luke ran a hand through his hair. The elevator hadn't moved, the doors still open. Although he was exhausted, he knew he wouldn't sleep. He needed something to take his mind from the woman upstairs. He'd been about to press the button for the penthouse; now he changed his mind.

He needed to work.

CHAPTER TWENTY

"We lost the men we sent after Carson's lead."

Lauren glanced up at the words. "What? How the hell could you lose them?"

Mark shrugged, a casual lift of his shoulder beneath the designer suit. "They didn't report in. We're trying to trace them now."

"Fucking brilliant. And?"

"Merrick is dead."

In the end, she'd decided the risk wasn't worth taking and had given the order to have him removed. "How?"

"Don't worry. It appears that the professor committed suicide. An affair with a male student gone wrong. The student killed himself tonight as well—tragic. The professor was distraught."

She studied her assistant, but his face remained expressionless. He could have been talking about a simple business deal. Mark was handsome, intelligent. He was also a sociopath, which was the characteristic that had landed him the job.

"Do you want any of the details?" he asked.

"No, this was more in the way of cleaning up loose ends that should have been cleared years ago."

He frowned. "Why weren't they? It's unlike

you to leave loose ends."

She gave a small smile. "Would you believe sentimental reasons?"

Mark's eyes flashed with amusement. "No."

His response didn't surprise her. "Show no weakness" was the motto she lived by. Today, people did not leave the Conclave unless it was in a permanent manner.

But she hadn't always been quite this hard, and Merrick had been a friend as well as a colleague. Back then, she'd allowed him to walk away when the project he was working on was terminated. Had even employed him since on a casual basis.

Why had he surfaced now? With Descartes coming to fruition, the timing was certainly suspect.

"So what have we got? A small town GP who carries out an internet search on Professor Merrick and Descartes. The doctor is interrogated but knows nothing. Or almost nothing. Just a single lead, who appears to be a nobody. Except our men disappear when they go after her. What's the link?"

She rubbed her hand over the smooth skin of her forehead. Mark moved to stand behind her, and his fingers massaged her shoulders, digging in to the solid muscle. For a minute, she closed her eyes and allowed the tension to drain away.

God, it felt good.

Another reason she had employed Mark—his magic fingers.

She opened her eyes and shrugged him off. He stepped back.

"Merrick didn't actually know anything about the current project." Lauren tapped her pen on the desk. "You had someone watching him? I take it there was nothing suspicious about his behavior?"

"Nothing obvious. He did have a visitor earlier today who didn't fit his usual pattern. I've sent the pictures to your monitor."

Her computer screen flashed to life as he leaned across and punched the keyboard. A photo of a woman filled the screen. She was beautiful, flawless, with pale blond hair pulled into a loose chignon that showed off her perfect bone structure, a full mouth, and blue eyes fringed with dark lashes. There was something familiar about her, though Lauren couldn't place her and was sure she had never seen her before.

"Who is she?"

Mark tapped a few keys. "Shit."

"Don't tell me—more good news?"

"Her name is Jenna Young. Which just happens to be the name of the doctor's patient—Carson's lead."

Lauren sighed. Loudly. "And no one put this together before now."

"The information just came through."

"What do we have on her?" Drawn by that sense of familiarity, she glanced at the photo again. "She doesn't seem the type to take on three of our men."

"She's twenty-six, lives in London, and works at the National Museum of Anthropology."

"Hmm. I suppose there might be a legitimate reason for visiting a professor of biochemistry."

"This is her companion, though the woman met with Merrick alone."

A photograph of a man replaced the woman on the screen.

"Nice," she said. He was somewhere in his thirties, tall, lean with a narrow, handsome face. Something clicked into place as she looked at his eyes. Shock rippled through her. She had an almost photographic memory, and a name flashed into her mind. "Lucien Hockley."

"Really?" Mark murmured. "We have him down as a Luke Grafton. Owner of Grafton Securities, a multinational security firm. According to Merrick's assistant, he arranged the meeting to discuss some research into biotechnology with the professor."

"No, that's definitely Hockley."

"So who is Lucien Hockley?"

"He's supposed to be a dead man." Her headache was back. "Sit down. We may have a problem."

Mark sank into the seat opposite but remained silent as he waited for Lauren to continue.

"Lucien Hockley supposedly died in a car explosion ten years ago along with his wife and baby."

She closed her eyes for a moment, getting her thoughts straight. Though she could have pulled up the file, she preferred to remember it for herself.

One of those little shivers of instinct ran through her—this was something important. Her skin prickled with reaction, and she rubbed her hands down her arms. "Lucien Hockley's father was one of the Conclave's mistakes. You know how we work. Each member identifies another potential member. That's how we grow. It's up to them to make the contact and to decide whether they are a suitable candidate for recruitment."

Pausing, she stared at the photo. Lucien was the spitting image of his father.

"James Hockley was identified. It was one of the few occasions where the system failed."

"Why?" Mark asked.

"On the surface, he was perfect. The Hockleys were old money, which James Hockley had multiplied many times over. The family was into everything—oil, property, even arms manufacture. Which is probably what made him appear the perfect candidate."

"But?" Mark prompted.

"James Hockley was one of those rare creatures, a wealthy man with honor." Lauren shook her head. "It was obvious if you did your research. The man was a goddamn war hero, but the member recruiting him was so sure he was landing a big fish he looked no further than the surface. Hockley pretended to go along with it long enough to find out about the existence of the Conclave, then threatened to expose us. He was dealt with."

"What happened to the member who tried to recruit him?" Mark asked with genuine curiosity.

Lauren's lips curved into a smile. "Oh, he was dealt with, as well." The Conclave didn't like mistakes and did not accept stupidity from its members.

"So how does the son come into this?"

"Lucien Hockley reacted badly to his father's death. He was eighteen at the time, and he left home and joined the French Foreign Legion."

Mark sat bolt upright in his chair. "How wonderfully melodramatic. I didn't know the Legion existed in real life. I thought it was just in the movies."

"No, it exists, and it's one of the toughest training grounds a soldier can have. By all accounts, Lucien thrived there. He joined at the lowest level, but a man like Lucien Hockley isn't born to be a private. He worked his way up through the ranks, got a couple of awards for bravery."

"You sound like you admire him."

"There's a lot to admire, if you like that sort of thing. Anyway, he obviously grew out of it. He returned home at twenty-four with a wife he'd picked up in England and a baby daughter. We kept an eye on him but never considered him a threat until he started asking questions. The decision was made, and we had confirmation of the hit."

"Instead, it appears he survived."

"Obviously. But his wife and baby were killed, and he's been out there all this time. A man with a mission." *Jesus, just what they needed.*

"So what do we do?"

"First of all, find him." She slammed her fist down on the desk. "Shit. Why did this happen now?"

Descartes was her baby. She'd planned it from conception. Despite those early, disastrous experiments, she'd seen the potential and persuaded the Conclave to go forward with this. Now only days from seeing the results, the whole project was in jeopardy.

A click to the next photograph showed the man and woman together against the backdrop of

the spires of Cambridge University, where she had
studied. Where she had met Merrick and John
when they had all been undergraduates.

The couple weren't touching but there was a
sense of togetherness about them. They were well
matched, both tall, good-looking. Her gaze was
drawn to the woman, and that same sense of
familiarity washed over her.

What was her role in this and her connection to
Hockley?

"I want to know everything about Jenna
Young. Get me a report by morning."

A ripple of unease ran down her spine. It
couldn't be.

That project had been terminated. Twenty-two
years ago.

CHAPTER TWENTY-ONE

Luke had spent much of the night working until the details blurred and Stefan had told him to piss off and get some sleep. He'd meant to take the elevator straight up to the apartment and his own room, but instead found himself heading back to the control center.

He had no intention of going to her again tonight. From now on, he'd maintain his distance. Callum was right. What did he really know about her?

Even so, he found himself switching on the monitor to her room, where she lay curled up on the bed, still wrapped in the towel. It looked like she hadn't moved in over three hours, her eyes wide open and staring.

A wave of tenderness washed over him. The feeling shocked him to the core. He wished he could deny it, but if life had taught him one thing, it was to face problems head on and never ignore them. Jenna Young was a problem. The question was — did he allow her to become a bigger problem? Or did he get rid of her before that could happen? He could hand her over to Callum. Callum would keep her safe if Luke asked him.

But he couldn't do it. He needed her close by.

Finally, he acknowledged that she moved something inside him, something he hadn't felt since Leah. He waited for the surge of pain that always accompanied thoughts of his dead wife, but the pain had become a distant memory muted by time into a dull ache.

Jenna was here, now, in the present. Maybe Callum was right — he was about to rejoin the human race, and his timing was as bad as it could get.

He wouldn't allow himself to care. That wasn't who he was, but at the same time, this didn't have to be a catastrophe. Jenna was involved with Descartes, and his best bet of finding out how, and using that to his benefit, was to keep her close and earn her trust.

He switched off the monitor and headed up toward the penthouse.

• • •

The door clicked open, and a figure stood silhouetted in the brighter light from the hallway. Jenna didn't move, but her pulse sped up, and every muscle locked rigid. But once she recognized Luke, the tight knot of tension inside her unwound a little.

She scrambled upright, holding the towel across her breasts, and glanced at the clock on the table beside the bed. Over three hours had passed, though that seemed impossible.

"Is everything okay?"

Luke didn't answer. He stepped into the room, and the door swung shut behind him, leaving them in the dim light spilling out from the bathroom. Hands shoved into his pockets, he crossed the room to stand beside the bed and stared down at her.

"What is it?" she asked. "Has something else happened?"

"I wanted to check you were all right. Are you?"

At the question, the tension inside her snapped. Apart from her father, in her whole life, no one had really cared how she was. That was her fault; she kept people at a distance. Her illness had always been a secret, an invisible barrier between her and anyone who might come close. But Luke knew. Although they'd known each other only a short time, he probably knew her better than anyone else alive.

Before, she hadn't been able to cry. Now, tears poured down her face. She sniffed, trying to hold them back.

Luke sank onto the bed beside her, pulled her onto his lap and into his arms as he had done the night before. That same sense of safety engulfed her, and she curled herself into a ball and gave in to the flood of anguish that washed over her.

He didn't move, didn't speak, just held her tight.

In the end, she ran out of tears. Exhausted, she leaned her head against his chest. The sense of safety vanished to be replaced by something new. A slow heat burned into life low down in her belly as she squirmed in his arms, needing to get closer, and for a moment, they tightened around her.

Loosening his hold on her, he sat up straighter. His hands slid around her waist so he could lift her and place her on the bed. Bereft, Jenna wanted to reach out for him, to hold on to him. It was more than not wanting to be alone; she no longer wanted sex with some anonymous stranger as she had in the past.

She wanted Luke.

He rose to his feet and peered down at her, his eyes gleaming in the darkness, and she stretched out a hand to him. "Don't leave me."

When he didn't move, she dropped her hand to the knot holding the towel at her breasts. Her fingers trembled, refusing to behave, but finally the towel loosened and fell away, leaving her naked before him.

Logically, she knew she was beautiful but had always felt flawed. Now she held her breath, waiting for him to respond, half expecting him to walk away.

"Please, Luke."

His hand went to the buttons of his shirt and slipped the top one open. Some of the tension inside her relaxed as he slowly stripped the shirt and tossed it to the floor. He was lean but powerfully built, the muscles ridged over his abdomen.

Some sort of scar ran down his right side, and a tattoo decorated his right arm, but she couldn't make it out in the dim light.

"Are you sure about this?" he asked.

At his words, her gaze flew to his face to find him watching her as though he could see inside her mind. She shook her head because she wasn't sure about anything anymore. But at the same time, she reached out for him…

Their lovemaking was hard and fast and fierce and forced everything else from her mind. Afterward, he collapsed and rolled onto his side, dragging her with him.

Normally at this point she would get up, leave the bed, and get away from the man as quickly as possible.

But not with Luke. Instead, she wrapped her arms around him and burrowed her face against his chest. Breathing in the musky scent of sex, she felt at peace for the first time since she had seen David's body two nights ago.

• • •

Luke felt her go soft and boneless against him. His body was totally relaxed, but something niggled at his mind, and he realized with a start that he felt cheated, used. The thought almost made him smile. Although he was all for role reversal, he wasn't sure he liked this one.

But he understood why she had acted as she had.

He'd used sex the same way, many times. Used it to block out the bad memories for a little while. But casual sex always left him with a feeling of emptiness, and now, he was filled with the need to make her see him as more than just a means to forget—he wanted to be someone she would remember.

She was the most beautiful woman he had ever slept with. Probably the most beautiful he had ever seen. As he pulled away to look into her face, a shiver of unease ran through him.

Truth was, she was almost too perfect. Her bone structure was flawless, her skin without blemish, her nose straight, her mouth ideally proportioned.

Her eyes were closed, and they blinked open as if she could sense his stare. "What?"

He smiled. "I was thinking how perfect you are."

Some emotion flickered across her face. "I'm not perfect. I might look okay, but it's a pretty, pointless facade that covers up the crap underneath. I'm flawed, about as far from perfect as it's possible to get."

The bitterness in her voice was clear. For a moment, he had no clue what she was talking about. Then he remembered. He hadn't thought much about her illness since she'd mentioned it yesterday, but now he realized how big a part it played in her life and in her perceptions of herself as a person.

"It's a small part of you. It's not who you are."

The moment she opened her mouth to protest, he stopped the words with a kiss.

This time their lovemaking was slow and erotic. And afterward, she fell asleep in his arms almost immediately. Luke held her close while her limbs relaxed.

He should get up, go do some research. Start analyzing the information they had retrieved from Merrick's house. Instead, as he had the night before, he held Jenna tight and closed his eyes.

CHAPTER TWENTY-TWO

Jenna awoke to bright sunlight.

She couldn't believe she had actually slept, but she must have drifted off right after Luke had made love to her for the second time. She smiled at the memory and wriggled under the thin sheet.

Her mind was clear, all her senses alert. For the first time, she could hear the muted hum of the traffic in the streets far below. Listening carefully, she heard someone moving around the apartment. Her body fizzed with energy, as if she could get up and run and fight and—

The thought of Merrick flashed through her mind, but she pushed it aside; she would think about it later. Right now, she felt too good and wanted to savor the feeling for a little while.

Even the pain from her broken finger had vanished. The dull ache faded to nothing. She held the splinted fingers up in front of her face and noticed the swelling was gone completely from her knuckles, the bruising cleared, leaving her skin once again flawless. Tentatively, she touched the broken finger, increasing the pressure when she felt nothing.

A fracture should take weeks to heal. On a sudden impulse, she picked at the end of the tape and unwound it, holding herself tense, waiting for the pain to strike. Nothing.

She removed the last of the tape, and the splint fell away. Her finger appeared perfect. She clenched her fist. Had they been mistaken? Had it never been broken? But she'd heard it snap, had seen the unnatural angle.

What the hell was going on? She'd always been fast at healing, but all the same, this was beyond weird.

After climbing out of bed, she padded naked to the bathroom. She glanced at her face in the mirror, not something she did often; she hated to see the perfection and know what lay behind it, but today something drew her.

She stared as though at a stranger. She looked the same, but somehow more sharply defined.

Maybe she was in love.

The stupidity of the thought made her grin. More likely, she'd just had a night of great sex. Anyway, she'd long ago vowed she would never fall in love. She didn't know what the future held for her, but she didn't think it was fair to inflict that future on some poor, unsuspecting man. But with Luke she felt safe, maybe because she doubted Luke was any more into commitment than she was.

In the shower, she turned the water on hot and hard, felt every drop against her skin. She rinsed away the sweat of the night with a hint of regret as the memory of the pleasure washed over her.

Eager to see Luke, she dried herself quickly and dressed in clean clothes packed in the bag Callum had brought for her.

Luke was in the kitchen, dressed in a pair of black sweatpants and nothing else, his chest and feet bare. She stood in the open doorway, watching him.

His expression was more relaxed than she had ever seen it, though disappointment flashed across his face as he observed her loitering figure.

"You're dressed," he said. "I'm making coffee. I was going to bring it to you in bed."

She closed the space between them, and she couldn't resist reaching out, placing her palm against the raised scar tissue that marked his skin from his collarbone to his chest. At her touch, he went still, and she shifted her hand, trailing it over the hard muscle of his upper arm where a tattoo showed dark against his skin.

"I saw this last night. What is it?"

"I got it when I was in the army. It's a flaming grenade." His lips curled in a rueful smile. "I was young."

"The words are in French. 'Legio Patria Nostra.' What does it mean?"

"The Legion is our Fatherland. It's the motto of the French Foreign Legion."

"You were in the French Foreign Legion? I thought that was only in stories."

"Oh, it's real. People join up from all over the world. They're a mixed bunch and on the whole pretty rough. It was an education, and I learned a lot." He shifted on the balls of his feet and shrugged again. "My father died suddenly when I was eighteen. I went slightly off the rails and ended up joining the Legion."

That explained a great deal about him. "Did you fight?"

"A lot of skirmishing. Mainly in Africa."

She ran her hand over a scar on his left shoulder. A souvenir from that skirmishing? "What made you give it up?"

"I grew out of it." He grinned. "It happens. Unfortunately, by the time I got out, the family business seemed a little tame. So I used what I knew and the contacts I'd made to set up the security business."

"What about your friend Callum?" she asked. "Was he in the army as well?"

"Not the same one, but I met him when I was stationed in Ivory Coast. He was in the British army—the SAS."

"Wow." Though she was not surprised.

"Yeah, he was good—the best. But he got disillusioned with the army, and when I set up the company, he came in with me. It's good to have someone you can trust."

"Yes, it must be." Even if Callum wasn't the most comfortable person to be around. Did Luke have anyone else? "What about your mother?"

"I never knew her. She died when I was two, and my dad brought me up."

"Something we have in common."

He laid his hand over hers, where it still rested against his shoulder. "Your mother is dead?"

"To be honest, I'm not sure. Apparently, she left us when my illness was diagnosed. My father would never talk about her. I was only four. Sometimes I think I remember, but..." She shrugged and decided to change the subject. "Hey, is there a gym nearby?"

"There's one in the building. Why?"

She rolled her shoulders. "I feel in need of a workout. Normally I'd run, but I'm not sure that's a good idea."

"The gym is in the basement. There's a pool as well." He stepped in closer. "But you don't need to go down there for a workout." His gaze dropped to her breasts. "I have a much better idea."

He moved suddenly, his hands shifting to her hips. Lifting her onto the counter, he stepped in between the *V* of her thighs. He flicked open the top button of her shirt and had progressed to the second one when a cell phone rang behind her, and he went still.

His expression was rueful, but he stepped away and reached for the phone. Though he turned his head as he answered, she clearly heard Callum's voice at the other end of the line.

"I'm on my way up."

Luke glanced at her, regret clear in his eyes. "Okay, I'll see you in five."

Jenna jumped down off the counter as Luke shoved the cell phone in his pocket.

"That was Callum. He's on his way up."

"I heard."

"You did? You must have good hearing."

She frowned. "This morning it seems I do. Does Callum live here?"

"He has an apartment a couple of floors down. He stays there when he's in the country." He made to leave the room but paused in the doorway. "I didn't use anything last night."

For a moment, she didn't understand what he was saying. Then she realized he meant no condom. "Is there anything I should know?"

"I'm clean. What about you, any chance there will be repercussions from this?"

"No. I'm on the pill."

She'd hated the idea of passing her disease to anyone and had seriously considered being sterilized, but strangely, it was her father who had told her to hold off. He'd said the advances in medical science were coming so fast, who knew what cures would be available in another decade?

"Good. I'll be back after I've dealt with Callum." His smile was apologetic. "Maybe you should go to the gym after all. I have a feeling this might take some time."

He closed the door behind him.

Her gaze settled on the coffee machine as the scent of fresh coffee teased her nose. Jenna poured herself a cup and sat at the table, sipping it. Even through the closed door, she could hear Luke moving around the apartment, and she frowned again.

The flavor of her coffee tasted more intense than she had ever noticed before. Everything appeared sharper, brighter. Was it some sort of relief that she was alive when others were dead?

Or was something else happening? Last night, for the first time in as long as she could remember, she hadn't taken any medication. But she didn't feel ill. She felt... She closed her eyes. She felt vital, alive, alert. Could it be some sort of side effect, a symptom that heralded much worse to come? Or had the medicine, while forestalling her illness, also dulled her senses?

The elevator door slid open. Presumably Callum arriving. Jenna sat back in her seat. If she closed her eyes, she could hear the conversation clearly.

"You look like you just got laid," Callum said

"Leave it." Luke's tone held irritation or guilt. Possibly both.

"Do you know what you're doing?" Obviously, Callum was unwilling to leave it. "This woman is a possible suspect, and even if she weren't a suspect, she's our only lead. She's bait, and you're losing focus."

"I said, leave it," Luke snapped.

"Damn it, Luke, this is my deal as much as yours. I have as much at stake as you. Leah was my sister."

Who was Leah?

"I know." He was silent for a minute, and Jenna strained to hear. "This way, Jenna trusts me. Don't worry, I'll do whatever's necessary."

What the hell did that mean?

Had Luke been playing her?

Who were they trying to trap? Presumably David's murderers. That had been Luke's purpose all along, so why did she feel betrayed?

Nausea churned in her stomach, and she swallowed the bitter taste that rose up in her throat. Footsteps approached the kitchen, and she forced her expression into blankness. Luke opened the door; behind him, she could see Callum. She pasted a smile onto her lips.

"What's going on?" she asked.

"Nothing. I'm just heading downstairs. We're going to continue work on the stuff Callum picked up from Merrick's place. See if we can extract any information from the hard drives." He crossed the room, came to a halt in front of her, leaned in close, and kissed her lightly on the mouth.

A rush of rage washed over her. She pushed it down.

"Will you be okay?" he asked.

"Of course." She twisted her lips into a smile. "I might go use that gym."

"Take the elevator straight down to the basement." He turned to go.

"Luke."

"Yes?"

"What's happening with the police? I should phone in."

His brows drew together. "No need. I talked to them yesterday. They haven't found any leads yet, but they know to call here if they need you for anything."

She studied his face, but it was back to its normal facade of blankness. Slowly, she nodded. "Okay."

He looked at her for long moments then flashed a smile, his eyes warming. "I'll see you for lunch."

Jenna stared at the closed door for long minutes after he had gone. A dull ache nagged at her chest, and she rubbed it with the palm of her hand. A memory of how he had made love to her the night before tore through her mind. Maybe she had initiated the first time, but he could have said no. The second time, he'd been so tender. Had it all been an act?

After all, he had warned her he didn't do relationships. She should have listened.

She forced herself to wait for ten minutes before she got to her feet and went back to the bedroom. After crossing to the window, she peered down at the city below. They were on the Isle of Dogs, and she could see the river Thames in the distance. They couldn't be far from the train station, where she could catch a train into central London and get to Scotland Yard from there.

She changed her jeans and shoes for sweatpants and sneakers, picked up her bag, and headed for the elevator, stabbing her finger on the basement button. Thirty floors down, the elevator opened into the underground parking area, but off to the side was a set of double doors, presumably to the gym.

Inside was a smart carpeted hallway with a number of doors leading off, each clearly labeled. Shooting range, gym, pool; the last one on the right had a picture of a staircase. Faint sounds came from the rooms as she passed, but if she concentrated, she could identify the individual noises. The splash of water, the muted pop of a silenced pistol, a murmured conversation. She passed the other doors and went through the last one. A concrete staircase led upward, and she followed it one flight, where she reckoned the ground floor would be.

The door at the top led into a large reception area with glass double doors at the front and a desk occupied by a uniformed security officer. He glanced up as Jenna entered the area.

Her heart pounded, but she smiled brightly and headed for the exit. He watched her but made no attempt to prevent her leaving. Out of the corner of her eye, Jenna saw him pick up his phone.

Her pace quickened, and she reached the doors as he rose to his feet.

"Miss?"

She ignored the call and pushed, half expecting the double doors to be locked, but they opened easily, and she was outside. As soon as her feet hit the pavement, she ran. Behind her, someone shouted, but she kept running. She was fast, and soon she'd put half a mile behind her. Her cell phone rang twice, but she ignored it and ran on. Finally, she slowed her pace, though she wasn't even breathing hard, found herself in a residential street and kept going at a slow jog until she came to an alley bisecting two rows of houses. Entering the narrow space, she glanced back, but no one had followed her, or if they had tried she had left them far behind. She pulled her cell phone from her bag and noted the two missed calls were from Luke. Ignoring them, she found the card Detective Mitchell had given her and punched in his number.

"Mitchell, here."

"Detective Mitchell, it's Jenna Young."

"Where the hell have you been? We've been trying to get hold of you for the last forty-eight hours."

"I've been with David's cousin. He told me he'd been in contact with you, and everything was fine."

"Everything is not fine, and I don't know who you've been with, but it isn't David's cousin. You know how I know that? Because Dr. David Griffith didn't have any cousins."

Shock slammed through her. She stood, her back pressed against the rough stone walls as she took in his words. While she'd doubted Luke's motives, she'd never doubted who he was. If he wasn't David's cousin, who the hell was he? And how was he involved in this?

Descartes.

Luke had said there was some sort of imminent terrorist threat, and Descartes was the code name. Had Descartes led Luke to David and then to her? If so, had he been responsible for David's death? Had it all been a setup? Her mind whirled, her stomach churning as she came up with possible implications.

"Jenna?" Mitchell broke into her thoughts.

"Yes." Her voice sounded weak, and she made an effort to pull herself together.

"Are you still with this man?"

"No."

"Where are you? I'll send a car."

She thought about it for a second but didn't want to hang around. "No, I want to keep moving. I'll get the train. I should be there within the hour."

Before he could say anything further, she ended the call and was about to put the phone away when she changed her mind. She phoned Luke's cell instead. He picked up straightaway as though waiting for her call.

"Jenna, where are you?"

"I decided to go for a run after all. I needed the fresh air."

"Come back, Jenna. You're not safe out there."

"And am I safe with you?"

He was silent for a moment. "I would never hurt you."

Suddenly, she was furiously angry with Luke and with herself for being such a gullible fool. "No? I just called the police. I wanted to check for myself, and guess what? It turns out David doesn't have a cousin. So who the fuck are you?"

"Come back, and I'll explain everything." He

sounded calm and reasonable, and Jenna bit back the urge to scream.

"Yeah, right. I'm heading for the nearest police station." The lie came easily. Luke had resources, and she'd bet he was already looking for her. She cut the call and switched off the phone, shoving it back in her bag.

Cautiously, she slipped out of the alley, but there was no one around and she headed, at a walk this time, in the direction of the train station.

CHAPTER TWENTY-THREE

Standing in the control room, Luke stared at the cell phone in his hand. Jenna wasn't answering.

What had made her suspicious? She'd seemed relaxed, more relaxed than he had ever seen her before.

He'd felt the same. For the first time in over ten years, he'd woken feeling at peace, but he should have known it wouldn't last. That the world would intrude.

If Jenna had gone to the police, he could be expecting them on his doorstep anytime soon, and he had no intention of being around when they arrived.

The search into Merrick had thrown up nothing at first. The investigation into Jenna's father had been much more interesting. Jonathon Young appeared fine on the surface; all the proper facts were there. He'd been born an only child in London to parents who were also alone. He'd gone to medical school in Edinburgh, then a residency in a London hospital, then spent time doing research before taking up general practice. He'd married a Sandra Leavsey. They'd had one daughter, Jenna, and divorced four years later. There were no details of his wife other than a name.

He'd almost told Stefan to stop the research, they were wasting their time—the man was obviously perfect. As that thought had crossed his mind, he'd paused.

No one was perfect. Jonathon Young's life had been totally uneventful, and that fact alone should have rung alarm bells.

Instead of calling off the investigation, he'd told the researcher to dig deeper, and Jonathon Young's life had unraveled. Until twenty-two years ago, he had not existed. His whole life was a web of lies.

Luke had read the reports from the accident. While Jonathon Young's life might have been a lie, his death appeared genuine. Just an accident.

So who was he? Who was Jenna?

Young was likely a real doctor. It was the weak point, and if the man had had any sense, he would have changed that. Maybe he needed the doctor thing because Jenna had this genetic illness. Maybe being a doctor gave him access to the drugs she needed. But why couldn't she have gone to a different doctor? Unless her actual illness revealed something her father had wanted kept a secret.

He crossed to where Stefan was working. "Found anything else?"

Stefan shook his head. "I've come to a halt

trying to work backward. It's a dead end. He's covered his tracks too well."

Luke pressed his fingers to his eyes. Maybe they needed to approach it from another angle. "Go back to Merrick. Back to twenty-five years ago. Where he was working, who he was working with—especially any medical doctors who could fit Young's profile."

Stefan glanced up after a minute, a grin lighting his face. "How did you know? There he is. Dr. John Creighton. The age fits. They went to university together—Cambridge. Merrick studied biochemistry, Creighton medicine. Creighton did a residency at a hospital in London but moved into research and got a job with Merrick a couple of years later. That's all at the moment. You want me to look into it?"

"Yes. Everything you can find about him." He thought for a moment. "Where were they working together?"

Stefan studied the screen. "Bentley Research, a biotech company."

"Find out everything you can about that, as well."

If they dug deep enough, they might find a connection between the Conclave and Bentley Research, although that didn't explain the tie to Descartes.

"Luke?"

Callum came to stand beside the desk, his face stamped with excitement.

"You've found something?"

"Ivory Coast."

"The Conclave's old haunt."

It was where Luke had first met his friend, back before he had even heard of the Conclave. Luke had been posted to Ivory Coast with his regiment, providing a peace-keeping force. Callum had been with his SAS unit, attempting to free some British aid workers who'd been kidnapped. His unit had come across something unexpected and had been wiped out. All except Callum, who'd been badly injured in the attack but had managed to crawl away and lasted two days alone in the jungle. Luke had found him and saved his life, and they'd been friends since.

Callum had left the army afterward, bitter at what he considered the lack of investigation into the death of his men, but Luke had kept in touch. Eventually, Callum had introduced Luke to his sister, Leah. She had been the catalyst that had changed Luke, made him see there was more to life than the exhilaration of danger and the excitement of a good fight. He'd given up the Legion and gone home with every intention of settling down.

That hadn't worked out well. Maybe some people weren't meant for a settled existence.

And now they were going back to where it started, Ivory Coast.

"One of our informants there has picked up a rumor," Callum said. "Apparently, some guy walked out of the jungle over a week ago, spouting a story that his whole village was dying. He'd gone out searching for work, came back and found the place surrounded by trucks and armed guards and everyone sick. He got out of there fast."

Luke had long ago learned to go with his gut instinct. Now, it was screaming at him that this was important.

"Where is he?"

"My guy is trying to find him, but it looks like he's vanished."

Luke got to his feet. He paced the room, every sense telling him to move fast. "We need to get out there."

"The plane's ready to take off when you are."

"Good." But thoughts of Jenna nagged at his mind, and he realized with a shock that he wanted her safe. He was sure she was caught up in the middle of something she couldn't understand and was liable to stumble into danger without knowing. She was naïve enough to think the police were the good guys. She hadn't yet learned there was no such thing.

He pulled his cell phone from his pocket and tried her again—still no answer—and he swore softly. Hoping she would read it and get back to him before she gave herself up to the police, he typed in a text message. Next, he called the man he'd had watching the local police station for any sign of Jenna, but she hadn't turned up, and Luke suspected she'd lied. The morning after Griffith's murder she'd spent a few hours at New Scotland Yard. It would make sense she'd go there now.

"Still no sign of the woman?" Callum asked.

"No, but everything's cleared here. If the police do turn up, they won't find anything."

"We've been friends a long time and I've never known you to make mistakes. If she'd been in one of the holding cells, this wouldn't have happened."

Luke didn't bother to deny it. "I'm going to call Scotland Yard."

"And tell them what?"

"I'll speak to the detective in charge. Tell him he needs to keep a close eye on her."

Callum frowned but didn't argue.

He looked up the number and then punched it in. "Could I speak with the officer in charge of the David Griffith murder? I have information."

Eventually a man answered. "Detective Inspector Mitchell."

"Do you have a Jenna Young, there?"

"Who is this?"

"She's in danger. Don't let her out of your sight. If anything unusual happens, question it."

There was silence for a moment. "I don't know who you are, but I suggest if you have any information pertaining to the murder of David Griffith, you get down here and make a statement."

Ignoring the suggestion, Luke ended the call.

CHAPTER TWENTY-FOUR

Jenna walked the last half mile and stood on the steps of the building, a wave of relief crashing over her. She'd spent the whole journey peering over her shoulder. Within seconds, she'd be safe.

At the last moment, she took out her phone and switched it on. There were five missed calls, all from Luke, and one text message.

You can't trust the police. You can't trust anyone.

Why shouldn't she trust the police? Then she remembered the conversation she had overheard that morning—she was nothing more than bait to Luke. Gnawing on her lower lip, she stared at the message then turned off the phone and headed into the building.

At the desk, she spoke to a uniformed officer. "I'm Jenna Young. I'm here to see Detective Inspector Mitchell."

As she spoke, Mitchell pushed through a set of doors behind her. A smile of relief formed on her lips, which faded when she saw his expression.

"Come through," he said, holding the door open. She followed him, and he indicated a counter to the right. "Would you like to leave your things at the desk?"

"Why?" She hadn't had to last time she was

here.

"Actually, it wasn't a request."

"Am I some sort of suspect?"

"Ms. Young, you phoned in a murder and then disappeared for forty-eight hours. We'd like to keep you around for a while this time. If that means treating you as a potential suspect, then yes."

She put her bag on the desk and signed the paper they handed her.

Don't trust the police, Luke had said. Suddenly she wished she'd spoken to him. It was too late now, but she would get one phone call. They had to give her that.

"Have you found the person responsible?"

Mitchell ignored the question. "Follow me." He led her down the hallway and into a small room that held a table and two chairs. The walls were painted beige, and one was taken up by a mirror. Jenna looked at it curiously. "Is that so you can watch me?"

He nodded.

"Am I really a suspect?"

"We're not sure what you are at the moment, but we'll hold you under the Prevention of Terrorism Act if we have to."

"What? Are you saying you've found David was connected to some sort of terrorist activities?"

"I can't reveal that to you. Now take a seat."

His face softened. "If it means anything to you, I don't think you're guilty of anything, but we have to be sure. Can I get you a coffee?"

"Please."

As he called out the door, Jenna sank into one of the hard metal chairs and rested her hands on the table. A minute later, the detective who had been with Mitchell the night of David's murder entered, carrying three coffees. She put two down on the table, took the third, and leaned against the wall, sipping it and watching Jenna.

Mitchell sat opposite her, placed a file on the table, and then picked up his mug. He pressed the recording device on the table. "Interview with Jenna Young, DI Mitchell, and DC Jameson, 11:15 a.m...."

Taking a sip of coffee, he studied Jenna. "So do you want to tell me what's happened between now and when you left here two days ago?"

Jenna took him through the initial meeting with Luke and answered his questions as best she could. She was finding it hard to believe Luke was not David's cousin. He'd been so convincing; even the photograph had appeared genuine.

When she got to the part about the attack on her father's house and the man she'd stabbed, Mitchell interrupted.

"You stabbed a man, and you didn't think you should report this to the police?"

Jenna shifted in her chair. "Luke said he'd taken care of it. He said he handed them over to some contacts he had in intelligence. It sounded so believable. I was in shock—I just wanted to get away from there."

Mitchell sighed and ran a hand through his hair. "We'll need a description of the men who attacked you later. Let's finish this up. These men who broke in, did they hurt you at all?"

"They said they'd do to me what they'd done to David. They broke my finger."

Glancing at her hand where it lay on the table, he raised one eyebrow. "They broke your finger?"

She realized how it must sound, but she didn't have an explanation, and frustration gnawed at her insides. "I'm telling the truth. My finger was broken. I removed the splint this morning, and it was fine. I don't know how, I—"

"Calm down, Jenna."

She knew he didn't believe her, and she didn't want to calm down.

When she mentioned finding Professor Merrick dead, he stopped her and turned to Jameson. "Sarah, go check it out." He turned back to Jenna. "Why don't you have a break for a minute, drink your coffee?"

His arms folded across his chest, he leaned back in his chair and watched her. "You think the guys who attacked you at your father's house were the same ones who killed your doctor friend?"

"Not the same people but from the same place."

"Hmm, you remember the artist's impression you did for us last time you were here?"

"You found him?"

"Maybe." He picked up a file, took out a photograph, and handed it to her. Shock churned in her stomach as she stared down at the image. The man was obviously dead, laid out on the slab in the morgue. She licked her lips.

"What happened?"

"We don't know. He was brought in as a possible hit-and-run on the same night the doctor died. When we posted your artist's impression, he was flagged immediately. You did a good job. Now, would you like to tell me what the hell's going on?"

Jenna's head was about to explode. None of this made sense. David's killer had died that same night. Had he been murdered, too? The men who'd broken into her father's house had acted as though they had killed David or at least knew his killer. She stared up at Mitchell. "I don't know. I just don't know."

He sighed then slammed the file on the table and sat, fingers drumming, a brooding expression on his face.

Jenna sipped her cold coffee. A few minutes

later, Detective Jameson came back. "The story holds up. At twelve fifteen the fire services arrived at this guy's house. The professor was found hanging from the banister. It's being treated as a suicide, but the house was completely destroyed, so it was hard to find any evidence to prove otherwise. The fire looked like it was set deliberately, but it could have been the professor, some sort of funeral pyre."

Mitchell studied Jenna. "I don't like any of this, and I don't understand it, except for some reason, you're right in the middle. You'd better finish your 'story' and we can try to see if there's some sort of pattern here."

Jenna swallowed and told him the rest without mentioning the fact she had spent the previous night with Luke. When she'd finished, Mitchell gazed into space for a few minutes and Jenna fidgeted.

"Well, first thing is we send someone over to this place and see if we can't pick up Luke Grafton, but I have a feeling we're not going to find anyone there. You have a cell phone number for him?"

"I'd give it to you, but it's in my bag."

He smiled the first genuine smile she had seen from him that day. "We'll need you to work with the artists again, get a mock-up of this guy and the ones who broke into your father's house."

"You know, I really have no idea what this is about."

"Funny thing is I believe you, and that's not something I say very often in this room. On the other hand, it's obvious you're involved in it all somehow. We just have to work out how."

On that point, she could agree. "So what next?"

"I'm going to set some wheels in motion." He stood and stared down at her. "We'll get to the bottom of this. I promise."

Behind him, Detective Jameson snorted and rolled her eyes. "He always resorts to clichés when he hasn't a clue what's going on."

Mitchell ignored the comment and crossed to the door. "I'll be back. Try not to worry—you're safe here."

The door clicked shut behind them. Jenna laid her head on her folded hands and closed her eyes. Her head ached. She'd woken that morning with a sense of well-being. Despite the circumstances, being with Luke had made her feel safe. How ironic was that?

The door opened and she jumped; she must have dozed off. Mitchell stood in the doorway, and he did not look happy.

Jenna straightened, smoothing a hand over her hair. "What is it?"

"There's been a change of plan. We're moving you."

"Moving me where?"

"To a safe house."

"You mean I'm not safe here? I'm in the middle of Scotland Yard. Where the hell is going to be safer than this?"

The frown didn't leave his face. "The orders came from high-up."

A flicker of foreboding tingled along her nerve endings. Luke had said she couldn't trust the police, couldn't trust anyone. "I don't want to go."

"You don't have a choice."

She searched the room, seeking some way out. All she could think of was letting Luke know where she was. "Do I get a phone call?"

"I'm afraid not."

She pressed the spot between her eyes. "More orders from high-up?"

He didn't answer, and she rose reluctantly. What would they do if she refused to move? Maybe she didn't want to find out.

"Mitchell."

"Yes?"

"Luke left me a text message on my phone, when he knew I was coming here."

"And?"

"He said don't trust the police. Don't trust anyone."

His brows drew together in a frown. "And what do you think he meant by that?"

"I don't know. But is this normal?"

"Nothing is 'normal' about this case." He shook his head as if undecided about something.

"There's something else isn't there?" Jenna asked.

"I think this Luke guy might have phoned here just before you arrived."

Hope leaped up inside her. "What did he want?"

"To tell me you were in danger." He sighed. "Look, if you are in danger, maybe a safe house is the best place for you. Don't worry. I'm going to send DC Jameson with you. She's good, she'll keep an eye on you. We won't let you out of our sight."

CHAPTER TWENTY-FIVE

Jenna glanced at the detective who sat beside her on the back seat of an unmarked police car.

"Do you do this sort of thing often, Detective Jameson?"

The woman turned from staring out of the window and grinned. "No, but it makes a change from the office. And call me Sarah. I have a feeling we're going to be spending a lot of time together."

Jenna sighed. The euphoric feeling she had awakened to had evaporated, leaving her lethargic and drained of energy. Should she mention her illness, in case she passed out or something?

Then again, she hadn't eaten anything since lunch the previous day. Maybe she was suffering from nothing more than low blood sugar, but she suspected not. She felt different, somehow changed inside, and her father's warnings niggled in the back of her mind. All the same, food might help.

"I don't suppose there's any chance of something to eat?" she asked.

"You hungry?"

"Starving. I haven't eaten today, and it's been sort of stressful."

"I bet." Sarah leaned forward and tapped the

driver on the shoulder. "George, isn't there a sandwich bar on the corner down here? If you get a chance, pull over."

Ten minutes later, Jenna bit into the chicken sandwich, a Styrofoam cup of coffee gripped between her knees. She could almost feel the energy flooding through her. Looking up, she found Sarah watching her, a smile curving her lips.

Jenna smiled back. "How come you got stuck babysitting me? Wouldn't you rather be out catching bad guys?"

"You're joking. The boys were fighting over this job. I got sent because Mitch didn't want any of them to spend time with you, and he's too busy to do it himself. Believe me, he would have if he could."

"He would?"

"Oh, yeah. Hasn't stopped talking about you since that night."

"He's your partner?"

"Yes, but strictly work-wise, and we've been together only a month."

"He seems like a nice man."

"He's okay. He's also single; he told me to make sure I mentioned that. But I'd never have anything to do with a cop outside work." She smirked as she studied Jenna. "So are you in any sort of relationship?"

Jenna had a memory of lying beneath Luke last

night. Heat surged at the memory, and she silently berated herself. He'd been using her, getting her to trust him, and she wouldn't be taken in again. "Is that a police question?"

"Nah, just told the boys I'd get the gory details." She grinned, but the smile turned to a frown as she turned to look out of the window. Jenna followed her gaze. Up ahead there was some sort of crash, and the car slowed to a crawl.

"Turn around, George." Sarah's tone was terse and urgent.

The car came to a halt. Jenna twisted in her seat to stare behind her. A dark van was coming up close, preventing them from turning.

"I don't like this." Sarah reached up and pulled a pistol from the shoulder holster beneath her jacket before turning to Jenna. "I want you to get down on the floor. Stay there until I tell you."

Jenna didn't move. She was staying where she could see what was going on.

"George, radio in."

"Not working." He glanced back at the two women. "I'll go see what's happening." He climbed out and hurried toward the crash. Sarah took a cell phone out of her pocket, pressed a button, and frowned. "I'm not getting a signal. That doesn't make sense." Her voice held the first hint of panic.

Jenna had a flashback to the night she'd been

attacked in her father's house. The phones hadn't worked then, either. The thought focused her mind. Fear clawed at her gut, but she forced it down. "We have to get out of here." When she reached for the door, Sarah stopped her with a hand on her arm. "No, we should stay in the car. Nobody's going to do anything, not in the middle of London."

Jenna gaped at her. Was she in denial?

Something caught the corner of her eye, and she turned to look out the side window. They'd stopped by the opening to an alley. Down it, Jenna could see a vehicle parked. As she watched, it began to roll slowly toward them.

She stared, mesmerized, as the car picked up speed. It was a black suburban of some sort, and she waited for it to stop, for something to happen. Instead, it sped up, and she grabbed Sarah and pulled her head down. "Get down," she screamed. "They're going to crash into us."

The next instant, the vehicle slammed into them side-on. For a moment, all was chaos; the airbags in the front exploded with a loud roar, and the air inside the car filled with thick white dust. Jenna choked then coughed, trying to clear her lungs. The car was moving sideways, groaning with the strain until it hit something solid, and the metal started to buckle. Panic flared hot and hard. They were going to be crushed, but there was no way out. The front and sides were blocked.

Finally, they stopped moving.

Beside her, Sarah bent over, coughing, still holding the gun in her hand.

"Sarah," Jenna shouted her name, and she looked up, her face white with dust and shock, a streak of blood on her forehead running down into her eyes.

"You need to shoot out the back window. We have to get out of here."

Sarah wiped at her face with the back of her hand. "What?"

Her teeth gritted. "The back window. Shoot it."

Sarah shook her head as though she couldn't understand the question. "I can't see."

When Jenna reached for the gun, Sarah released her hold, and Jenna pulled the pistol from her fingers and pointed it toward the back. She fiddled with the safety and aimed the gun, but before she could fire, the side door was wrenched open from outside. Hiding the gun by her side, she dropped her arm.

A man Jenna had never seen before crouched by the door. He was dark-haired with olive skin. He studied the two women, drew a pistol from his waist, and shot Sarah once through the forehead. The detective fell back, her eyes staring, instantly dead.

Jenna's mind froze. Then she was filled with a

fury so strong it cleared the fear from her mind.

"Get out," he said.

She kept her right arm by her side as she climbed slowly out of the car. Up ahead, the crowd milled around the crash. Their driver had vanished. Had he been part of the trap?

Don't trust the police.

The man grabbed her left shoulder and pulled her forward, toward the dark vehicle. Jenna took a deep breath and swung her right arm up, pushed the gun into his side, and squeezed the trigger.

He went rigid beside her, and she pulled her arm free, twisted out of his grasp, stepped back, and kicked him in the chest. As he collapsed to the ground, she was off and running. Somebody was behind her, but she didn't turn, just kept going.

Something slammed into her thigh, and she stumbled. She reached her hand down—it came up wet. She'd been shot. There was no pain yet, but she could feel a numbness washing through her. It spread from her thigh, up through her body. Though she tried to keep going, her leg gave out beneath her, and she crashed to the concrete sidewalk. Her vision blurred, darkening at the edges.

A man stood over her. Jenna concentrated on his face, but her field of vision got smaller and smaller until it flickered out, and she was left in darkness.

CHAPTER TWENTY-SIX

The plane landed on an unmarked airfield outside the city of Diva.

Worry nagged at Luke. He couldn't get the idea out of his mind that Jenna was in danger. He pulled out his cell phone, called Scotland Yard, and was put through to Detective Inspector Mitchell straightaway.

"Are you going to tell me what the fuck's going on?"

Luke heard the tone of voice and knew something had gone wrong. "What's happened? Where's Jenna?"

"Mr. Grafton, or whoever the hell you are, my partner has been shot dead, Jenna Young is missing, and you're my only lead."

"Shit. When did this happen?"

"I'm not going to discuss the case with someone who I think is involved right up to his neck. Get in here, and maybe we'll talk about it."

Luke glanced out of the plane window to the red dusty scenery of Ivory Coast.

"That's not possible."

He ended the call before Mitchell could say any more and made a second call to a contact in the police force. They knew nothing and he frowned as he put the phone back in his pants pocket.

"What is it?" Callum asked from beside him.

"They've got Jenna."

"The Conclave?"

He shrugged, trying to calm the rage inside him. "We have to presume so. Sounds like she was ambushed. The police were moving her to a safe house, and the car was attacked. The officer with her was shot dead. It was a setup—it had to be."

"At least it sounds like she's alive. You know the only thing we can do is follow this through. You've got to put her from your mind. Concentrate on what we're doing here."

Callum was right. The information they found here might be used as a bargaining chip. If the Conclave wanted Jenna dead, they would have killed her at the scene rather than take her, so she was probably still alive. Although, by now, she might be wishing she wasn't.

That they hadn't killed her meant they believed she had information. Or they also didn't have a clue how she was involved.

Fear and frustration waged inside him. For the first time in ten years, he was thinking of something other than finding the people in charge of the Conclave and bringing them down. He wasn't sure it was an improvement.

Where was she? Was she scared? In pain? He

hoped she wouldn't try to hold out, but he truly believed she didn't know anything. They would keep up the questioning until they had drained her of everything and they were sure she knew nothing more.

But while he had no clue where she was, there was nothing he could do back in London. He'd just have to hope they found something out here that would lead them to the Conclave and Jenna.

The heat hit him as he stepped out of the plane. He'd changed into lightweight camouflage gear, as had Callum. Climbing down the steps, he breathed in the remembered smell of Africa—heat, dust, and a subtle scent of decay.

Thick, scrubby brush surrounded the airfield; a red dirt track was the only route out. As he stood, a cloud of dust formed in the distance. A land cruiser emerged out of the bush, coming to stop by the plane. Luke greeted the driver, a local man named Jacob whom they knew well from their time in Ivory Coast, and climbed in the back. A cold waft of air conditioning enveloped him. Callum got in beside him, and the car pulled away without a word being spoken.

The plane turned and taxied to the end of the runway, where it would wait for their return.

Once clear of the airport, the vehicle came to a halt, and Jacob swiveled in his seat to face them. He lit a cigarette. "I found him."

"And?"

"He's dead. He was dead days before I got to him."

"You got the body?"

"Still in the morgue. Wasn't nobody going to touch him. He'd bled out from everywhere."

Luke frowned. "Some sort of Ebola?"

Jacob took a drag of his cigarette and shrugged. "We should have the autopsy results sometime today."

"You identified him?"

"Yeah. I traced the rumors back, found someone who knew him. He didn't want to talk, but in the end, I persuaded him. I take it you want to see where the dead man comes from?"

"Yes."

"It's three hours away, in the bush."

"Then we'd better get moving."

He started the vehicle, and they drove in silence for a few minutes.

"So tell me what you know," Luke said.

"Not a lot more than I've already told you. This guy turned up and started raving about how his whole village was sick. He'd been away, said he was looking for work, but most likely poaching. Anyway, he comes back to find the place surrounded by trucks and a load of guys in weird outfits—I'm guessing Hazmat suits—and a lot of dead and dying bodies around the place. Somehow he avoids getting picked up, maybe luck or just that he knows the area, and he gets the hell out of there fast."

"And didn't have the sense to keep quiet."

"I doubt he was exactly thinking straight by the time he wandered into Diva. Bordering on delirious, the guy I talked to said. He was dead by the following morning."

"What made you think the Conclave is involved?"

"Just a hunch. You were the one who taught me to trust my hunches." He shrugged. "You think I'm wrong?"

"No, I suspect you're spot-on. I just wish I knew what it all means."

Perhaps this was an exercise, a testing ground for some sort of biological weapon, but he doubted they would find much evidence. Still, it was impossible to carry out an operation of that size without leaving some clue behind. He needed something, anything.

As the vehicle bumped over the uneven road, he tried to sleep. In the end, he gave up and stared out of the side window. Much of the country was agricultural, but here the land was arid, sparsely populated, and the scenery unchanging, dry bush and more bush. Luke swigged from a bottle of cold water and willed the time to pass.

Finally, they pulled off the dirt road and came

to a halt under the shade of a huge tree.

"You go on foot from here," Jacob said. "There are Hazmat suits in the back."

Luke climbed out and opened the trunk. He passed one of the suits to Callum, then stripped off his jacket, his weapons belt, and boots, and pulled on the aluminized bodysuit.

"Shit, this is going to be unpleasant," Callum said from beside him. "Like being inside an oven."

"You'd rather go in there without one?"

"Hell, no."

Luke turned to Jacob. "We'll be back within two hours. If we're not, you get out of here."

"No problem."

Luke pulled down the face mask and switched on the breathing apparatus. "You hearing me okay?"

"Yeah, I've got you. Let's get this over with."

It felt strangely isolated within the suit; sounds filtered through the microphones. Callum had left his radio open, and Luke could hear his even breathing. A trail led away from the dirt road, into the bush. It was marked clearly by the wheel tracks of some sort of truck, and Luke photographed the prints then followed them, with Callum close behind him.

Half a mile on, the track they followed led straight to the village — or rather, to what had once been a village. Nothing remained but blackened markings where the huts had stood. Stepping closer, Luke studied the dark powdered remains, kicking the ash with his boot. There was nothing left, nothing bigger than dust. Sweat trickled down his body inside the suit and rolled down his forehead, stinging his eyes. Outside of blinking to clear his vision, he could do nothing about it.

"They must have used some sort of incendiary agent. This wouldn't happen in a natural fire." Callum's voice came through his headphones, and Luke nodded.

"Get some samples. If we find out what was used, we might trace it."

Callum placed the case he carried down on the ground, took a small plastic bag from inside, scooped a sample of the black powder, and stored it away. "Christ, I'm hot," he muttered.

Luke wandered around the village, photographing the remains. There were probably around fifty huts in all. How many people? What had happened to them?

The areas between the huts were marked with the same tire tracks, as though the trucks had driven intricately around the village. On the far side, he saw where they had exited. He called to Callum, and together they followed the marks. Luke was expecting it, but still a shaft of shock pierced him in the gut as he came to an abrupt halt at the edge of a black circle.

He leaned down, picked up a pinch of black ash, and rubbed it between his fingers. There was a greasy feel, and it smeared on his gloves. Nausea roiled in his stomach. Stepping back, he watched in silence as Callum collected samples.

He had no doubt they had found the remains of the villagers. "Jesus, a whole village."

"Yeah, it sickens me, as well, but we'll get them this time." Luke could hear the barely suppressed excitement in Callum's voice. "I'm guessing they tested some sort of bioweapon on the people and burned the evidence. You can't do that sort of operation without somebody noticing. Either the stuff is made in country—and there can't be many places capable of doing that—or it's been brought in recently. Either way, we'll find it."

"I know." Luke took a deep breath of stifling air and tried to feel some of Callum's excitement, but he couldn't get the image out of his mind. A whole village—men, women, and children. How had they died? Had they realized what was happening?

But he could do nothing for them.

All he could do was get the people who had done this.

CHAPTER TWENTY-SEVEN

Jenna came awake slowly. She lay on her back on a narrow cot in a small, square room that looked like a cell. A white cotton sheet covered her, scratchy against her bare skin. Her whole body throbbed, not with pain, but with a sensation she couldn't define.

Pulling herself upright, she clutched the sheet to her breasts and peered around. There were no windows except for a small square of glass in the steel door. The walls and ceiling were painted white, and the only furniture was the cot attached to one wall and a toilet pan in the corner opposite the door.

Someone had removed her clothes; she was naked beneath the sheet except for a bandage around her left thigh.

There was no pain even though she'd been shot in the leg. The center of the bandage was blackened with dried blood, but she could feel nothing beneath it. She picked at the edge of the tape and unraveled the bandage. The skin of her thigh was smooth, unmarked, no sign of any bullet wound.

Wrapping the sheet around herself toga-style, she rose to her feet and crossed to the door.

Through the small window, she could see nothing except a short stretch of corridor painted the same featureless white as her cell. With her forehead pressed against the coolness of the glass, she stood and listened.

If she concentrated hard, she could hear the distant murmur of voices, the moan of someone in pain, and a door clicking open. She knew she shouldn't have been able to hear these things. Something was happening to her. Her senses were stronger, her hearing and her vision clearer than they had ever been. Even her sense of smell was sharper. Breathing in, she caught the whiff of disinfectant from the toilet in the corner and the faint tang of chemicals in the paint. Beneath the external smells, she could scent a faint, sweet odor emanating from her own body, oozing from the pores of her skin, vaguely familiar as though remembered from a dream.

She glanced down at her hand where she clutched the sheet. Only days before, her finger had been broken, but it had healed far faster than should have been possible, and she knew it had something to do with the medicine. Or rather the lack of medicine.

Her father had listed the symptoms in an endless promise of misery to come, but never this. Had he known? Could she be experiencing the side effects of some experimental drug? Again, her thoughts turned to the notes she'd found in his office.

Her watch was gone, and she had no clue how much time had passed or where she was. Would Luke have heard about her abduction? Would he come looking for her? Ultimately, she sensed he was a good man and was overwhelmed with a longing to see him, to touch him.

Shock had sent her running from him. Shock and disappointment. She didn't want to be bait.

She'd thought they had a connection.

Instead, she had discovered she was just a pawn in a game she suspected he had been playing for a long, long time.

But how tenderly he had held her through the night. And she realized that while he might be willing to sacrifice her to gain his ends, the decision would never be easy.

It didn't matter. No one knew where she was. Whoever had her were probably the same people who had killed David. They had shot Detective Jameson without a flicker of remorse, and they would do the same to her.

First, they needed something from her. Information, she presumed. Information she didn't have, but that wouldn't help her. And they would use any methods available to get her to talk.

Though she should have been terrified at the prospect, instead she felt calm. Returning to the cot, she sat, hugging her knees to her chest. Everything had happened so fast, and she hadn't had a chance to analyze it or try to make sense of it.

Her father's death had set something in motion. Or rather, *she* had set something in motion. If she'd done what her father had requested and not told anyone, just gone directly to Professor Merrick, would any of this have happened?

Descartes was the answer, but she couldn't imagine how a twenty-five-year-old secret tied in with an imminent terrorist threat or what part she played in that secret. Had everything her father told her been a lie? She'd always believed he loved her and had her best interests at heart.

She still believed that. But he'd been hiding something.

Her head began to throb again with all the unanswered questions. She rubbed her temple with the tip of her finger and pressed her eyes, pushing away the questions.

Leaning back against the cool concrete wall, she closed her eyes and pictured Luke. Behind her lids, an image of him flickered through her mind. He was somewhere hot and dry. The sun beat down on him. His mind was full of horror as he stared at...

She blinked. Had she really seen him?

Footsteps sounded down the corridor, and her body tensed. They were coming for her. She concentrated and picked out two sets of feet and the low murmur of voices. Wrapping the sheet tighter around her, she waited.

The footsteps came to a halt in the corridor outside her cell, and she glanced at the small window. Memories prickled along her neck; this wasn't the first time she'd been in a room like this while people studied her through the glass.

Someone peered back at her, the lock clicked, and the door swung open.

CHAPTER TWENTY-EIGHT

The drive back to the airfield seemed to go on forever, and the sun was setting by the time they pulled up beside the plane, one of those fantastically dramatic African sunsets that paints the sky in scarlet and burnt orange.

Luke couldn't get the image of the charred ring of greasy ash out of his mind. How many had died there? Two hundred? More? It was hard to believe so much human life could be reduced to so little. Luke had seen some bad things in his time in the Legion, but he'd never managed to acquire the cavalier attitude to human life and death that so many of his fellow men quickly developed.

He felt filthy, the dust sticking to his sweat-soaked skin, and he wanted to stand under an icy cold shower and wash away the sensation of death that clung to him like a miasma of evil.

Callum climbed out of the vehicle behind him. "We'll find them," he said.

"Yeah." It was true. The trucks had to come from somewhere. Whatever had been used to kill those people had to be brought into the country. He turned to Jacob. "I want you to get back to Diva. See if the doctor's finished with the autopsy report, and I want samples, blood, sweat, everything sent to the UK tonight. Get rid of the body, pay off the doctor, and then I suggest you get out of here. We're going to start digging, and once we do, you can bet they'll come searching for where the original leak came from. They'll be coming after you."

"I'll be on a plane out of the country tonight."

"Make sure you are," he said and slapped him on the shoulder. "You did well. This may be the break we've been looking for."

He climbed the steps into the plane and poked his head through the cockpit door. "We ready to go?"

"Yeah, just waiting for you to get on board."

"Good. Take us home."

He unfastened his weapons belt, and tossed it on the seat behind him then sat down next to Callum, rested his head back against the seat, and closed his eyes. Images of Jenna filled his mind. Where was she? Had they harmed her? An intense sense of urgency filled him. They had to find her, but in the ten years investigating the Conclave, they'd never gotten close. He would never discover where they had taken Jenna unless he could find someone with enough to lose that Luke could convince them that talking was worth the risk. And he had to do it fast.

Beside him, Callum opened his laptop and powered up.

"We need satellite photographs of the area," Luke said. "There were a number of trucks. We need to see them, identify them. They had to come from somewhere."

"I'll get someone working on it."

"We also need a list of international companies working over here. Cross-reference them against Conclave profiles. See if we can't narrow it down. I want to know who their contact is in Ivory Coast before we land, and I want to know everything about them."

Callum typed into the laptop, but it would be a while before the information started coming in. Luke stretched out on the row of seats at the front of the plane. Again, behind his closed lids he saw an image of Jenna, her beautiful face twisted in pain. The thought of her suffering filled him with anguish.

He sat up and pulled out his cell phone, punched in the number of Scotland Yard.

"Could I talk to Detective Inspector Mitchell? It's about the murder of David Griffith."

A moment later, the call was transferred. "Mitchell, here."

"Luke Grafton."

There was a moment's silence. "I hope you're calling to tell me you're coming in."

"Is there any news of Jenna?" He knew the answer before Mitchell spoke.

"No. It's as if she's vanished in a puff of fucking smoke."

Luke didn't bother saying anything else, just ended the call and laid his head back. Finally, he drifted off into a restless sleep.

"Luke?"

As Callum spoke his name, he woke abruptly.

"The satellite information has come in. I think we may have found something, a convoy of trucks setting off from Diva, fitting the time schedule."

"Any clue who they belong to?"

"They were aid trucks, supposedly taking building materials inland, but they were provided by one of the companies we've been investigating, a big international drug company, Flexley International. Stefan told me to tell you something."

"What is it?"

"He said Flexley is owned and run by a Gordon Haughton. Haughton used to own a research company a couple of decades back — Bentley Research."

"The company Merrick and Jenna's father worked for." Sitting back in his seat, he grinned. "It's him. It's got to be. Get me everything there is on Haughton."

CHAPTER TWENTY-NINE

Jenna backed away from the door as it was pushed open from outside. Two men came in, one dressed in black pants and a black sweater, the other in a white lab coat. She hugged the sheet tighter around herself as the first man's gaze ran over her, lingering on her breasts, and something flickered to life in his eyes. He was good-looking in a hard way, his dark hair cut military short above a bony face, narrow lips, and pale eyes. Out of the two, he appeared the more human. Jenna instinctively caught the bundle he tossed at her and found it contained a pair of gray sweatpants and a white T-shirt.

"Get dressed."

She searched the room for some privacy, but there was none. So she turned away and drew on the pants under the cover of the sheet, then dropped it to the floor and tugged the T-shirt over her head. Turning back, she found them watching her.

"Hold out your hands," the man in black said, his face expressionless.

Jenna's hands went automatically behind her back and she took another step away, only to come up against the wall of the cell.

The man followed; he moved in close and grabbed her upper arm, his fingers biting into the muscle. He pulled her hand from behind her back and slipped the bracelet of a set of cuffs around her wrist, yanked out the other arm, and fastened it so her hands were tied in front of her.

"Where am I?" Jenna asked. "Who are you?"

The man didn't answer, just turned away. "Follow me."

Jenna didn't want to. A hollow feeling settled in her stomach.

A smile curled the corners of his mouth as he turned back. It didn't reach his eyes, which remained cold as ice. "Do as we tell you and nothing will happen."

Jenna searched his face but found nothing to reassure her, then glanced at the other man, the one in the lab coat, and a shiver of revulsion washed over her. He had white skin and pale hair and studied her out of bulging eyes as though she were some sort of specimen. He licked his lips, and Jenna looked quickly back at the first man and nodded once. She had no choice. At least if she got out of the cell, she might have some chance of being able to work out where she was and seeing if there was any way to get out of there.

They led her down a corridor of white walls and bright fluorescent lighting. There were no windows, and she realized they must be underground. A sense of claustrophobia tightened around her. Fear clogged her insides. David's bloody remains flashed through her mind. That would be her in a few minutes, because she could not tell them what they wanted to know.

When she dragged her feet, the man behind shoved her none too gently in the lower back. She flashed him a look of hatred, and he frowned as though puzzled by her response.

Finally, they stopped by a metal door that led into a room only slightly larger than her cell. It reminded her of a doctor's surgery, and the comparison did nothing to calm her fears. Swallowing the dread that rose up in her throat, she halted in the doorway. A hand touched the small of her back, and she jumped. It lingered for a moment, fingering her flesh, then shoved hard, causing her to stumble into the room.

A steel table stood in the center, with buckled straps fastened at each corner. Jenna stared at it, mesmerized, as a shudder of horror ran through her. Her gaze darted around the room, searching for anywhere to go, but there was no escape, and dread locked her muscles rigid.

They could do anything to her, and she was powerless to stop them. At the thought, the anger rose inside her, momentarily overcoming her fear. She thought about fighting, but with her hands cuffed in front of her, she had no chance. Still, she would fight rather than get on that table. They would have to drag her there kicking and screaming.

But the man in the lab coat pointed to a leather chair to one side. "Sit," he said.

She sat. The other man approached her. "Hold out your hands."

She didn't move, and a slow smile curled his lips. His hand moved fast, his fist crashing into her face. Everything went black as her head slammed into the back of the seat. Sparks flashed in front of her eyes, and something warm trickled from her nose to her mouth—she tasted the sharp, metallic tang of her own blood. When the pain subsided, she blinked her eyes open. That small smile was still on his face but not reflected in his expressionless eyes.

"Hold out your hands." He repeated the words.

Jenna licked the blood from her lip, but this time she raised her cuffed wrists while he unlocked the restraints and tossed them on the table.

Her head swam. The blow had shaken her, and not just physically. She knew it was meant to affect her psychologically, was meant to make her realize her vulnerability. Show her she was helpless, and they could do whatever they wished with her. Instead, it concentrated the hard little knot of hatred that twisted in her belly. She stared up at him, memorizing his face as he strapped first one wrist and then the second to the arms of the chair.

Reaching across, he swiped his finger over her chin and wiped the blood on her T-shirt, the crimson stark against the white cotton. For a moment, his hand cupped her breast and squeezed hard, and her gaze flew back to his face.

"Later," he murmured and crouched down in front of her to fasten the straps around her ankles.

As she realized what he meant, she promised herself she would fight him before she let him touch her like that. The straps held her tight; there was no escape. Panic flared, and she forced it down, breathing slowly, deeply. She stared at the man and allowed her hatred to show in her face.

He straightened and backed away, leaning against the far wall with his arms folded across his chest. "She's all yours, Doc."

Jenna's gaze darted to the second man in the room. The doctor approached, and she flinched as he wiped the blood from her face with a paper towel, his touch almost gentle. He rolled a trolley close beside the chair, and she peered at it out of the corner of her eyes. It contained electronic equipment and a set of needles and bottles.

He patted her lower arm below the elbow and inserted a needle into the vein to collect blood. After he'd filled two small bottles, he labeled them and put them on the counter across the room.

Jenna concentrated on his actions, preventing her mind from thinking about what was to happen. He came back, looked at her for a moment, then hooked a finger in the neck of her T-shirt and tore it, exposing the tops of her breasts. Her eyes snapped closed, but she forced them open and watched as he taped two monitors to her chest. He fiddled with the dials of the machine and stepped back.

"Your name?"

Her gaze darted to the other man, who raised an eyebrow and made a move as though to straighten.

"Jenna Young."

At the soft chuckle across the room, her hatred rose.

The man in the white coat took her through a series of questions about who she was and what she did, and she answered them truthfully. There was no reason not to—she was sure they must know this stuff already. They were calibrating some sort of lie detector. For a moment, she allowed herself to hope they would believe her when she told them she knew nothing—that they wouldn't resort to torture—until her glance flicked again to the man leaning against the wall. His eyes followed the rise and fall of her breasts, and for the first time his expression was clear: he looked eager.

"Okay, it's ready." The doctor stepped away from her.

Though she hated to beg, she knew she had to try. "Please, don't do this. I don't know anything. I can't tell you what I don't know."

The man in black moved to stand in front of her, but she couldn't tell what he was thinking. "Tell the truth, and this will be all over."

"You really believe that?"

When he glanced away, she knew there was no help. This was going to happen, and she could do nothing. All the same, she couldn't stop herself fighting against her bonds. It was futile and left her panting with frustration.

"Tell me about Descartes."

The voice was soft, reasonable. She opened her mouth to answer, to tell them about the letter from her father, but couldn't make the words come out. Her mind screamed at her to tell them whatever they wanted to know, whatever it took to stop them from hurting her. But she couldn't do it. Something inside her would not allow her to give in to them; some stubborn, stupid streak would not give them the satisfaction. She glared into his eyes.

"Go to hell!"

He turned to the doctor. "Hook her up."

The doctor selected a needle from the trolley. He tapped her arm again and inserted the needle into her vein, attaching it to an intravenous bag before nodding to the two men, who crouched down in front of Jenna.

"This is something Doctor Smith here has been working on for us. Just so you know, it's a combination of truth serum and pain inducer." He reached across and stroked a finger down over the skin of her cheek. "It's very effective. You'll want to pass out, take my word for it, but you won't. So, you have one more chance. What do you know about Descartes?"

Goddamn fucking Descartes. She was beginning to hate the name.

She clamped her lips together and looked away.

"Go ahead, doctor."

CHAPTER THIRTY

The pain was instantaneous, sending burning needles of agony through Jenna's arm, filling her whole body with fire. Every muscle locked against the pain, her back arched, and she couldn't prevent the scream tearing from her throat.

The pain lasted for an age, finally ebbing to a throbbing ache. Her head fell forward, and she gasped in air.

"Feel like talking now?"

The words came from a distance. Her mind was clouded, hazy.

"Tell me about Descartes."

She opened her mouth to answer, the words rising up in her throat, then she swallowed them down and took a deep breath.

Not wanting to see the pain coming, she closed her eyes tight. It hit her again like a sledgehammer, slamming into her. The torture was unbearable, but how could something be unbearable when you had no choice but to see it through? She heard her own screams as if from a distance, her mind spiraling out of control, closing in, red splashes on her closed lids shrinking to blankness.

Then she was floating.

The pain vanished, and she blacked out.

And she was dreaming. At first, she was flying through total darkness. Then small pinpricks of light appeared on the black landscape. They were stars, and she was hurtling through space. She had been traveling longer than she could remember, had lost control a long time ago, but now she could sense her ship losing strength, and she knew it would be over soon. A deep sadness filled her. She was so far from home, a home she would never see again.

In the distance, a blue-green planet gave her a flicker of hope. Would she make it? Then the ship sputtered beneath her, and she knew it was over. Instead, she was heading toward an orbiting satellite. Lifeless, bare rock. The land came toward her, slowly at first as the ship tried to regain control, then faster as it lost the battle. They crashed into an outcrop, the ship disintegrating beneath her. The last life-force dwindled to nothing, and she was alone in a barren land.

There was no life around her and soon she would also be gone. Would she go to join her people? Would they find her so far from home?

Jenna came back to herself, sobbing. Not from the pain that lingered in her body, but from the memory of overwhelming sadness. She'd been dreaming, but of what and where she wasn't sure.

She lay curled up on the tile floor. Her face was

wet; she was crying for something she didn't remember and couldn't understand. As she moved, everything hurt, so she wrapped her arms around her stomach and blanked her mind. Finally, she drifted off into a light sleep.

When she opened her eyes again, she had no clue how much time had passed. Her cheek pressed against the cold floor. A dark smudge of crimson stained the white tiles where she'd lain, but when she put her fingers to her face, it felt fine.

Pushing herself up, she stumbled to her feet and steadied herself with a hand on the steel table. The pain was gone completely, wiped away, though her limbs were stiff from lying on the cold floor, and she stretched. She crossed the room to a small sink against the far wall, the strength returning to her limbs, and ran the tap, putting her mouth to the water, spitting it out then swallowing. When she straightened, she peered at herself in the mirror and splashed water over her face before wiping it clean with the paper towels. Reaching up, she stroked a finger down her nose. Earlier, she'd heard the crunch as it broke, but now her face was perfect; even her split lip had healed.

What was happening to her?

She whirled around at the sound of the door opening. The running water must have masked the footsteps. A man entered the room—the man in black — and her stomach clenched.

The door clicked shut behind him, and she glanced over his shoulder.

"Don't expect any help there. You can scream, and the guards won't come. No one will come." He examined her; his gaze sliding over her body then back to her face, a small frown forming between his brows. "You look surprisingly good. I was sure I'd broken that pretty nose, and your heart stopped beating there. We thought we'd lost you." He took a step toward her. "And that would have pissed the doc off. He's never lost one. Well, not without meaning to, anyway."

She clamped her lips between her teeth but didn't speak. Her mind worked furiously. He was one man. If she could catch him off guard she might have a chance, but she had to bide her time.

He reached out, grasped the torn edges of her T-shirt in his hand, and ripped it open, baring her to the waist.

"Very pretty," he murmured, his voice thickening.

Jenna swallowed her nausea.

"You going to play nice?" he asked.

She nodded.

"Had enough? Well, you're still going to have to talk, but you be good and we might come to some arrangement."

One hand cupping her breast, he stepped in

closer and squeezed her nipple between his thumb and finger. A stab of pain shot through her, and he smiled.

"I wouldn't want you going too docile on me—I like a little fight."

He released her breast, his hands moving to grip her shoulder. Whirling her around, he slammed her face-first into the wall, then came up close behind, pushing his body into hers. His erection pressed into her buttocks, and she clamped her teeth together to stop the scream of rage.

He shoved his hand down the waistband of her pants, dragging them down over her hips. One thigh pushed between hers, spreading her legs. Jenna swallowed again, holding herself still.

Not yet.

She whispered the words inside her head while she waited for the best moment, when he was fully aroused and off guard.

When he stabbed one finger hard between her thighs, something exploded in her head. Her whole world faded to crimson, and a strength she hadn't known existed welled up inside her. Heaving backward, her elbow caught him across the throat, tearing herself free of his grip, and he crashed to the floor behind her. She yanked up her pants, turned around, and strode to where he lay. He stumbled to his feet, but she felt no fear now.

Her mind clear, her body strong—invincible—her vision narrowed to the man in front of her. Almost as if she moved in slow motion, she whirled and kicked. Her heel caught him in the chest, and his ribs caved beneath the force of the blow with the snap of broken bones.

Shock flashed across his face, blossoming into pain. He stared at the dark wet stain of blood seeping over his shirt and clutched his hands to his chest, backing away as the pain merged with horror.

She stalked him then, until he came up against the chair she'd been strapped to earlier and fell back onto it.

Jenna came to a halt beside him, leaned down close to his face, and whispered in his ear. "The guards won't come if I scream, but how about if *you* do the screaming?"

She reached out a hand and pressed his chest, heard the grating of broken bones. He opened his mouth to scream, but only a gurgling sound emerged from his damaged throat, and she swore. "Scream, goddammit!"

Loosening his shirt, she tore it away from his chest, but it was too late. White bone stuck out from his shattered rib cage. As she watched, he choked, his lungs filling, his hand clawing at his throat as he drowned in his own blood.

She stared down at his dead body and felt

nothing but fury.

After crossing the room, she peered out the window, but the corridor was empty. She rattled the door, but she'd known it was locked. Finally, she went back to the body and searched through the pockets.

Nothing.

Returning to the door, she banged on the metal. "Help, he's collapsed." No one came.

After searching the room, she spotted the small surveillance cameras in each corner. Were they watching her? She sank to the floor, leaning her back on the door. The adrenaline seeped from her system, leaving her drained and shaky. A few minutes later, a sickly sweet smell filled the room. She tried to rise to her feet, but her limbs felt too heavy, and she crashed back to the floor. Her mind clouded, and eventually the shadows engulfed her.

When she woke again, she was on the steel table, her arms and legs strapped to her sides. The body was gone and the blood cleaned from the floor.

She tugged at the restraints, but they were steel, and there was no way she could free herself. Despair threatened to overwhelm her. She tried to concentrate on something good, and an image of Luke flashed into her mind. But he didn't care about her. He'd been using her—nothing more.

With the death of her father, she was truly

alone. She had followed her father's lead and never let anyone close. Now it was too late, and there would be no one to mourn her.

Though while Luke had been willing to use her, for two nights he'd held her close while she slept, soothed away her nightmares.

She had to believe he cared.

She had to believe somewhere, someone was thinking about her.

CHAPTER THIRTY-ONE

An image of Jenna flashed across his mind as Luke climbed out of his vehicle in the car park of the Flexley research headquarters.

The image was so strong that he paused, his hand on the car door. He closed his eyes, trying to capture the picture, but it was gone. He shook his head and slammed the door.

The building was in one of the industrial parks on the outskirts of London. It appeared prosperous; the gardens surrounding the area were well maintained. The car park almost full.

Gordon Haughton, the CEO of Flexley, came from old money. He had inherited the company thirty years ago after his father died in a boating accident—a rather convenient boating accident—that had handed the family fortune and companies over to Haughton at the age of twenty-eight.

He'd prospered suspiciously well since, which was one of the first things Luke's team looked for when profiling companies for possible Conclave involvement. Luke had no doubt Haughton was involved with the organization; the doubt was whether or not he would talk.

The secret was finding something the person cared about more than their own life and wealth.

Haughton had a wife and a six-year-old daughter. Rumor had it he doted on them. Luke hoped the information was true.

The reception area was huge, obviously set up to impress customers and potential investors. Luke knew the company was doing well despite the current state of the economy, again, another good indicator of the Conclave's backing.

He approached the young man at the reception desk, who glanced up at Luke with a professional smile. "Can I help you?"

"I'd like to see Gordon Haughton."

"Do you have an appointment?"

"No."

"I'm afraid Mr. Haughton will not be able to see you. Could I ask the nature of your business? Perhaps one of our managers could help you."

Luke stepped in closer. "Phone Haughton and tell him there is someone to see him relating to his recent business endeavors in Ivory Coast."

"I'm afraid we don't have any connections with Ivory Coast."

"Do it," Luke growled.

The young man glanced toward the doors where a security officer loitered.

"Call security, and I'll find another way to contact Haughton, and you will lose your job."

His hand hovered over the telephone, and then he picked it up, punched in a number, and held a murmured conversation Luke didn't even try to pay attention to. He was certain the mention of Ivory Coast would get him the interview he needed.

"That was his assistant. She'll give Mr. Haughton the message and get back to us. If you'd like to take a seat."

"No."

He leaned on the counter and waited. His cell phone rang. He pulled it out and checked the caller ID. Callum.

"It's done," Callum said, and Luke ended the call.

Across the room, a set of elevator doors opened, and a smartly dressed woman emerged. Somewhere in her forties, slim, beautiful, and he'd bet super-efficient.

She came to a halt in from of Luke and held out her hand. "I'm Juliana Wade, Mr. Haughton's assistant, Mr.?"

"Hockley, Luke Hockley."

"Well Mr. Hockley, if you could tell me what this is about, I could perhaps schedule you an appointment, but I'm afraid Mr. Haughton is very busy. So it would probably not be until next week."

"You came down here just to tell me that?" He gave her a slight smile. "Look, we both know Haughton will see me. Could we take that as a given and move on?"

She raised an eyebrow but nodded. "Follow me."

He could feel her giving him sidelong glances in the elevator as they rose to the top floor, but she didn't speak again.

Once out of the elevator, she led him through an outer office, knocked on a set of double oak doors, and opened them without waiting for an answer. A man was seated behind a desk, and he rose to his feet as Luke entered the room. The woman left, the door clicking shut behind her. The man was tall and lean, with a thin face and dark hair streaked with gray. He didn't smile, and he didn't hold out a hand, just gestured to the chair on the other side of the desk and sat back down.

Luke took the seat indicated and waited for Haughton to speak. He needed the man off guard, and the best way to do that was to keep him guessing.

Obviously, Haughton had the same idea. For a minute, they sat in silence. Luke stared out the floor-to-ceiling windows and stifled his impatience while he waited for Haughton to break.

Haughton cleared his throat.

"Luke Hockley?" Finally, Haughton broke the silence. "I'm afraid I don't know the name."

"You wouldn't," he replied. "It's not one I use these days."

Luke had decided to use his own name; it felt strange hearing it after so long, but the time of hiding was almost done. It was likely someone in the Conclave had identified him by now, probably from surveillance feeds on Merrick.

If this thing worked out, the Conclave would fall, and as far as Luke was concerned, all those involved in it would also fall. It wouldn't matter who knew his real identity.

And if the Conclave didn't fall, the chances were Luke would be dead anyway.

"Hmm, Hockley." The man's brows furrowed in concentration. "There was a company we did some business with, must be fifteen years ago."

"That would have been my father. He's dead."

"I'm sorry." Haughton was more at ease now. He sat back in his seat. "So, how can I help you?"

Luke allowed a small smile to curve his lips. "I'm looking for a friend of mine. She's gone missing."

Haughton frowned. "I'm not sure I understand. My assistant mentioned you had information regarding a business deal in Ivory Coast."

"Not a business deal." He studied the other man's face to see if there was a reaction to his next words. "More in the way of a massacre, a whole village reduced to ashes. Does that sound like something your company might be involved in?"

If the shock was there, Haughton hid it well.

His expression hardened. "I think you're wasting my time, Mr. Hockley."

"I hope not. As I said, I'm looking for a friend of mine."

The change of subject seemed to throw Haughton. He shook his head slightly, and his frown deepened. "How could I possibly help you find this friend?"

"Let's go back to the massacre."

Haughton rose to his feet again and shoved his hands in his pockets. He turned to stare out of the window for a moment before turning back to Luke.

"I agreed to meet with you because—"

"You agreed to talk with me because I mentioned Ivory Coast. You don't believe I know anything, but you can't afford to let it pass. The Conclave doesn't react well to stupidity in its members."

Haughton swallowed—a telltale sign of nerves—and satisfaction washed through Luke. He realized deep down there had been a small niggle of doubt that they were wrong. That Haughton's seeming involvement was nothing more than coincidence. Now he was certain Haughton was in this up to his neck.

He had to play him right, and maybe he would lead them to Jenna. Hopefully she had held out and they hadn't broken her yet. She had to be alive, and while she might not know it, she had the answers.

But he needed more time. He would break Haughton and get Jenna back. They would uncover the secrets of Descartes and stop the terrorist attack. And then he would tear the Conclave apart.

Haughton was staring at him, shock stamped on his features. "I don't know what you're talking about." But for the first time, Luke heard a tremor in his voice.

"The Conclave."

Haughton sank down into his chair.

"To get back to my friend," Luke said. "I know the Conclave has her, and I want her back."

"I can't help you."

"I think you can."

Haughton shook his head. "You can't have any proof about my company's involvement in any massacre."

"Not yet, but we'll get it."

Haughton ignored the comment. "I know nothing of any Conclave."

"You don't know much, apparently. Tell me, do you know what it's like to lose someone you love?" Luke's tone was gentle.

Haughton's gaze shot to his, but he didn't answer.

"To know they might be in pain? Terrified?"

Haughton glanced away. When he turned back, his face was hard. "I'm sorry you've lost your friend, but I can't help you."

"Oh, you *will* be sorry. And you *can* help me. You won't want to, but I'm hoping you'll find the alternative harder."

"The alternative? Are you threatening me?" His voice held a faint tinge of anger. The man was an arrogant fool. Maybe he thought he was beyond the things that affected normal people, but he'd soon find he was wrong.

"Yes."

"I'd like you to leave."

"Not just yet. You see, I'm going to give you a glimpse of how it feels."

"How what feels?"

"I'm going to give you a glimpse of what it's like to lose someone you love. To worry that at this moment someone could be hurting them. Of course, that is presuming you love your wife and daughter."

"What?"

Luke allowed a small smile that didn't reach his eyes. Haughton had to believe he would go through with this. The truth was Luke wasn't sure what he'd do. He'd done some hard things over the past ten years. He'd killed, and he'd condoned the torture of men, but they had always been who he considered the bad guys. Most of them had been murderers or worse. Haughton's wife and daughter were innocents.

But so was Jenna.

Forcing the concern aside, he faced Haughton. "A colleague of mine is holding your wife and daughter. If you do not cooperate fully with me, he will cause them pain. Now the question you need to ask yourself is, are you willing to sacrifice them? Because, if you don't cooperate, it will come to that."

The color drained from Haughton's skin, leaving him pale. "I don't believe you." But his voice lacked conviction.

Luke pulled his cell phone out of his pocket and punched in Callum's number. "He needs convincing."

He handed the phone to Haughton, who raised it to his ears with a trembling hand.

From across the desk, Luke heard the scream that shrilled down the phone. Haughton's hand tightened until his fingers looked like claws.

"Rachel?"

She must have spoken. Luke couldn't hear the words, but Haughton went from white to a sickly shade of green. He pressed the phone against his ear. "Rachel, just be strong. I'll get you out of there." He glared at Luke. "I don't believe you. They're innocents. You're bluffing."

The bastard was willing to risk his loved ones.

Either he didn't love them enough, or he was too scared. Or he didn't believe Luke was serious. He grabbed the phone from Haughton.

"He needs a little more convincing." He held the phone out to Haughton's face.

This time the scream lasted for long seconds. Afterward, the room was silent except for Haughton's labored breathing.

"Next time it will be your daughter," Luke said. "What is she, six? Seems a pity she should pay for your mistakes."

Sweat beaded on the man's forehead; his eyes darted around the room as though he could find a way out. "You're animals. You have to let them go."

Unexpected fury whipped through Luke. "Animals? Yesterday I stood on the remains of an African village. All that was left of over two hundred people was ash. How did they die? Was it quick? Painless? Do you care?" He ran a hand through his hair. For ten years he'd pursued this, but he'd always felt so cold, emotionless. Now red-hot rage burned through him. "Do you even fucking know?"

Emotions always got in the way, and he swallowed the anger. He waited as Haughton also brought himself under control.

"I can't tell you anything. They'll kill me."

"And if you don't tell me everything, I will kill

your wife and daughter and make you watch. So you have a dilemma. Your death, perhaps at some unknown time in the future. Or your wife and daughter's death very, very soon."

"My daughter's only a child. I don't believe you'd do it."

Luke considered the other man for a moment. "Perhaps I could tell you a little history, Mr. Haughton, to convince you of my sincerity in this matter." He sat back in his chair. "This is a matter of public record, so you can check I'm telling the truth. Ten years ago, I, too, had a wife and daughter. My daughter was a baby, only three months old. A few years earlier, my father had died under suspicious circumstances. I started asking the wrong questions of the wrong people, and they decided to get me out of the way. So they blew up my car. Obviously, I survived; my wife and baby didn't. They were torn to bloody little pieces. I came around with bits of them plastered to my skin." He allowed the hatred to fill his eyes. "Now, you're the one thing standing between me and getting the people who did that to them. Look at me and tell me you really believe I'm not sincere."

Haughton was silent for a minute. Luke raised the phone. "Callum—"

"No, wait," Haughton held out a trembling hand, and the tension inside Luke relaxed.

He kept his face expressionless as he lowered

the phone. "Yes?"

Haughton sagged as though his bones crumbled. Then he nodded, a quick jerk of his head. "I'll tell you what I can, but I don't know much—none of us do. It's the way things work."

Luke smiled. "Let's hope you know enough." He thought about what to ask. There were two strands of information he needed to pull together. The first was the terrorist attack, the when and the where. The second was Jenna. There was one thing that tied them together.

"Tell me about Descartes."

Haughton's eyes widened at the name. "How—" He broke off and closed his eyes for a moment. When he opened them, Luke knew he had won. "Descartes is the name of an ongoing project."

"Its purpose?"

He shrugged. "As far as I can tell the purpose is twofold. The technology used is new; they're still testing it."

"What is it?"

"I don't know, and I'm telling the truth. Some sort of bioagent, but I've never seen anything like it."

"You haven't tested it here?"

"It wasn't in my remit."

"So Ivory Coast was a test?"

"Yes. We needed to know how effective the chemical would be when used out in the open.

Whether it would travel. Whether it could be contained. And the tests went perfectly. The chemical was one hundred percent lethal. No survivors, and it cleared from the atmosphere in under twenty-four hours, leaving no trace."

"And they plan to use this chemical in some sort of terrorist attack over here?"

"I'm not sure where. I don't get told the details, but from the quantity involved, it's something big."

"Why?" Luke said. "What can they gain from it?"

"Do you understand anything about the Conclave, Mr. Hockley? Do you know why the Conclave exists? Power. That's what we want. What's the most powerful struggle in the world? Life and death. My bet is the Conclave is proving to the world they have that power and are willing to use it." He smiled. "It sort of puts us on par with God, don't you think?"

"You're insane."

"Perhaps."

A shrill ringing sounded in the room.

Luke's eyes narrowed. "What is that?"

"The fire alarm."

CHAPTER THIRTY-TWO

Haughton pressed the console on his desk. "Juliana, what the hell's going on?"

Her voice came back slightly panicked. "I don't know. I'm looking into it."

Luke stood up and came around the desk. "You have CCTV?"

Haughton switched on the monitor on his desk. He pressed a few buttons, and the reception area came up on the screen. People were streaming out of the stairwells and heading for the doors.

"Could you have been followed?" Haughton asked.

"Maybe. It's more likely you're being watched. Come on, we have to get out of here." He gripped Haughton by the arm. "Just a warning. If I don't call in every thirty minutes, my people have orders to kill your wife. Another thirty and your daughter will die. It's in your best interest that I get out of here alive. Are we understood?"

Haughton nodded. He stood up and walked, not to the double doors Luke had entered by, but a smaller one at the back of the room. It led into a bathroom, a farther door opposite led out of this. Haughton took a key card from his pocket and swiped it through the lock.

Luke drew the pistol from his shoulder holster and switched off the safety. "Where does this lead?"

Haughton glanced from the gun back to Luke's face. "My private quarters. We can get up to the roof that way. I have a helicopter up there."

"You can fly it?"

"Yes."

"Go on."

Haughton pushed the door open, and Luke followed him through into a luxurious hallway. Haughton might have said money wasn't his motivating force, but he was certainly fond of the trappings of wealth. He led the way along the hall to a steel door, swiped the card again, and then they were in a narrow stairwell. They climbed up and finally came out onto the rooftop of the building.

Luke placed a hand on the other man's arm, preventing him from stepping out. His gut was telling him this was too easy so far. Straight ahead, through the open doorway, stood the helicopter—a small four-seater. Between them lay an open stretch of concrete.

"We're going to run for it." If they stayed up here any longer, they would never get off this roof alive. He'd been stupid not to realize they'd be watching Haughton and couldn't afford to make such mistakes. His mind wasn't focusing.

"Go."

Pushing Haughton in the small of the back, he shoved him out in the open, with Luke just behind.

Gunshots sounded, and Luke's muscles tensed, waited for the tear of bullets into his flesh. Instead, Haughton staggered and went down.

"Shit."

Haughton was a liability now, expendable to the Conclave, whereas they would want to take Luke alive to find out who he was working with and how much he knew.

Whirling around, he squeezed off some shots and saw two figures dive for cover behind a small concrete wall. He didn't look at Haughton, but a groan told him the man was still alive.

Without pausing the shots, Luke reached into his pocket and pulled out a stun grenade, glad he'd come prepared. He pulled the pin and tossed it over the wall, then reached down, grabbed Haughton by the upper arm, and dragged him to his feet.

A brief examination revealed he'd taken two shots, one in the leg, one in the stomach, but he was capable of moving, and Luke ran with him in the direction of the helicopter.

There was no sound from behind them and when they reached the cover, he turned to Haughton.

"How badly are you hit?"

"I'll live. Let's get out of here."

He opened the door and managed to scramble into the pilot's seat. Luke strode around to the other side and climbed in as the blades started to whir. Haughton was pale, his face set, but he appeared in control. For a short while, he'd be okay, not that they had any choice. There was no movement from across the rooftop, but they would doubtless have reinforcements on the way.

He took out his cell and punched in Callum's number. "They're after us. We're leaving Flexley by helicopter, and we'll need picking up. I'll leave my phone on—you can track us on the frequency. Haughton's been shot, so we'll need medical supplies."

He put the phone away as they rose into the air. They hovered for a moment, and he looked down onto the roof, finding two men down. "Head out of the city. North."

He kept his eyes peeled for any likely place to land. They were on the outskirts of London, so soon the buildings gave way to farmland. After ten minutes, he called Callum again. "Do you have us?"

"Yeah, Talbot is the nearest. He's heading in your direction. Should be close in another fifteen minutes."

"Okay. I'm going to find somewhere to go

down. Haughton doesn't look good."

Sweat beaded on the man's forehead, and his right hand trembled where it gripped the stick. Luke turned to stare out of the glass and spotted a large flat field that might be a possibility. He touched Haughton's arm and pointed down.

Haughton adjusted the steering so they banked, before leveling up over the center of the field. The helicopter lurched to a landing, but they were down. Haughton switched off the engine and slumped over the controls. Leaning across, Luke placed his fingers to the other man's neck; the pulse was steady, if a little weak.

He unstrapped himself and climbed down, noticing a busy road alongside the field about fifty meters away. On the other side was woodland. He carried the injured man to the shelter of the trees where he could watch the road. After laying Haughton on the ground, he tended the man's wounds with a medical kit he'd pulled from the helicopter.

"Can you walk?"

"I think so."

Luke pulled Haughton to his feet, but when he tried to take a step, the leg gave way beneath him. Luke swore, but caught him before he hit the ground, and pulled him upright. "Keep your hand on my arm. We've only got to get to the road."

There was a ditch between the field and the road,

and he knew Haughton wouldn't make it, so he hefted him over his shoulder and climbed down into the ditch and up the other side.

A helicopter droned in the distance off to the south, giving them only minutes before they were discovered. He put Haughton down; the man swayed but managed to keep to his feet. At that moment, a black truck pulled up beside them, and the door opened. Luke pushed Haughton onto the back seat and climbed in behind him. "Drive."

They pulled away and slid back into the flow of traffic. If the helicopter had satellite coverage of this area, they would pick them up sooner rather than later. At least the traffic was busy. Up ahead was a tunnel.

"Pull over in the tunnel," he told the driver.

• • •

Lauren rested her head against the back of her chair and rubbed her eyes. She hadn't slept in two days, but there was little else she could do now. Everything was in place. Tonight she would move out of the city. London was not somewhere she wanted to be once they released Descartes.

A low knock sounded on the door; she sat up straight as Mark entered. He appeared hesitant, and her eyes narrowed on him. She remained silent as he stopped in front of her desk and stood before her, shifting from one foot to the other.

"You might as well get it over with and tell me," Lauren said. "What's gone wrong?"

"We don't really know."

She gritted her teeth. "Tell me."

"We got the woman, Jenna Young. She's being interrogated at headquarters."

A flicker of unease ran through her. She remembered the photograph of the woman, that hint of recognition. Who was she? And how was she tied in to Descartes? "Has she talked yet?"

"No, but there's something else."

He paused, and her unease flared into anger. "For Christ's sake, Mark, tell me."

"She killed Lynch during the interrogation."

Shock tore through her. Lynch was a sadistic son of a bitch, but he was an excellent interrogator who never took undue risks. "How?"

"I've sent the security film to your monitor."

Lauren leaned across and switched on her computer. Mark came around to stand behind her. The screen flickered to life. A woman lay curled up on the floor of a white tiled cell, her long blond hair covering her face. She wore gray sweatpants and a white T-shirt, torn and stained with blood. "She fainted during the interrogation," Mark said. "Which is itself odd—the drugs should keep her conscious." He leaned across and fast-forwarded the film.

Lauren watched as the woman rose to her feet,

crossed the room, and rinsed her face in the small sink. She was easily recognizable as the woman in the photo—Jenna Young. Lynch entered the room, spoke briefly, ripped her T-shirt, and felt her up. Mark slowed the film again as Lynch pushed her face up against the wall and pulled down her pants.

Jenna moved incredibly fast, whirling and jabbing her elbow into Lynch's throat. Lauren frowned as Lynch was thrown across the room. She pressed the pause button and glanced up at Mark.

"Could the drugs have done something? Given her some sort of adrenaline flash that enhanced her strength?"

"Not according to the doctor. He's never known any reaction like this."

Lauren reached across and restarted the film. Lynch rose to his feet; he looked pissed but not badly hurt. Jenna spun and kicked out, hitting him squarely in the chest, and he went down again. This time he did appear hurt, and Jenna stood back and watched as he stumbled to his feet and collapsed back into the chair. She leaned toward him and spoke.

"What's she saying?" Lauren asked.

"She wants him to scream."

It was obvious he was in no state to make any noise, panic clear on his face as he struggled to breathe. Jenna ripped his shirt and Lauren saw the blood and the white bone protruding from his chest. He died moments later. Jenna banged on the door, finally sliding to the floor. Mark pressed fast-forward, and she watched as Jenna passed out.

"The guards put gas into the room. She lost consciousness."

"Is she alive?"

"Yes. They have her in full restraints, though."

"Did she say anything during the interrogation? Anything at all?"

Mark shook his head.

"A lucky strike?"

"The doctor examined Lynch's body. She broke eight of his ribs. Hardly lucky for Lynch."

Lauren stared at the screen showing the frozen image of the blond woman slumped against the wall, hair falling forward over her face. That same sense of recognition niggled at her insides.

"Do we have a background file on her yet?"

"They've been working on it. I'll go see what they've come up with and send it through to you."

Lauren waited until he'd left the room then got up and poured herself a whiskey. She stood at the window, peered at the bustling city, and gulped the drink in one swallow. When Mark came back into the room, she was pouring a second.

"It should be there now."

After returning to her desk, she scrolled through the report. Jenna Young, twenty-six years old. Mother: Sandra Leavsey, deceased. Father: Dr. Jonathon Young, deceased. She noticed the date of death was recent. A coincidence? She clicked on his name and brought up a photograph.

Shock hit her in the solar plexus, and she released her breath on a gasp.

"What is it?" Mark asked from beside her. "Have you found something?"

For a minute, she couldn't speak while she studied the photograph. He was older, but it was definitely John. She switched to the photograph of Jenna Young and immediately saw the similarities in the bone structure. The narrow nose, the wide generous mouth—but her eyes didn't come from John, they came from her biological mother. She tried to tell herself she was wrong, but the ages matched. Jennifer would have been twenty-six now. If she had lived.

If she had lived? She shook her head. Here was the proof she *had* lived and that John had lied to her.

After they'd terminated the original Descartes project, John had wanted nothing more to do with them or her, and for the first and last time in her life, Lauren had done something not in her or the Conclave's best interests.

She'd let him go, told him how to hide himself, and given him the means to change his identity and become a new man. Merrick had continued to work for them on and off, but John had wanted out. Lauren had helped him because she understood his bitterness. She'd been bitter, too, though she'd never felt the personal connection John had—she'd never allowed herself to.

John hadn't been so important that the Conclave would waste their time hunting him down. Besides, she'd vouched for him and then put him from her mind.

Christ. All this time, and it had never occurred to her that he'd lied.

Twenty-two years ago, he told her he'd terminated the Descartes project. Now here was the proof it still existed. She stared in fascination at the woman on the screen.

"Jesus Christ," she muttered. "What have we made?"

CHAPTER THIRTY-THREE

Luke checked Haughton's pulse as the truck parked in the underground garage of an office block in Canary Wharf not far from their main headquarters. Luke owned the building through a number of untraceable intermediary companies. While most of the floors were rented out to other businesses, the ground floor contained a private clinic and an apartment, and the lower levels holding cells and a secondary control center. Callum waited by the elevator but hurried over as Talbot turned off the engine.

"How is he?"

"Alive but unconscious," Luke answered. "And I need him conscious sooner rather than later."

"The doctor's waiting for him."

Two men wheeled up a trolley, and Luke stepped out of the way, watched as they pulled Haughton from the vehicle and laid him on it. His head rolled to the side and his eyes fluttered open. "My wife? Can I see her?"

Luke stared down at him but felt no pity for the person responsible for the death of hundreds and involved in a plan that would potentially kill thousands. Maybe millions. He had given up the right to be pitied. "Once you've told me what I need to know."

Haughton didn't speak again as they disappeared into the elevator.

Luke ran a hand through his hair and pressed his fingers to his eyeballs.

"You look like shit," Callum said.

"Thanks. I could do with coffee and some food before we start the interrogation."

"You think he'll talk?"

Luke led them into the second elevator and pressed the button for the ground floor apartment. "Hell, yes. He knows he's got no options left. They tried to take him out back there. All he can hope for is to make some sort of deal with us."

"And will you deal?"

"Yes." To get Jenna back he would make a deal with the devil. "How's the wife?"

Callum shrugged. "She's good. I didn't even have to touch her. Just threatened to hurt the kid if she didn't scream nice and loud."

"Where are they?"

"Down in the basement cells. They're fine. You can bet your life they're a damn sight more comfortable than your lady friend right now."

The doors slid open, and he led the way into the kitchen. Luke didn't want to think of where Jenna might be or what she might be going through. His job was to concentrate on getting her back and stopping Descartes. At least now they had a chance. While Haughton wasn't top level, Luke was pretty sure they would get something useful from him that would lead them to Jenna. Hopefully in time.

He'd seen minds totally torn apart by the drugs the Conclave used, and once they decided she knew nothing else, they would kill her and dispose of the body, and he would find no trace of Jenna Young.

By the time the doctor called up to tell him Haughton was stable and they could talk to him, he was on his second coffee.

He stepped into the clinic. Callum followed him and leaned against the door just inside the room. Haughton lay on a trolley with his arm hooked up to an IV; a doctor stood at his side. "My wife?"

Luke shrugged. "She's fine. Frightened but unhurt. So far. When I see my friend, you'll see your wife."

"I told you—I don't know anything about your friend."

"Well you'd better start thinking of a way to find out." He needed to discover where Jenna was being held. Even if Haughton knew nothing about her, there must be a way he could obtain that information. "How do you contact the Conclave?" he asked.

"I don't. They contact me."

Luke wiped all expression from his face, leaned down close to the other man, and whispered in his ear. "You'll get your wife back in pieces if you don't cooperate. I know how that feels. Believe me, you do not want it to happen."

He stepped away, shoving his hands in his pockets as he waited for Haughton to decide. "You'll let us go if I talk?"

Luke shrugged. "If you tell me anything useful."

Haughton took a deep breath. "I have a contact. If anything goes wrong, I have a number I can call."

"What is it?"

He reeled off the number.

"Got it," Callum said from behind him. "I'll go get working on a trace."

"You ever called it?" Luke asked.

"Once."

"Why?"

"I thought someone was investigating the company. Poking their noses where they didn't belong."

"What happened?"

"I rang the number, and the problem went away."

Luke paced the room. The number wouldn't help, but he was sure a man of Haughton's position and intelligence wouldn't blindly follow an organization without at least attempting to discover who was in control.

"And you've never tried to find out more about the Conclave? You've never been curious? Come on, Haughton, you know the number's not going to give us anything."

For a second, some of the old arrogance flashed across his face. "Do you know who and what you're dealing with? How many people are involved in the Conclave? And you expect me to find one woman?"

"If you want to live, you will. Yes, the organization is huge, but I'm guessing there has to be somewhere central, somewhere they do their dirty work, where the low-level soldiers hang out."

Haughton licked his lips "Was she taken in London?"

"Yes."

His gaze darted to the doorway and back to Luke. "Maybe...there might be one place."

"Go on."

"After I phoned in that problem, I had him tailed."

"And?"

"The problem was killed. The men I hired followed the killers."

"What happened to them?"

"I received a phone call." He swallowed nervously. "From my contact at the Conclave. He said my men had been taken care of. They sent me a picture. They'd been tortured, mutilated. They said they would pass on it this time, that it was human nature to be curious, but if I ever got 'curious' again they'd do the same thing to me and my family."

"So, I'm guessing these men passed on some information before they were taken."

Haughton nodded. "They were wearing tracking devices, which they destroyed just before they were captured."

"So the Conclave are unaware you know this location?"

"As far as I know."

"You've never been tempted to make a visit?"

"No."

"The address?"

Luke tried to subdue the excitement rising inside him. He didn't know this was where they were keeping Jenna—it could be a complete waste of time—but his gut instinct told him he'd found her.

He left Haughton and made his way down to the control center, where he found Callum.

"The number's a dead end," Callum said. "It was cancelled an hour ago."

"That makes sense if they know we have Haughton. But he's given us an address. I think it might be a lead." He sat down and tapped in the address. "I want to know everything about this place. I want satellite images, building specs…"

"Do you want me to send someone over there?"

"No. I want nothing that might tip them off. Keep it low key, but get me the information." He glanced at his watch. It was late afternoon; they had only a few hours to prepare this. "We're going in there tonight."

Surprise flared briefly in the other man's face, but he nodded. "I'm on it."

"I'll go back and see what other information we can get out of Haughton. Call me when we have what we need."

CHAPTER THIRTY-FOUR

Was she still alive? Would she even be here, or was he chasing shadows?

Luke willed his mind to blankness. So many thoughts whirled in his head, and he needed to focus. This was the closest he had ever gotten to the Conclave, and Jenna had led him here.

As the vehicle came to a halt, he glanced out of the darkened windows. They were in a parking lot a couple of blocks down from the building. Callum slouched beside him, and on the bench opposite sat three of their best men, all veterans of either the Legion or the British SAS.

They were dressed in full combat gear, with Kevlar vests and weapons belts, carrying silenced weapons and stun grenades.

The back door opened, and Talbot, who was going to be coordinating the attack from the vehicle, jumped in. He made his way between them to the far end and punched a button, and a console swung out from the front of the space, the monitors flickering to life.

"Are you all online?" Talbot spoke softly.

Luke heard him clearly through the comm unit in his ear and nodded. One by one, the other members of the team gave the thumbs-up. Beside him, he could sense Callum's barely leashed excitement.

For many men—Luke included—combat was in their blood. Like a drug, you got so you craved it, and some men reached the point where they couldn't do without the rush. Luke had never gone so far but he, too, felt the stirring of the adrenaline in his veins. A dark excitement that tightened his gut, clenched his muscles, and focused his mind so everything became clearer.

Luke led the way, jumping down from the van into the shadows of the warehouse, before pausing at the edge of the wall to study their target.

The building appeared to be an ordinary office block, but from the intel it went far beneath the ground. No doubt the cells and interrogation units would be beneath them.

So close.

But if Jenna wasn't here, he was back to nothing.

They had identified a point of entry on the third floor. A few lights were dotted on here and there, but the third floor was in darkness. He led the way along the side of the building to where the metal fire escape clung to the wall.

Stefan had hacked in and pulled off the override codes for the security system, and Luke sent up a silent prayer that they were still valid. He pressed the nine-digit code into the keypad, waited until he heard the lock click, and pushed the door open. His shoulders twitched as he waited for the alarms. Nothing happened.

They were in.

"Is there anybody on this floor?" he spoke into the comm unit.

"Not that I can see," Talbot replied. "I'm sending a thermal imaging shot to your cell. I'll update it every thirty seconds."

Luke pulled his cell out of his pocket, punched it on, switching to the incoming image, and flashed through the floors. The imaging showed nobody on either the first, second, or third floors, although there were three people on the ground floor, probably manning the security station. The imaging would not reach underground. Gesturing to the others to follow, he turned and made his way along the corridor to the stairwell.

He reached the door to the ground floor and held up a hand to halt the others, then slipped open the door a few inches and peered around. Three men in security uniforms stood at the far side, faces turned away, talking among themselves. Security was slack, but he reckoned they mainly relied on secrecy to keep this place safe.

Luke slipped the night-vision goggles on. "Now," he murmured down the comm unit, and the building went dark. Outside, through the glass walls, the power had gone off all around them;

even the streetlights were out. The guards might not believe it was a power cut, but the confusion would give them a better chance.

One of the guards stepped up to the glass doors and peered out. He spoke into a radio and then came back to the reception desk, picked up the phone, and made a call.

A minute later, Talbot spoke. "I intercepted a call to the power company. They think the grid is down. You're on."

Luke turned to the others, held up three fingers, and made a cutting motion with his hand.

Callum remained at his side as the other three entered the reception area. They crossed the room silently, each picking a target, and the guards were dispatched, the bodies lowered to the floor and dragged behind the counter in the center of the room.

Luke turned to Callum and nodded. They had thirty minutes until the guards were due to call in, and Luke needed to be out of there and clear by that point. The hum of the backup generator came on. According to their intel, it would cover the elevators, but the cameras in the main building would be down.

Crossing the floor, he punched in the security code and followed Callum into the elevator. They drew their silenced weapons as the doors shut.

He raised his pistol as the elevator came to a

halt. The doors slid open, revealing three security officers. Luke aimed at the one on the right, pulled the trigger, and moved smoothly to the next. Beside him, Callum took out the third, and they dragged the bodies inside and out of sight.

A long corridor stretched ahead of them, the walls white and the lighting a dim orange glow. Luke led the way, hugging the wall as the murmur of voices drifted toward them from up ahead. They came to a doorway and he peered around; four men sat at computer screens. He and Callum pulled gas masks on as he rolled a gas grenade into the room. It went off with a quiet *pfft* of gas and a few seconds later, the men slumped down over their terminals.

He turned to Callum. "Okay, you go for the hard drives and anything else you can find. I'm going to search for Jenna."

A door a little farther on opened into a stairwell to the lower level. At the bottom, he took out another guard. Down here, the air was clean, and he removed his mask while he searched.

The first two rooms were laboratories; he passed them and continued on to a row of cells. All were empty, and he swore softly. She *had* to be here. The alternative was she'd never been here or they had already killed her and disposed of the body. That thought was unbearable, and he pushed on.

At the end of the corridor, he found the interrogation rooms. Jenna was in the second. He peered through the small glass pane in the steel door, and his heart stopped beating. She lay on a steel table in the center of the white-tiled room with her eyes closed, but he could make out the shallow rise and fall of her chest, and some of his tension drained away. Her wrists and ankles were fastened with steel cuffs to the corners of the table, her white T-shirt stained with darkened blood and torn to the waist, exposing her breasts.

He drew his pistol, shot out the lock mechanism on the door, and kicked it in. Her head rolled to face him as he entered the room, and her eyes fluttered open. They widened as she took him in. "Luke?"

"Are you all right?"

She blinked a couple of times. "I'm alive."

He smiled and crossed the room. "I'm glad. We're here to get you out."

Doubt flashed across her face. "Why? I heard you talking to Callum. I was bait, nothing more. Well, it looks like it worked—I got you here."

He could hear the bitterness in her voice. "They have to be stopped. Besides, while I might have started out with the intention of using you, that's not the only reason I'm here. You matter. I don't know why, and it's bloody inconvenient. But you do." He ran a hand through his hair. "Look, we'll talk when we're out of here. I promise, I'll tell you everything I know."

She studied him for a long moment. "Okay."

Luke strode to the foot of the table, unlocked the ankle restraints, and moved to her wrists. She sat up slowly, rubbing her arms.

"How do you feel?" he asked. "Are you okay to get out of here?"

CHAPTER THIRTY-FIVE

Jenna stretched experimentally. The truth was she felt fine, so filled with energy she could almost feel the blood flowing through her veins. She glanced down and saw she was virtually naked from the waist up. Luke's gaze lingered on her, but she didn't bother covering up.

They'd left her alone since she regained consciousness. She'd known it couldn't last, but somehow a strange sense of fatalism had overcome her fear when she'd heard footsteps. Her whole body had tightened in anticipation. Then she'd opened her eyes to see Luke standing in the doorway, and a feeling of overwhelming relief had washed through her body. He had come for her.

Saved her a second time.

Her mouth curved up of its own volition, and he frowned as though she wasn't behaving as expected.

"I'm fine," she said.

"They didn't hurt you?"

She remembered back to the drugs and the agony that had engulfed her body. "A little. I'm okay. I just want out of here. Are we going to make it?"

"Yes."

The soft tread of footsteps sounded. "Luke?" He looked up and caught her eye. "There's someone coming." She nodded to a spot behind him, and he turned slowly.

"Lie back down," he whispered. He drew his pistol and moved so he stood to the side of the door.

Jenna lay back on the cool steel and peeked out from beneath her lashes.

A man hesitated in the open doorway. He wore a shiny silver protective suit and a full face mask. Behind the mask, she recognized the doctor from her interrogation and had to fight the urge to leap up and rip out his throat. A flashback washed over her to how good it had felt as her heel had crushed the other man's chest. How good this would feel, and she had to lock her muscles to stop herself from moving.

The doctor stared at her for a minute, and she held still. He took a tentative step through the door, no doubt wondering why it was open. When he was in the room, Luke moved swiftly. He pressed his gun up against the doctor's side. "Freeze."

The man froze, and Jenna glared at him, allowing the hatred to show clearly in her eyes. Horror blossomed on his face. After swinging herself up into a sitting position, she jumped lightly onto her feet and stepped toward him. Above the mask, his eyes widened until she thought they might bulge out of his head. She liked the idea and allowed a small smile to curve her lips.

When he tried to step back away from her, Luke jabbed him hard with the pistol so he had no choice but to stand his ground.

"Who is he?" Luke asked.

"Doctor Smith. He's the one who carries out the interrogations."

"He hurt you?"

She nodded.

"Take off the mask," Luke said.

The doctor swung round. "What?"

"The mask. There's no gas down here."

"Gas?"

Luke reached across to pull off the mask, and Smith struggled, his hands snatching at his face as he tried to hold it in place. Luke ripped it from him and threw it on the floor. Smith lost control. Ignoring the pistol, he sank to his knees, scrabbling for the mask, which he grabbed at and covered his face with. His breathing was short and sharp, and he stayed on his knees and backed away until he was in the corner of the room, as far from Jenna as he could get.

She took a small step toward him, and he pressed back against the wall. Jenna turned to

Luke and shrugged. A small frown played across his face as he studied the doctor.

"It's safe," he said again. "There's no gas down here."

The doctor's gaze shifted for a fraction of a second to Luke and back to her as though he couldn't look away. His voice came out muffled from behind the mask. "Not gas. It's her." He lifted a trembling finger and pointed at Jenna. "She's poison."

• • •

"Lauren."

She'd dozed off as the car drove them out of London. Now she opened her eyes as Mark spoke her name. He sat on the seat opposite her, a laptop open on his knee, and from his carefully blank expression, something had just gone badly wrong.

"What?"

"The woman, Jenna Young, she's escaped."

She came fully awake "Tell me."

"They broke into the facility where she was being held."

"Who broke in?"

"We don't know. They stole the security feeds and the hard drives."

Lauren's mind raced, working through the implications. Did this compromise the attack? Should they call it off? Her whole mind protested at the idea.

"How did they find her?"

"We don't know."

"Well, what *do* you know?"

"Hockley went to see Gordon Haughton earlier today. When it became obvious Haughton was leaving with him, I gave the order to take him out. The hit failed, and they got away."

"Jesus."

"We didn't think it mattered. Haughton shouldn't have known anything, certainly not the location of headquarters."

"Well, obviously he did. There's something else, as well, isn't there?"

"Smith's missing. We think he was taken at the same time the woman escaped. Either that or he's gone into hiding."

"The doctor? Shit. How the hell did this happen? It must have been Hockley. Goddamn it!"

"It's not so bad. Smith knows very little about the actual attack."

"He knows enough, and he can guess more. Put extra security on the storage facility, just nothing too overt. I don't want to draw attention to the place."

"We have helicopters stationed nearby. I'll put them on alert. They can be there within minutes."

"Good. But let's see if we can find them before

it comes to that."

She sat back. What was the relationship between Jenna Young and Hockley? Had he gone in tonight to save her, or was the doctor his real target? Trying to ease the ache before it could take hold, she pressed her fingers to her forehead. One thing was sure—they needed to get Jenna Young off the streets.

"The woman—I don't care how, but I want her found. And if Hockley goes anywhere near the storage facility, kill him. And this time, make sure he stays dead."

CHAPTER THIRTY-SIX

"Where are we going?" Jenna asked. "Back to the apartment?"

She felt sick and shaky. She hoped it was just a reaction to getting out, a sort of relief, but Smith's words echoed through her mind.

She's poison.

He'd refused to say any more and had gone into a fit of panic when Luke had forcefully divested him of the mask. After that, he'd made no sense. Luke had cuffed him and dragged him along with them. He was somewhere in the vehicle following.

Beside her, Luke glanced away from the road. He frowned. "No. The apartment's been compromised."

"That was my fault, wasn't it? I told the police. I should have trusted you."

He shrugged. "Why should you? I lied. In the circumstance, I would have done the same. But tell me, how did you know? I thought we were close, but you vanished."

"I overheard you talking with Callum. You said you were using me. As bait."

This time he turned and stared at her. "How? We closed the door. You couldn't have overheard us."

"I don't know, but that morning I woke up and everything felt different. All my senses more acute. I thought maybe my medication had been having some sort of effect, suppressing my senses, and I was hearing normally for the first time."

His eyes narrowed as he considered her. "Being able to hear through a concrete wall is *not* normal."

She laid her head against the back of the seat. "Then I don't know, but I did hear. I got out of there and phoned the police. They told me David didn't have a cousin." She studied his profile, the lean, handsome face. "Who are you, Luke? For that matter is your name even Luke?"

"Almost. Lucien Hockley. Look, I'll tell you everything when we get to a safe place. Why don't you rest for now?"

She closed her eyes but saw again the terror on the doctor's face. "What did he mean? That I'm poison?"

"I have no idea, but we'll get the truth out of him. Did they use any drugs on you?"

"Yes."

"Well that's probably it. Maybe there's some residual effect as the chemicals clear from your body."

If that had been the case, the man she had killed would have worn a mask. He certainly hadn't thought she was poisonous. In fact, he'd been quite willing to get very close to her. No, something had happened between then and when the doctor had come back. He had found out something that terrified him.

Something about her.

• • •

"How is she?" Callum asked.

"She seems fine. Physically at least." Luke frowned. The Conclave had held her for nearly two days, yet she seemed to have suffered no physical harm. She said she'd been interrogated, they'd used drugs, yet there was no evidence of any intravenous injections.

"So, why don't you seem happy about it?"

"I am, I just don't understand, and I hate it when I don't understand."

"You think she might be some sort of plant? That she's working for them? Could they have let us take her?"

"I've thought about it, but the fact is, if she *were* a plant, they would have made it far more convincing. She would have looked like she'd been interrogated." He ran a hand through his hair. He was getting a weird feeling about this. "What about the doctor? Where is he?"

"Locked in one of the basement rooms. Screaming we're all going to die, that we have to let him out. He's babbling. He claims some guy called Lynch broke her nose."

Luke's fists clenched at his side. "Where is this Lynch?"

"Well that's the other thing. Smith claims your girlfriend killed him. He reckons he's never seen anything like it."

"Well, let's give him an hour or so to calm down, and then we'll question him. Have you started going through the stuff you picked up?"

"No. I'd rather leave it to the experts. If the hardware's been encrypted or booby-trapped, Stefan is more likely to pick it up. You know, they're going to be on to us by now."

"I figure they've been on to us longer than that, but we should be okay here for a while. This house is hard to trace back to us."

• • •

Jenna lay curled on the crimson velvet cover of the four-poster bed, huddled in a robe she'd found in the adjoining bathroom. Luke had told her to rest, but there was no way she was going to sleep, and besides, she didn't feel tired; she felt alert, wide awake, and hungry. She wanted food, and then she wanted to know what was happening and why. Luke had promised he would tell her what he knew.

When she was about to get up and go hunt for

him, there was a quiet knock on the door, and Luke poked his head in. "I thought you might have trouble sleeping."

"You thought right."

He came in and shut the door behind him. He'd showered, his dark hair damp, and he'd changed into faded jeans and an olive shirt. Something warm stirred to life deep in the pit of her stomach when she looked at him. He might have set out to use her at the start, but he'd saved her last night. "Thank you," she said.

A startled expression flashed across his face. "For what?"

"For saving me. A second time." Something that might have been guilt flickered across his features, but he shrugged it off. Crossing the room, he placed a mug of coffee on the table beside her and stared down at her for long moments. "You look good," he said.

"I feel good. And I don't understand it."

"What don't you understand?"

"This, for a start." She lifted her hand and waggled her fingers at him. "It should have taken weeks to heal."

His face was blank for a moment, and she realized he'd forgotten about her broken finger. Then shock flashed across his features. He reached out and took her hand in his, turned it over, and studied it, a frown forming between his brows.

"How long has it been like this?"

"Since the morning after…" She paused. She'd been going to say the morning after they'd made love, but suddenly she felt shy. "Since the morning I went to the police. I woke up, and it was fine."

"This ties in with something *I* didn't understand. You were interrogated, but there's not a mark on you." He stroked a finger down over her cheek. "Smith said you had a broken nose."

"They used drugs, and one of them hit me. I thought it was broken, but…" She trailed off. "Has the doctor said anything else?"

"Nothing that makes sense. Yet. We'll talk to him later."

She remembered the red-hot agony as the drug had coursed through her body. "Good." She picked the mug up from the table as Luke sat on the bed at her side. "Where are we?" she asked. "I couldn't tell in the dark last night."

"We're about forty miles south of London. We should be safe here for a while, but they're going to come after us. We need to find out how you're connected or this thing will never go away."

She sipped her coffee. "I was lying there thinking about it, and the more I think, the more it doesn't make sense. I feel like my head is about to explode, but otherwise, I feel fine. Really great. Which doesn't make sense, either." She bit her lip. "There's something else—I killed a man."

"Smith mentioned it." Head cocked to one side, he considered her. "How are you with that?"

She searched inside herself. Did she feel any guilt? "I feel good. He deserved to die, but that's not it. I killed him with one kick. I shouldn't be able to do that."

He didn't answer, and she finished the coffee and put the mug down. "Will you tell me what you know? Tell me who you are?"

"Of course."

"But first, do you think I could have some food? I'm starving."

He grinned. "You want to get up?"

"Yes, please."

Rising to his feet, he held out a hand. "Come on, then. We can talk in the kitchen."

She followed him through the house and down the broad stairway. The place appeared to be some sort of manor house, beautifully decorated in period style. It felt like a home and not a hideaway.

Finally, they entered a big open kitchen, and Jenna sat on one of the seats around the wooden table. Luke placed crusty bread, butter, and cheese in front of her. Jenna's stomach rumbled, and she tore off a chunk of bread, spread it with butter, and bit into it.

After pouring them both more coffee from the machine, Luke sat down opposite her. She ate in silence for a few minutes, and when her immediate hunger was satisfied, she sat back, cradling the mug of coffee. "Tell me," she ordered.

A flicker of amusement flashed across his face. "Tell you what?"

"Everything. Who you are, for a start. How you got involved in all this."

He stared into her face, as if unsure where to start.

"At the beginning would be good," she said.

Surprise flared in his eyes. "From the beginning, huh? Well, you'd better make yourself comfortable."

Jenna made to settle back in her seat but changed her mind, got up, and refilled her cup. She brought the pot to the table and refilled Luke's then sat back down. "I'm ready."

"I come from a wealthy background. My mother died when I was young, so my father brought me up. We were close. I was supposed to go to Harvard when I was eighteen, but my father killed himself a month after my eighteenth birthday."

Shock ripped through her. "What?"

"I was…surprised. I just couldn't believe he wouldn't have talked to me. I went a little off the rails for a while."

The connection clicked in her mind. "You joined the French Foreign Legion."

"I was a hotheaded idiot, but the Legion was good for me. It taught me discipline. After I got out, I visited Callum in London and met his sister."

He paused and took a drink of coffee.

"Callum has a sister? I somehow can't picture him with family."

Pain flashed in his face. "*Had* a sister. Leah is dead."

"How?"

He gave her a small smile that didn't clear the bleakness from his eyes. "You're getting ahead of yourself. Leah and I were married a month after we met and a year later, she gave birth to our daughter—Madeleine. Things were going well until I had a visit from an agent with the CIA. She claimed my father hadn't committed suicide but had been murdered. I called Callum, asked him to come over, help me look into it. We started digging into everything—my father's last months, his business dealings, his personal life. At first we didn't find much, but then I was given a letter. My father had left it for me in the event that I was investigating his death. In it, he told me he'd been approached by someone to join a group. A group whose sole concern was the amassing of wealth and power."

Luke rose to his feet. He ran his hands through his dark hair then shoved them into his pockets and paced the room. Coming to a halt across from her, he leaned against the counter and continued.

"Once we knew where to search, we found signs of an organization—the Conclave—that had a hand in everything; government, policy making, military. I knew I couldn't take it on alone, and we were no longer safe. We set it up that I was going to 'die,' along with my family, and we'd take on new identities."

Jenna felt a sense of dread rise up inside her. She knew where this was going. "What happened?" she whispered.

"We didn't move fast enough. They set a car bomb. It was supposed to kill me. Instead, Leah and Maddy were killed."

Jenna pushed out her chair and stood up. She crossed the room, wrapped her arms around Luke's waist, and hugged him close. For a minute, his arms tightened around her, then he held her away gently. "We need to finish this."

She nodded.

"They were killed outright. Callum was in the car behind. He managed to pull me out, but there was nothing we could do for them." He rubbed at the back of his neck, and Jenna could see the remembered agony in his eyes. "With the help of a CIA contact, we faked my death. Lucien Hockley died and Luke Grafton was born."

"I'm sorry. About your wife and baby."

"It was ten years ago. In the past."

"There are some things you never get over." At least that explained his aversion to relationships. It was probably just as well.

"Maybe." He shrugged. "Anyway, we've spent the last ten years going after them, but the whole setup is based on secrecy. At the lower level, no one knows anyone but their immediate contacts, above and below. People are recruited, and they themselves select a suitable candidate."

"Do you think that's what happened to your father?"

"Without a doubt. But if they'd researched him closely, they would have known he would never be involved in such an immoral organization."

Jenna frowned. "But what do they want? Is it political? Religious?"

"Neither, as far as we can tell. From the intel we've gathered, the Conclave crosses all political beliefs and religions. I've come to believe their only creed is power."

"I still don't understand where I come into this. And how did David get involved?"

"A few weeks ago, we captured a low-level soldier of the Conclave. There was little he could tell us—"

"You tortured him?"

He looked surprised at the question. "We persuaded him that it was in his best interests to talk. Do you think that makes us as bad as them?"

She thought about the question, about what had been done to David. What they had tried to do to her and to Luke, whose whole life had been changed beyond comprehension by their activities. How good it had felt when she killed the man who tried to rape her, and she realized she would do it again in a second. They needed to be stopped, and somebody needed to have the guts to stop them.

"No. You got no pleasure from whatever you did." A shudder ran through her as she remembered the sadistic pleasure in the doctor's eyes as he injected her with his chemicals.

Luke studied her, his face serious. "You know that for sure?"

She smiled. "Oh yes." She sat, and Luke followed her and sank down opposite. "Go on," she said.

"He told us something big was going down, code-named Descartes. He didn't know what or when, just that it would be soon, and he also gave us the name of his contact in London, a Lee Carson. When we picked up Carson's trail, he was following a man. A Dr. Griffith."

"David," Jenna murmured. "But that still doesn't explain why."

"I presume he must have done an internet search and it was picked up. Carson questioned him about Descartes. Under torture, Griffith revealed it was somehow linked to a patient. You. I assumed the identity of his cousin—"

"You had photographs of the two of you together." He raised an eyebrow and she scowled. "Okay, I'm being naïve. I guess that sort of thing is easy."

"Very easy. I went to see you. Unfortunately, you refused to cooperate. I had to find some way to make you trust me. I sent some of my men in to frighten you, with the intention of rescuing you and gaining your trust, but they got there too late. When they arrived, you already had visitors. We came in as fast as we could."

"Would your men have tortured me?"

"No. You were never supposed to be hurt. I haven't sunk that low yet."

"Because I'm a woman?"

"No, because you're an innocent."

He fell silent. Why was she so shocked? Why should he have thought twice about frightening her when he didn't even know her? When she was his last lead on a mission that had driven him for ten years?

And really, if he hadn't sent his men after her, they wouldn't have found her in time and likely she'd be dead by now. It wouldn't have been an easy death. All the same, she couldn't quite shake the sense of betrayal or completely ignore the tears that burned her eyes. She blinked and forced the feeling down.

He reached across the table and took her hand in his, stroking his thumb against her palm. "If it makes you feel any better, for the first time in over ten years I actually felt guilty. I was furious with myself. I should have never let you out of my sight after the first moment I met you. I knew you were involved, and I put you in harm's way."

She thought about pulling her hand free, but it felt too good. "Yes, it makes me feel better. Finish the story. Did you find out anything when I was gone? Did you get anything valuable from the place I was held?"

"We got the hard drives from the facility where you were kept; they're being analyzed now."

"How did you find me, anyway?"

"After you went to the police, we got some information that something relating to the Conclave had just gone down in Ivory Coast. We followed the lead and found a whole village had been wiped out by some sort of bioweapon. We think it was a test for something bigger."

"A village? How could they do that?"

"I don't know. We were able to follow the trail to a company in the UK. The owner fit the Conclave profile perfectly—"

"They have a profile?"

"Yes. It's not foolproof, but it allows us to pinpoint probable members. We persuaded this man to talk, and he gave us information that led us to you."

"Thank you. I know you didn't have to come for me."

His hand tightened on hers. "Yes, I did."

He was silent for a moment, but she sensed there was more. "What is it?"

"You remember we were investigating your father?"

She'd hated the idea, but she realized her father must be tied in to Descartes somehow. He'd been there at the start of it all. She rubbed her arms, suddenly chilled. "Did you find anything?"

"Yes. That up until twenty-two years ago Dr. Jonathon Young did not exist."

"I don't understand." Whatever she'd been expecting, it wasn't this.

"Oh, it was cleverly done. He must have had help. We had to dig deep to get the truth."

A sudden coldness filled her with dread. "So who was he? And why did he have to change his identity?"

"His name was John Creighton. We traced him through Merrick. They both went to Cambridge University—your father studying medicine, Merrick biochemistry—and later they worked together in a research facility."

"Are you sure it's him?"

Luke nodded. "We have photographs of

Creighton and Merrick."

She picked up her empty cup, got up, and filled it with coffee, more for something to do than because she wanted it. Her whole background was a lie, and suddenly she was scared of what she might discover. Then something else occurred to her.

"My mother? Who was she? Was my dad married at the time?" Had he left his wife behind when he took on the new identity? Is that why he would never talk about her mother?

Luke got up and came to stand beside her. "There is no record of John Creighton ever marrying."

"That doesn't make sense."

"There's more, Jenna. There's no record of him ever having a child. There is no record of your existence at all."

CHAPTER THIRTY-SEVEN

Jenna stepped backward and sank into the chair behind her. "Are you saying I don't exist? That he wasn't my father?" She searched Luke's face for the truth.

He shook his head. "That's what we originally thought, but we ran both your photographs through facial recognition software, which can be used to compare features and pick up similarities. There's no doubt your father is a close relative. In fact, if you study the pictures we have of John Creighton, you can see the resemblance, the bone structure especially. We can maybe try to find a source of DNA for him, but I don't think the relationship is in question."

"So where did I come from? Why is there no record of my birth?"

"We don't know, but we're researching it. We're also looking into what your father was working on with Merrick. We're pretty sure the company was a cover for the Conclave, but we still don't know what sort of research they were doing."

The information was going around and around in her head. A sudden jab of pain stabbed at her temple. Jenna pressed a finger against the point, but the pain only intensified. She rose shakily to her feet.

"I think I need to lie down. I don't feel so good."

Luke reached out a hand, but it dropped back down to his side before he touched her. "Jenna, none of this has any bearing on who you are."

"Yes, it does. It has every bearing."

Without waiting for him to say anything further, she turned and left the room.

She made her way back up to the bedroom and lay down on the bed, her eyes screwed up tight. Rolling onto her side, she hugged her knees to her chest.

What was happening to her?

Inside, she was changing. But into what?

Who was she? She flexed her fingers, feeling the strength. *What* was she?

She burrowed her face into the softness of the pillow.

"Jenna?"

She hadn't heard the door open.

Luke stood just inside the room, hands shoved in his pockets. "Are you okay?"

"I honestly don't know. I don't know what's happening to me."

"You need to forget for a while."

She gave a small rueful smile. "Forgetting would be good."

He took a few steps closer so that he was standing beside the bed, looking down at her through half-closed eyes. Something hot awoke deep inside her, uncoiling in her belly and clenching the muscles tight.

He held her gaze as his hands went to the buttons of his shirt. "I can make you forget."

Jenna sat up, peeled the robe from her body, and dropped it on the floor at his feet. Swinging her legs from the bed, she stood up and took a step toward him.

"Make me forget, Luke."

Jenna's face pressed up tight against his chest, and she smiled into his skin.

Her whole body tingled with the aftermath of pleasure, her limbs boneless, her mind at peace. For a little while at least.

Soon she would have to think again, try to unravel the secrets of the past. As Luke had said to her earlier, until she did that, she would never be free.

"You're thinking again," he whispered into her hair.

"No, I'm not." She pushed herself away slightly and came up on one elbow, allowing her gaze to wander over the length of him. Here and there were the scars of a life spent fighting. A raised burn ran down his right side, she guessed from the crash that killed his wife. She stroked her finger along the scar that ran down over his left shoulder.

"What's this?" she asked.

"Machete cut."

She winced. "Nasty. And this?" She pressed her palm over a small round scar an inch to the right of his navel. "Let me guess—bullet—must have hurt."

"Didn't feel a thing."

"Liar."

He cupped her face in his hand. "I just want you to know, I've been honest with you. From now on, I'll keep you safe. I won't put you in harm's way again."

She frowned. "Yes, you will, if that's what it takes to stop this thing."

"We'll find another way."

"No. We have to finish this."

"I won't lose someone else I care about to the Conclave."

At his words, her gaze flew to his face, and she saw the sincerity in his eyes.

"You won't lose me," she said, though she suspected the words were a lie. She knew she would do whatever was necessary to find the truth, and there was a good chance one or both of them would not come out of it alive.

Always in the past, she had held herself aloof from any man whom she might come to care for. She'd considered herself a liability, hadn't wanted to fall in love and have that love tested when she became ill, which had seemed inevitable. How could she have asked any man to put up with that?

But her father had lied about everything else. What if he had also lied about her illness? What if she didn't have a genetic disorder, but the medicine he gave her was for something else, something he hadn't wanted to explain? How better to get her obedience than to terrify her with promises of dire consequences should she fail to take it.

The phone beside the bed rang. Luke gave a rueful smile and picked it up. Jenna heard Callum's voice on the other end of the line.

"There's a video I think you should see, and we've found the security tapes on the hard drive. You need to come and look."

Luke sighed. "I'll be there in five minutes." He put the phone down. "I have to go."

"I heard, and I'm coming with you."

He opened his mouth to argue but must have seen the determination in her face, because he shut it again. Standing up, he stretched and held out a hand to her.

"We've no clothes for you, but come along to my room. I'll find you something to put on, and I'll get someone to pick up some things up for you." He pulled her in close and breathed in. "Hmm, you smell of sex. We can shower, as well. No reason to give Callum any more cause to piss me off."

CHAPTER THIRTY-EIGHT

Callum glanced up as they entered the room. His eyes narrowed as he saw Jenna, but he didn't say anything. He was seated at a computer and gestured to the chairs next to him.

Jenna hitched up her black sweatpants. They were rolled over about four times at the waist but the oversized T-shirt hung almost to her knees and covered them.

Sinking into a chair, she waited, anxiety gnawing at her insides. Callum had mentioned the security tapes, and she knew he must mean the ones of her interrogation. Did she want to see them and bring it all back?

Luke sat next to her; Callum pressed a button, and the monitor flickered to life.

"Ivory Coast. Field Test Four. Day One 1000 hours."

The screen switched to show an African village. The villagers were all huddled in the center, crouching in the dirt. Women, children, men. They didn't appear alarmed but were chatting and laughing among themselves. The camera panned out. Men in silver Hazmat suits, masks covering their heads and faces, surrounded the village. They all wore what she guessed were breathing apparatuses strapped to their backs.

One of them moved forward into the center of the village, carrying a cylinder. When he set it down inside the circle and flicked open the top, a faint trail of gas spiraled into the air.

The villagers stirred uneasily. A man rose to his feet and backed away. One of the guards surrounding them approached him and spoke, and the man returned to the circle.

Jenna felt a hard ball of fear twist in her guts. She didn't want to watch but couldn't make herself look away.

"Ivory Coast. Field Test Four. Day One 1400 hours."

Most of the villagers were down, lying prostrate in the dirt. One rose unsteadily to his feet and stumbled out of the circle. This time the guards made no pretense, just knocked him with the rifle butt so he collapsed to the ground. The camera closed in on him, showing bloodshot eyes, crimson seeping from open sores on the dull black skin.

"Ivory Coast. Field Test Four. Day One 1800 hours."

There was virtually no movement now. They lay either dead or too sick to move. Jenna blinked back the tears that stung her eyes. The men in suits walked among them, occasionally removing a body, dragging them away as though they hadn't been living, healthy human beings only hours earlier. She watched blankly until the final moments when the bodies were all cleared and the village was set alight.

Doctor Smith's face appeared. "Field test four was a complete success, one hundred percent mortality rate. Within twelve hours, all participants were dead. We tested the area at hourly intervals; all traces of the chemical were gone within a further six hours. It is my recommendation that the product is ready for active use."

The screen went blank. This time it stayed blank.

Jenna leaned back against her seat. Who were the people who had done this? What did they want so badly that life became meaningless?

She turned to Luke. "He said field test four. Does that mean they did this before? Why?"

"We think they plan a major attack on one or more of the big cities—London, probably, and maybe New York. As a statement. 'Show the world what we can do' sort of thing, but there has to be a bigger plan behind it. We just can't see it yet." He swiveled his chair to face Callum. "What else have you got?"

"Now for something more entertaining," Callum said. "We'll start with this one. There are earlier ones but nothing much happens. The one in the lab coat is our friend currently residing downstairs; the other man is named Lynch and, according to the doctor, he's dead." His gaze shifted to Jenna. She kept her face expressionless. "There's one interesting thing—neither the doctor nor Lynch are wearing masks here. So whatever made the doctor decide you were poisonous came after this."

Jenna watched the screen, wincing only when Lynch punched her in the face. After what she had seen in the African village, her interrogation seemed almost trivial, but beside her, Luke's hands tightened on the arms of his chair.

"Bastard," he muttered.

Callum paused the film and turned to her. "Your nose is definitely broken." He frowned and studied her closely. "You don't have a double, do you?"

"Not that I know of."

He shrugged but switched the film back on. The drugs hit her system and she screamed. Beside her, Luke tensed again but didn't move. She kept her attention on the screen—this was the part she didn't remember.

She went crazy, thrashing and fighting the restraints. First one of the straps holding her into the chair snapped, and the doctor and Lynch backed out of the room.

"Do you remember this?" Luke asked.

She shook her head. The second restraint

broke, and she hurled herself to the floor, finally curling into a fetal ball and going still.

"Anything to say?" Callum asked.

"No."

He reached across and pressed a couple of buttons. "Well, if you liked that, you'll love this one."

The screen came to life. Jenna saw herself standing at the sink in the white tiled room. She swallowed the lump in her throat as she realized what was coming next.

Her hands gripped the arms of her chair as the door opened, and Lynch walked in, locking it behind him. Watching the scene play out, she felt again the rage that had built up inside her. She moved incredibly swiftly, the force of her first blow knocking him off his feet. Keeping her gaze fixed, she watched the rest of the film. When she slumped unconscious against the door, Callum switched it off and turned to her.

"What the hell are you? Some sort of bionic woman?"

"Leave her alone," Luke snapped.

Callum shoved his chair back and rose to his feet. For a minute, he paced the room, and Jenna could sense the frustration emanating from his tense figure. Finally, he came to a halt in front of Luke. "You've got to admit, that"—he waved a hand toward the blank screen—"is not normal."

"No, maybe not. But it's also not Jenna's fault. She's as much in the dark about this as we are."

"Maybe." Callum turned to her, one eyebrow raised. "I'd like to try something."

He sat at a small table, glanced at Jenna, then at the seat opposite. She frowned but got to her feet, crossed to the table, and sank onto the chair indicated. Until he put his right elbow on the table and flexed his fist, she had no clue what he intended.

She stared at him in amazement. "You want to arm wrestle?"

"Let's just say I'm interested."

"Callum…" Luke spoke warningly from behind her, but she shook her head.

"No, he's right. It is weird, and I want to understand what's happening."

She put her elbow on the table and slipped her hand into Callum's, and his fingers tightened around her. He didn't trust her, and she didn't blame him, but she felt instinctively that he would like to hurt her. Not like the doctor. Callum didn't usually enjoy causing pain, but he would make an exception for her, because he felt she jeopardized their work, and how could she blame him? And maybe he was a little bit jealous that she had some of Luke's attention.

"Ready?" he asked.

When she nodded, his hand tightened on hers.

She allowed him to move hers a little just to get the feel of him. Then she stopped him. It was so easy. One minute her hand was being lowered, the next it...stopped.

She stared into Callum's face, saw his eyes widen in shock, as she gently but inexorably pressed his hand onto the wood of the table.

Pulling her hand free, she looked at him steadily. "Best of three?"

"What are you?"

She rubbed her palm down her pants. "I don't know—that's the truth."

A hand touched her on the shoulder, and she glanced up to see Luke standing over her. "Have you always been this strong?"

"No. I woke up the morning after Merrick's death, and I felt wonderful. My hand was healed, my senses were more acute."

"That's how you overheard the conversation between me and Callum."

"I also noticed when I ran away that I could run faster, for longer."

"But you don't know why?" The question came from Callum.

She took a deep breath. "I think it's to do with the medicine my father gave me. He told me it was treating a genetic illness, but I think he lied. The night Merrick died I didn't take any for the first time in as long as I remember. It must have been suppressing this." She gestured to the table. "That's all I can think of."

"I've never heard of any pill that could do this," Callum said.

She gave him a nasty look. "That doesn't mean it doesn't exist."

Callum's cell phone rang, and he picked it up and listened. "The doctor's ready for interrogation."

"Good," Luke replied.

Prickles of ice shivered across her skin. What did the doctor know about her? What would they discover? Part of her wanted to run and hide and pretend all this wasn't happening. But the rest of her knew she had to discover the truth, however difficult it was to take. "I'm coming," Jenna said.

Luke studied her for a moment then said, "Let's go."

CHAPTER THIRTY-NINE

The basement had been transformed into a series of cells. Luke led them through a steel door and into a room about ten feet by ten feet. A chair stood in the middle, into which the doctor was strapped.

He looked up as they entered, panic flaring as he caught sight of Jenna.

"Don't let her in here. I told you I'd talk—just get her out."

Luke turned to her. She glared at the doctor with hatred in her eyes. This wasn't doing her any good, and they needed the doctor's cooperation sooner rather than later. "Jenna, come with me?"

She frowned but followed him out of the room and through a second door.

"This is an observation room." He pressed a switch and a window appeared in the far wall. It looked into the cell where the doctor was secured. "You can see and hear everything from here." He picked up one of the comm units from the counter and slipped it in his ear. "If you want to ask anything, hold this button down, and you can talk to me."

He turned to leave.

"Luke?"

"Yes."

"Will you ask him about me? About what he said?"

"Of course."

She caught her lower lip between her teeth and chewed. Suddenly he had an inkling of how she must feel. Jenna was one of the strongest people emotionally he had ever met, but right now she was confused and afraid. He crossed the room and wrapped his arms around her, held her close. "We'll get to the bottom of this. There will be an explanation."

She pulled free and stepped back, a rueful smile on her lips. "I know—but not, I suspect, one I'm going to like."

He forced a smile of his own. "Look on the bright side. At least it looks like you don't have Huntington's."

"You're right. Now all we need to find out is what I do have."

"It will be all right."

He turned and left the room, wondering what he'd discover about her. He forced aside his worries over Jenna. They were close. He could feel it. This was their chance to cut off the hydra's head and end the Conclave forever. If Dr. Smith could lead them to Descartes, they would have a bargaining chip.

He reentered the cell and nodded once to

Callum.

Callum was more experienced at interrogation techniques, but Luke didn't think they were going to have to get nasty with the doctor, which was unfortunate.

He wondered how much pain the man had dispensed in his time working for the Conclave. Luke had seen his pleasure as he injected Jenna with his chemicals. Leaning against the wall, he fixed his gaze on Smith's face.

"Tell us about Descartes," Callum said.

Shock flared in his face as though he hadn't been expecting the question. "Descartes?" His voice caught on the word. "I thought you wanted to talk about the woman."

"Descartes and the woman. How are they linked?"

His gaze darted around the room, came back to Callum. "I don't know."

Luke pushed himself off the wall, crossed the room, and crashed his fist into the doctor's face. The bone crunched beneath his knuckles, and blood spurted from the broken nose. "That's for Jenna. To start with."

Callum stepped closer and leaned his face close to Smith's. "You agreed to talk. So talk. Or we will find a way to make you." He lifted his hand to show a syringe filled with a pale yellow liquid. "We took this from your lab, and I'm dying to see how it works."

Smith stared at the syringe as if mesmerized. "I'm telling the truth. I don't know the link. That's why we had her, why Lynch had orders to interrogate her. She was somehow tied into Descartes. She knew the name when she shouldn't have, but we didn't know how. And she didn't talk."

"Right, so tell us about Descartes. What is it?"

"I told you—I don't know."

"We've just watched a video of you in Ivory Coast. Ring any bells?"

"If you saw the film, you know I was there, but that's not Descartes, or at least, I'd never heard it called by that name. I'd never heard the word Descartes until Lynch started the interrogation of the woman. It meant nothing to me."

Luke frowned. Perhaps the doctor wasn't aware of the imminent terrorist attack—that would fit with the way the Conclave usually worked—allowing the players to know only what they needed and no more. "So what was the gas, where did it come from?"

"I was told it was a by-product of some other experiment, produced by accident, and they needed to know what it could do."

"What did they plan to use it for?"

"I don't know. That's not my job."

Callum leaned in closer. He lifted the syringe,

reached across, and pushed up the man's sleeve, baring his forearm. Smith stared at it, for the first time fighting against his restraints.

"No, wait. That's not how we work. You must know that. Nobody knows the full picture."

"Nobody?"

"Well, somebody at the top, but we never see them, never hear from them directly."

Luke stepped up close, and the doctor eyed him warily. "I don't believe you."

His eyes bulged. "What?"

"Even in an organization as secretive as the Conclave, things get out. Nothing can remain that secret. Somebody always talks."

Smith remained silent. Luke looked at him, pictured his smug face on the video in Ivory Coast. Rage rose up inside him, and he leaned in close. "If you don't tell us what we want to know, I'll let Jenna continue this interrogation. I'll lock you in here with her for as long as it takes."

When the doctor remained silent, he straightened and turned to the two-way mirror. "Jenna, would you like to join us?"

"No, I'll talk. Keep her out of here and I'll talk."

"Good. Perhaps we can start again. What do you know about Descartes?"

"Okay, I'll tell you what I've heard over the years. The rumors started in the 1970s. I know that much."

Luke frowned at the words. He hadn't realized Descartes went back so far.

He'd found evidence the Conclave went back hundreds of years in one form or another, and he believed it was headed up by hereditary members. It had started with one powerful family, and today, at its head would be the last of that family. But why did the 1970s sound important? What had happened back then? He concentrated hard, running the information he had learned over the past few weeks about Descartes. There was something important, and he remembered.

In April 1972, Apollo 16 had touched down on the Descartes Highlands on the moon.

He ran a hand through his hair, trying to tie that in with everything else he'd learned. He didn't believe in coincidences. He turned back to the doctor.

"What else?"

"Not much, and I'm telling the truth. The only other thing I heard was…" He paused. "It's a rumor only. I never heard anything to substantiate it…"

"Get on with it," Callum said.

"I heard it all began with something they brought back from one of the lunar landings."

"What?"

"I don't know." He glanced at the two-way

mirror. "I really don't know."

Unfortunately, Luke believed him. Maybe there was some other way to find out. Perhaps it was part of public record, something they had brought back, some mineral or chemical found only on the moon. If not public record, perhaps one of the astronauts could tell them what had been found.

It didn't help answer the question of how Jenna fit into all this, though. Maybe it was time to find out.

"What do you know of the woman, Jenna Young?"

The doctor's gaze flashed to the two-way mirror as though he could see Jenna sitting on the other side. His face twitched and his hands tightened on the arms of the chair. "Nothing."

"Come on, you told us she was 'poison.' Hardly 'nothing.' If you'd never seen her before or heard of her before, why would you say that?"

He licked his lips. "After she killed Lynch, I sent the tapes upward. I don't know where they go, but we have a protocol we follow if we want to move information fast."

Luke made a mental note to get the details of that protocol, but he didn't want to interrupt the doctor's flow. "Go on."

"I got a call back within the hour. They said to test her, but to take maximum precautions, to presume she was toxic. I was on my way to start the tests when you took me."

Luke glanced toward the two-way mirror. "You have any more questions?" he asked.

Her voice came through the comm unit. "Ask him what sort of poison he was testing for."

Luke turned back to the doctor. "What were you to test for?"

He appeared surprised at the question. "A variation of the same poison we used in Ivory Coast."

"That doesn't make sense. Jenna hasn't been exposed to the poison. Why should she be infected?"

"I wasn't to test for infection. I was to test for production. I was told she could be producing the poison."

Shock numbed his mind for a moment. He shook his head. It didn't make sense. Or maybe it did. Maybe she was somehow involved in the original experiment; she would have been a child, only four when her father did his vanishing act. Would she remember anything? He glanced again at the mirror, forced what he hoped was a reassuring smile.

"How do you do this test? Can you do it here?"

"Yes. But I need certain chemicals."

Luke shoved his hands in his pockets and

turned away while he thought about where to go next. He decided to leave the Jenna question for the moment.

"You worked on the poison?"

Smith looked wary, but he nodded.

"Where are the stocks kept?"

"Usually they're spread around the country, but they've been moving them recently to a secret location."

"Where?"

"I don't know. I didn't need to know." He blinked rapidly, his eyes flickering to the mirror. "But there's a laboratory outside London. It's the only place with storage facilities for larger amounts. It must be there."

"We believe the gas is going to be used for an attack on London sometime in the next few days. Would you say there's enough for that?"

"There's more than enough to take out a whole city. More than one. We were told to put together two separate shipments."

"Can you give us the location of the laboratory?"

"Yes."

"And is that the only stock of the poison?"

"I don't know. It's the only one I know of, but they could have been developing it elsewhere."

"Tell me a bit about it. I saw the film—it resembles some sort of Ebola derivative."

"The symptoms might seem like Ebola, but it isn't. It's like nothing I've ever seen." He looked up and met Luke's gaze. "Like nothing on Earth."

Luke considered the words. "You think they first found it on the moon."

"Maybe. There are molecules in there I've never seen before."

"Is there a cure? Once a person has been exposed, is there anything you can do to stop the progression of the symptoms?"

"No. We were specifically told never to investigate a cure."

Which didn't mean there wasn't one.

He glanced back at the mirror. Was she poisonous? If so, was he already infected?

He turned to Callum. "Get the details. Everything he has on this lab facility and get the protocols for sending messages up the chain of command. And find out how we get rid of the stuff. We're going to destroy their stocks of the gas, and we're going to send them a message."

Callum followed him to the door. "Are you thinking what I'm thinking?"

"How the hell would I know that?"

"Come on, Luke. You reckon we've been infected?"

He shrugged. "I don't know. If we have, it's not the same thing we saw in Ivory Coast. The first symptoms showed almost immediately. You feel anything?"

Callum shook his head. "Nothing."

"Me neither."

"Which doesn't mean a thing."

"Hmm." He thought for a moment before turning back to the doctor. "The chemicals you need for testing Jenna. Tell us exactly what they are. If it's possible we'll get some."

He left the room and went back to where Jenna waited for him. She backed up when he entered. Strain showed in her eyes.

"Maybe you shouldn't be anywhere near me," she said.

He ignored the words, stepped toward her, and took her in his arms. She resisted for a moment, pulling back, but then sighed and leaned against his chest.

"I reckon if you're giving anything out, I've already got it. But I feel fine. We'll worry about it later. First thing is to stop the terrorist attack."

"You're going to this lab."

"Yes. We'll go in and destroy the stocks. There may be more, but it's all we can do at the moment."

"What will you do with him?" She nodded to the window where he could see Callum questioning Smith.

"I don't know. Maybe hand him over to the authorities when this is all over."

She looked up into his face. "What do you think is wrong with me?"

"I don't think there's anything wrong with you. You're perfect."

"You know what I mean."

An idea had been growing in his mind. "I think maybe they did some sort of tests on you when you were a child. The drugs your father gave you suppressed the effects of those tests."

"But where did I come from?"

He stroked the hair from her face, studied the perfect features, the flawless skin. A small frown furrowed the space between her brows. He decided not to share what he thought about that.

"I don't know," he replied. "But we'll find out. We're going to break this thing wide open. For the first time we have a means of communicating with someone in the Conclave, maybe not the head, but very close. We'll uncover all their dirty little secrets."

Her frown deepened. "I don't want to be anybody's dirty little secret." She bit her lip. "I think I should keep away from people for the time being. I don't know if I am poisonous, but I'd rather not risk infecting anyone else. I'm going to go back to my room."

"I'll get the stuff the doctor asked for. He can do the test when we get back. We'll find out one way or the other. Until then, yes—it might be a good idea to stay in your room. I've sent for some clothes, and if you're hungry, dial the kitchen. They can leave the food outside your door."

She nodded, her eyes still shadowed, and he had an almost overwhelming urge to hold her tight, never let go. Instead, he forced himself to take a step back. His hands fell back to his sides. "Come on, I'll see you to your room. Then I need to talk to Callum, go over the intel, make some plans."

They were silent as they made their way upstairs and through the quiet house. Luke cast her a sideways glance but could tell nothing of her thoughts. He stopped in front of her door and pushed it open.

"Try not to think about it."

A wry smile curled the corners of her lips. "Right. Like that's going to happen. Will I see you before you go?"

"Yes. We'll wait for darkness. I'll come back before we leave."

She stepped through the door and shut it behind her, leaving him staring at the dark paneled wood and wishing he could stay with her.

He couldn't begin to imagine what she must be thinking, but the best way he could help her was to bring down the Conclave and expose their secrets.

Including Jenna.

• • •

Jenna lay back on the velvet coverlet and stared at
the crimson-and-gold canopy above her head. The
color reminded her of blood. She rolled her head
to one side and looked out the window instead,
wishing she could sleep to make the time pass, but
if she closed her eyes, she saw an image of those
people dying. Their pain and despair as they must
have realized they'd been tricked, and no help was
coming.

Was she poison?

The image of the villagers was superimposed
with a different one—Luke, his life and vitality
drained away, his skin slick with blood.

She'd always held herself off from getting close
to anyone, hadn't thought it fair when she could
get ill at any time.

But this was worse.

Now, it appeared she could actually kill those
close to her.

CHAPTER FORTY

"So how do we do this?" Callum asked.

"They must know we have Smith; they'll be expecting us. We need to go in fast, blow the place, and get the hell out of there."

"And what about the woman?" Callum's expression was blank.

"Tell me what you're thinking," Luke said.

Callum shrugged. "I'm thinking we're almost there. We've worked at this for ten years, and at last, we're close, but you're not thinking straight. That woman has you tied in knots."

Luke wasn't going to deny it. For the first time since this whole nightmare had started, he was looking beyond the end of the mission, actually contemplating an existence after they destroyed the Conclave. Always before he'd known he would give his life for the cause. He still believed that, but now the difference was—he didn't want to die, he wanted to live. But Callum was involved in this as well. "So what do you think we should do about Jenna?"

"I think we should lock her in one of the cells. Keep her quarantined. At the very least, keep her confined to her room. If she is somehow poisonous, chances are we're already infected, but there's no need to risk anyone else."

"She's staying in her room. It was her idea." He stared Callum straight in the eyes. "She's not the enemy."

Callum ran a hand through his hair. "I know. I just want to be sure that your priorities are right. Hell. What are you going to do if we get this stuff and the doctor tells us she is toxic?"

"I don't know. Search for some sort of cure, I guess."

"For her, or for us and every other poor sod she's been in contact with?"

"Both. Look, we know she's been fine for the last twenty-six years. There's no reason why she can't be fine again, why we can't reproduce the drugs her father gave her. Now drop it."

Luke knocked on the door and pushed it open without waiting for an answer. Jenna lay on the bed facing him, her eyes wide open. She blinked as though coming out of a trance, and he crossed the room, putting the bags he carried on the floor by the bed.

"Some clothes for you. I guessed the sizes, but they should fit."

"Thank you." But she made no move to look inside the bags. "If you find out I am poisonous, will you do something for me?"

"What?"

"Kill me." She held up a hand to stop him interrupting, and he bit back his words. "I saw the film. I couldn't bear to be responsible for doing that to anyone. Really, I'd rather be dead."

"It won't come to that. Besides, we can quarantine you until we find out the cause. Or until we can get a supply of whatever it was your father was giving you."

"Maybe, but you must keep the option open."

"I will," he lied. "Now come here."

She rose to her feet and stepped into his arms. After a minute, he released her. "I just came to say goodbye. We'll be heading out in a few minutes. I'm leaving two men here—use the internal line if you need anything."

"Will it be dangerous?" she asked.

"Shouldn't be, if the doctor's given us accurate intel on the place and the security."

"Could he be lying?"

"He could be, but I doubt it. Let's say it's in his best interests for us to succeed. I've sent him back to London—we have a holding facility there. He knows if we fail, they'll release the poison, and he'll die along with everybody else. He didn't change his story, so I think the intel is good, and we have all the security codes, the guard positions, and so on. Should be easy." He didn't add "as long as the Conclave aren't waiting for us."

She forced a smile. "I'm glad. I want this to be over."

"Me too." He reached out and stroked a stand of silky hair from her cheek, tucked it behind her ear. "I have to go."

CHAPTER FORTY-ONE

Jenna watched as his tall figure strode from the room and the door closed behind him.

Luke had said the attack wasn't dangerous, but she'd known he didn't want to worry her. How could it not be dangerous?

She wished she were going with him. A horrible feeling of doubt nagged at her mind. Something was going to go terribly wrong; she knew it but felt helpless to prevent it.

Crossing over to the window, she drew back the curtains to peer down onto the curved gravel driveway below. A minute later, a black van drove up and parked directly beneath her. Luke and Callum stepped out onto the wide stairway, both dressed in black combat pants, boots, and Kevlar vests. They wore weapons belts with pistols, and a shiver of unease ran through her. She'd led such a sheltered life with her father, and she found it hard to believe the man who cared for her for all those years could have been part of this world. Why had he never told her, never prepared her... Unless he'd done things he was ashamed to tell her.

Luke glanced up at her window as if he could sense her presence, but she stayed still and a second later, Callum spoke to him, and he turned away. They climbed into the back of the van, the double doors slammed, and the van pulled away.

After waiting until it had disappeared around a curve in the long drive, she sank down onto the bed. She sat for a long time, her mind blank, then gave herself a small shake. Reaching for the bags Luke had brought her, she tipped them onto the mattress next to her, finding underwear, jeans, T-shirts, and a pair of sneakers. She dressed quickly then paced the room.

Restlessness gnawed at her. She recognized the feeling—it was a familiar companion. In the past, she had always run it off, and perhaps that's what she needed to do now. Go run off some of her excess energy. Run until she was so exhausted she couldn't think of anything else.

She went back to stand beside the window and peered down. Only one floor up; she could jump from here, go running and be back before anyone knew she was gone. She fiddled with the catch. They were old-fashioned sash windows that slid up smoothly when she pushed. The night air was cool against her skin, freedom beckoned, and without thinking any further, she slipped a leg over and sat perched on the ledge.

The harsh shrill of the phone rang on the bedside table as she was about to push herself off. A light flashed on the handset—an internal call, presumably one of Luke's men. She swung her legs back into the room and crossed to the phone, picked it up.

"Lock your door. We may have a problem. I'll call when we have the all clear."

After placing the phone gently on the table, she stood for a few seconds, slowing her breathing. She reached out and switched off the light, leaving the room bathed in moonlight, then crossed to the door and cracked it open an inch. From somewhere below her, she caught the muffled pop of a silenced pistol and the sound of footsteps running down the hall. She closed the door and turned the key in the lock.

Luke should be at the laboratory facility by now. Soon he would blow the place and end the threat of the bioweapon being used in London. After that, it was only really her life involved. She just needed to stay free for a little while longer. And warn Luke.

She picked up the phone again and started to enter the number he'd left her before she realized the line was dead. Nothing but an ominous silence. She tried the internal line, but no one picked up.

She was on her own.

They'd cut her off. Just like the night at her father's house. A cold lump settled in her stomach, and panic rolled over her in waves, threatening to suck her under, fogging her thoughts.

She tightened her fists until her nails cut into her palms, and the sharp sting brought her back.

No way.

She had to get out of there.

Keeping close to the walls, she edged around and peered out of the open window. Nothing moved.

Should she go find a weapon? Why hadn't she asked for one?

But she didn't want to be cornered inside the house. At least outside she could make a run for it. Without giving herself any more time, she swung herself out over the ledge and hung down by her fingertips, dangling for a moment before releasing her grip and dropping to the driveway below. Shock ran through her ankles as she landed. She rolled, came up onto her feet, and stood for a moment, testing that everything was fine; there was no damage.

As she turned to run, a jolt punched her in the back and pain erupted inside her, driving all coherent thoughts from her head. Agony radiated outward, contracting her muscles to solid steel. Her knees gave out, and she collapsed to the ground.

Then the pain vanished.

She pushed herself up onto her hands as it came again. Her body snapped rigid, and her cheek hit the gravel.

This time when the pain stopped, she lay still.

"Well, she's a fast learner, anyway," a woman said from somewhere behind her. "Don't move." A toe nudged her in the side as hands grasped her wrists, pulling them behind her. Cold metal snapped around them, and she was caught. Jenna dragged her gaze upward. A woman stood before her, tall and blond, her elegant appearance at odds with the weapon in her hand. "Taser," she said, aiming it at Jenna. "Very effective."

"Who are you?"

The woman pursed her lips. "Let's just say I was a friend of your father's."

"My father is dead."

"I know, and I'm sorry. As I said, we were friends."

Jenna's mind raced. "Were you also friends with Professor Merrick?"

"A long time ago."

"He's dead, as well."

"I know. A tragic loss."

Was there a faint thread of amusement in the voice now? A flash of humor in her eyes?

"Who are you?" Jenna asked again.

"My name is Lauren; that's all you need to know."

"And what do you want, Lauren?"

"Why, to help you, of course."

"Do I need help?"

She gave a soft chuckle. "Oh, yes. I imagine you're feeling a little strange right now. You feel like you're changing. Would you like to know why you are changing? And even what you are changing into?"

"Do you know?"

"Yes, I know."

"So tell me."

"Later. But I will tell you that if you stay out here, you will eventually kill every person you come in contact with. So you could say I'm doing the world a service." Lauren was silent for a moment before continuing. "By the way, how is the handsome Mr. Hockley? Is he showing any symptoms yet?"

The voice held such certainty. An image flashed through her mind of Luke dead, blood oozing from open sores that blossomed across his skin. Nausea roiled in her stomach. "Do you have a cure?"

"Yes, and maybe I'll give it to you. If you cooperate." She turned to the man who stood behind her. "Is Hockley here?"

"No. We've cleared the place."

"Shit. Then we have to assume he could already be at the storage facility. Damn. Time to call in that backup."

"I'll get on it."

Hard hands dragged Jenna to her feet, and she

stood swaying in their grip.

Lauren gave a rueful smile. "I'm sorry, but I've seen you in action, so…"

Something struck her from behind, and the world went black.

CHAPTER FORTY-TWO

"Are the perimeter sensors down?" Luke spoke into his comm unit.

"All done, boss."

"Okay, I'm going in."

He scaled the wall, jumping lightly down on the other side, and stood for a moment in the shadows, surveying the compound. The place was a converted country estate, and three hundred feet of lawn separated him from the main building. Floodlights lit the immediate area, and he could make out the guards moving about, six at the front. More than Smith had said, but they'd expected that. At a guess, there would be at least the same number at the rear.

"Are you in place?" he asked into his comm.

He waited while he received an affirmative from the four men situated on the walls surrounding the house then pulled the night-vision goggles over his eyes.

"Okay, take them out. On my count. One, two, three."

He heard the muted thud of the silenced sniper rifles. The first shots shattered the floodlights, plunging the area into darkness, and moments later, the guards crumpled to the ground.

"All clear, boss."

In the silence that followed, he held himself motionless, but nothing moved. "Callum, we're on."

Callum appeared on top of the wall. He carried the large rucksack containing the explosives, which he lowered gently to Luke. They ran across the open space, stopping once they reached the shelter of the building, while Luke oriented himself with the information the doctor had given them. According to the intel, the house should be empty, but there would be more guards inside the storage unit situated at the rear.

All was quiet as they made their way around the side of the house. The storage facility was obvious—a stone-built barn, but the doors had been replaced with steel. Callum placed a charge on the lock then they stood to the side, backs pressed against the stone.

The force of the blast blew out the door. Seconds later, two guards appeared, weapons in their hands, only to be taken out by the snipers still on the perimeter walls.

"Okay, let's do this."

He followed Callum through the door. The snipers would keep watch outside; his job was to ensure no one interrupted while Callum set the explosives. The building was one large room, a huge steel vault in the center. Callum worked quickly, setting the charges around the base.

"Boss?" Talbot's voice came through his comm unit.

"What is it?"

"There's a call for you. You need to hear this. I'm patching it through."

Luke frowned. What was so important Talbot would interrupt the mission? "Yes?"

"Mr. Hockley, I presume."

A woman's voice, but one he'd never heard before. "Who the hell is this?"

"My name is Lauren, and I'm here with a friend of yours."

After a moment's silence, Jenna's voice came down the phone. "Luke? Whatever she asks, don't agree. Finish this. Remember what I—"

She was cut off, and Luke swore softly. What the hell had happened at the house?

"What do you want?" He kept his voice controlled while inside he was raging, his mind frantically searching for options.

"I want you to stop what you are doing. Get out of there with my chemicals intact, and perhaps I'll let your friend live. In fact, I'll definitely let her live. I can't wait to get her into the lab and find out what makes her tick."

"Don't touch her."

She laughed softly, and Luke gritted his teeth together to stop himself from ranting.

"I'll touch her, but I won't hurt her. In fact, I'll help her. I'm probably the only person who can at this point."

"What do you mean?"

"If you come out of this alive, I might tell you. Before I kill you. For a second time."

"A second time?" The words made no sense to him. Then it all became clear, and a tidal wave of black hatred flooded his body. "You murdered them."

"If you're referring to your wife and baby, yes. Not actually by my hand, but I gave the order. I suppose I was also responsible for your father. I'm telling you this because you need to know I'm sincere in my threats. You have five minutes to get out of there. Any explosions, and she dies instantly."

The phone went dead. Luke stared at it for long moments then forced himself to move. They had to get the hell out of there. All he could think of was Jenna; she filled his mind.

"I heard," Callum said.

"We're getting out of here."

"The hell we are. The explosives are nearly set. I'm finishing this."

"I gave an order. Stand down."

"What the fuck are you thinking?"

"She has Jenna."

"Yes, and I heard what Jenna said to you.

Finish this. It's what she wants."

"She doesn't understand."

"Of course she does. She saw that film. Would you want to live knowing you were responsible for the death of thousands, maybe millions? Think!"

Slowing his breathing, Luke tried to shift his brain from the fog of panic, and Jenna's words came back to him.

I couldn't bear to be responsible for doing that to anyone. I'd rather be dead.

He smashed his fist into the wall.

"Luke?"

"Get on with it," he snarled. "And fast. They'll be coming for us."

Off to the south, the rising drone of helicopters told Luke time was running out. He spoke into his comm unit. "Everyone stand down. Get back to the vehicle."

Callum set the last charge and ran toward him. "Let's go." He raised his hand, showing a small rectangular detonator. "We have ten minutes to get out of here."

"Callum, they'll kill her."

For a moment, Callum's face softened. "Maybe. Maybe not. You heard what that woman said. They want to study her."

He was right—they might not kill her straightaway. If they got out of this alive, and if he could track her down a second time...

Too many damned ifs. But hadn't he always known this would never have a happy ending?

The hum of the approaching helicopters was louder. As the lights of the first burst out from behind the cover of a steep hill, he stared off to the south.

"Too late."

The shots tore up a strip of ground in front of them as they dove for cover behind a low stone wall.

"Fuck," Callum groaned.

Luke turned sharply. "You hit?"

"Yeah, lower leg. It's okay."

Luke peered over the wall. The helicopters were nearly on top of them. "If they land, will they have time to deactivate the explosives?" he asked.

"Maybe."

Luke thought of all he had tried to do, how many years he had spent chasing the monster. At least he could finish this one thing. They could still do this...if they manually detonated the explosives. Of course, that was likely to be fatal for both of them. "Give me the detonator."

Callum shook his head. "No way. You have a woman to rescue. And I can't run. At least one of us can get clear. So piss off out of here."

Luke's gaze flashed to the detonator. Callum's finger hovered over the switch. From here, he would be caught in the blast. There was zero chance of survival.

"What's the range of the detonator?"

"A mile."

"Let's go, then." He grabbed Callum by the shoulder and hauled him to his feet. The bullets chased them across the open ground, and he felt the moment Callum was hit again as he sagged against him, and Luke nearly went down. They weren't far enough, but they'd run out of time.

He crashed to the ground with Callum beneath him. For a second they locked gazes. Luke gritted his teeth. "Do it."

The roar of an explosion filled his head. The blast slammed into him like a solid wall of darkness as the building disintegrated in a ball of fire, hurling debris through the sky.

Luke covered his head with his arms, but it wasn't enough. Something hit him from behind, and everything went black.

CHAPTER FORTY-THREE

They were driving through country lanes in Lauren's huge limousine. One guard sat on the seat beside Jenna, his grip hard on her upper arm as though he expected her to dive out the window. A second man sat facing her, a gun pointed directly at her head. She could have taken the man who held her—could probably have taken both of them—except she was cuffed, and she was pretty sure she couldn't take a bullet in the brain.

"Shit," Lauren said from her seat opposite Jenna.

She closed the lid on her laptop and looked across at Jenna, her eyes narrowed.

Jenna had heard Lauren's ultimatum to Luke and could only hope he would go ahead. He must know she wouldn't want any more deaths on her conscience.

From Lauren's furious expression, she presumed he must have succeeded and blown up the stock. Jenna's muscles tensed as she waited for something to happen. Would they kill her straightaway?

Christ, how far had she come that she could consider such a possibility and not be reduced to a quivering heap of fear?

Too far.

Lauren frowned at her for a moment. "Let her go." She spoke to the man who sat beside Jenna, and the grip on her upper arm loosened.

"Don't worry," Lauren said. "I'm not going to kill you. Though I have to admit it goes against my better judgment to not carry through with a threat." She drummed her fingers on the top of the laptop and stared out the window. After a moment, she picked up her cell phone and hit speed dial. "Mark, did you see that?"

Her ear close to the phone, she listened for a moment so Jenna couldn't catch the other side of the conversation.

"Send in a cleanup team. If Hockley is alive, keep him that way." She ended the call and placed the cell phone on the laptop.

Had Luke been hurt? She forced the question out. "What happened?"

Lauren pursed her lips. "To your boyfriend? We'll have to wait and see, but from my experience, he's not that easy to kill. No doubt, he'll turn up again."

Jenna pushed down her panic but sent up a silent prayer that Luke was alive and unhurt. Then she put the thought of Luke aside. If she was going to die, at least she wanted the truth first.

"I don't suppose you'd uncuff me?"

"Why not? You might be strong, but you're

intelligent enough to know you won't survive a bullet." She nodded to the guard, and he pulled a key out of his pocket.

Jenna shuffled around so he could reach her wrists and a moment later, she was free. She sat back and rubbed at her arms through the thin material of her T-shirt as she studied the other woman. It was hard to believe she was a contemporary of her father's. He would have been fifty-six this year. This woman appeared nowhere near that age, with her smooth skin, pale blond hair pulled up into a perfect chignon, and dark blue eyes.

She caught Jenna's stare and raised an eyebrow. "So, tell me, what's been happening to you?"

The question took Jenna by surprise. "What? Aren't you going to torture it out of me?"

Lauren laughed, genuine amusement in the sound. "You are so like your father."

"How did you know him?"

"I met him when we were at university in Cambridge. He was a brilliant student."

"Were you...?" She paused, not sure whether she wanted to know the answer.

"Were we what?"

"Lovers?"

Lauren frowned. "Hardly. Your father was gay. He was sleeping with your friend Merrick at the time. I believe they resurrected the affair later when they were working for me." Lauren studied her. "You seem shocked. You mean he never told you?"

Jenna admitted it to herself—she was shocked. Not that her father was a homosexual, but that he had kept it a secret from her for so long. Christ, she'd been a fool. But he must have had a relationship with a woman at some time, otherwise where had she come from? Unless he wasn't actually her father. She was finding it hard to believe her father's whole life had been a lie.

"Was he really my father?"

"Oh, yes. You can see it clearly in your face. Your bone structure comes straight from John."

"My father was dark. His eyes were brown."

"Your hair and eyes come from your mother."

Jenna bit her lip. "Who was she?"

A small almost mischievous smile curved the corners of Lauren's lips. "Well—" She broke off as the car slowed to a crawl. "We've arrived. I think this conversation will have to wait until later."

Jenna wanted to scream her frustration, but she knew it would do no good. The car came to a halt in front of a set of double steel gates that slid open, and the vehicle drove through. Jenna peered back over her shoulder and saw the gates close behind them.

She should be afraid, but instead, a sense of

fatalism settled over her. If she was to die, so be it. At least Luke had succeeded, and the poison was destroyed, so they had done some good.

They drove slowly along a curved drive and finally pulled up outside a large Georgian manor house. It stood four stories high, and lights gleamed from the ground-floor windows.

A man hurried down the stone steps in front of the house and opened the car door. Lauren stepped out and gestured for Jenna to follow. She did, climbing from the car and looking around her. The grounds were set in smooth lawns dotted with oak trees. The gates had disappeared around a curve in the long drive, but she could see a tall stone wall that ran around the property.

Could she make it to the wall if she ran?

Her muscles tensed. As if sensing the movement, Lauren's head swung around. She stared at Jenna, one arched eyebrow raised. "Don't," she said, and Jenna took a deep breath, felt the tension drain away.

The man who had opened the car door was late middle-age but looked lean and fit in a dark suit, white shirt, and tie.

"This is Summers," Lauren said. "He takes care of the house for me."

The two of them set off up the wide stone steps. Jenna hesitated a moment before following. At the top, a set of oak doors led into a hallway, while off to the right a sweeping staircase hugged the wall. Lauren came to a halt at the bottom.

"Show Ms. Young to the blue room, Summers."

"Yes, ma'am."

She turned to Jenna. "There are a few things I need to do. Your friend has made life a little difficult for me. My people do not take kindly to failure, and Hockley has managed to delay our timetable considerably."

Jenna frowned. "So you're not in charge of the Conclave."

Lauren glanced away as if deciding how much to reveal. Then she shrugged. "Some of it. Some of the time. Maybe one day I'll explain how it works, but not right now."

Five minutes later, Jenna stood in the center of a large, elegant bedroom. The walls were a pale eggshell blue, the carpet and soft furnishings a deep, rich sapphire. After waiting until the door closed behind Summers, she crossed the room and pulled aside the brocade curtains to peer out into the darkness. There were bars on the windows, and through them she spotted an armed guard directly below her and another under the trees a little way off. Dropping the curtain back in place, she sank down onto the bed.

The world had taken on a surreal quality. She was being treated like a guest, but that could change any moment—she was pretty sure those guards would have orders to stop her should she try to leave — so it looked like for now, she was stuck here. But she desperately wanted to know how Luke was. Was he even still alive?

The strange thing was she felt no fear of Lauren. She had to remind herself this was the woman directly responsible for the murder of Luke's family. That she had been part of a plan to release a poison into London that would have killed thousands, if not millions. Yet she didn't seem evil.

Leaning her head against the bedstead, she hugged her knees to her chest and waited.

CHAPTER FORTY-FOUR

Luke regained consciousness slowly. He lay facedown on the hard ground, his cheek tacky with drying blood. His whole body ached from the force of the blast, but he couldn't identify any specific problem areas.

Intense heat bathed his right side. He forced his lids open, the lashes sticking together. The buildings were engulfed in flames. At least Callum had succeeded—the poison was destroyed.

Closer, he could see the mangled remains of a helicopter still burning, but over the crackle of flames, the roar of others grew louder. They were close, the drone of the engines changing as they hovered, ready to land. He peered upward as they backed off slightly, no doubt looking for a safe spot, and he knew he had to move.

Rolling onto his side, he saw Callum.

His friend lay a few feet away, sprawled on his back, his eyes closed. Luke stumbled to his feet and lurched across, collapsing to his knees beside him. Pressing his hand to the warm skin of Callum's throat, he felt the faint, unsteady pulse against his fingertips.

A long shard of steel stuck out from his chest, and a pool of dark blood surrounded his friend.

When Luke drew his knife and cut away the material around the wound his breath hitched, and he sat back on his heels and stared. The entry was to the right of Callum's heart, but directly over his lungs. He daren't pull the metal free.

"Luke?" Callum's lashes fluttered open. His eyes slowly focused, and he turned his head to the side to stare at the burning building. "Did it work?"

"Yes, it worked. The chemicals are destroyed. Now lie still, while I work out what to do."

Callum laughed softly, but the sound held no humor. "You're wasting your time, and we both know it. You need to get away from here."

"Not yet."

"We had to do it."

"I know." And he did. He just wished it hadn't ended like this.

"But I hope they haven't killed her. I hope you find her." Callum swallowed, and a grimace of pain passed across his face. "Maybe I didn't want you to have a normal life, but I was wrong. Leah would have wanted you to be happy."

He fell silent.

Luke clasped his hand. He sat for long minutes, his mind numb. Callum had been a part of his life for so long—the only family he'd had left after Leah.

Across the lawns, the first of the surviving

helicopters had landed, and its cargo of men was fanning outward. But he couldn't seem to care. He stayed unmoving, Callum's hand held tightly in his, until he knew his friend was gone.

Rage seeped into his mind, overriding the mind-numbing sense of shock. The Conclave had taken somebody else from him.

The men had spread out from the helicopter, and in the flickering light from the fire, he saw them clearly. Staggering to his feet, he cast one last look at Callum and turned and ran for cover, crouching close to the ground. He heard no commotion to signal he'd been spotted, and he made it to the relative shelter of the main house.

Was Jenna alive? Or had that evil bitch carried out her threat and killed her when the laboratory exploded? He didn't think she could be dead, because he was sure he would feel something. He had to keep believing. The alternative wasn't acceptable, and until he knew for certain, he would presume she was alive.

As he made his way around the house and back through the woods to where the vehicle was parked, Talbot stepped out of the shadows of the trees.

"Where's Callum?"

"Dead."

"Shit."

Talbot had served with Callum in the British

army for many years. The men had been friends, and Luke knew this must hit him hard, but the time for grieving would be later, after he had Jenna back. He needed a bargaining tool. He needed a plan.

"Let's get out of here."

Talbot hesitated.

"Look," Luke said roughly, "if we want any chance of getting the fuckers who killed Callum, we need to get away from here now." He put his hand on the other man's arm. "It's what Callum would have wanted."

Talbot glanced back the way he had come, nodding. They climbed into the dark vehicle and drove away, leaving their friend behind.

Was it all worth it?

Then he remembered the African village and imagined the devastation the same poison would have caused in the densely populated city of London.

He slumped on the seat, his elbows resting on his thighs, his head drooping from exhaustion, and for the first time in his life, he prayed. Prayed that Jenna was still alive.

CHAPTER FORTY-FIVE

Lauren sat in a red brocade chair, a laptop open on the coffee table in front of her. She glanced up as Jenna hovered in the open doorway and tilted her head at the laptop. "I thought you'd like to know, I've heard back from the clean-up team. They found one body."

Jenna stepped into the room, holding her breath as she waited for Lauren to go on. The woman was a sadistic bitch. Lauren smiled as though she could read Jenna's thoughts. "Not your Mr. Hockley, you'll be pleased to know."

Relief washed through her so strong she sank down onto the seat behind her, her legs trembling with shock. "Who was it?"

"They don't know, but perhaps you do." She reached down and turned the laptop so Jenna could see the screen. It was Callum, clearly dead. Jenna closed her eyes briefly against the image.

"I take it you know him."

"His name was Callum, but I don't know any more than that."

"And no doubt wouldn't tell me if you did."

Rage exploded inside her. Jenna clenched her fists at her side and fought the urge to leap up and punch the woman who sat across from her so complacently. If she did, she'd be dead before she could sit back down. She had an idea Lauren was the sort of woman who would leave nothing to chance.

The rage drained from her as suddenly as it had come, leaving her lost. She was out of her depth. The information about her father had hit her harder than she realized, and she still didn't know who her mother was, or what was happening to her. Or why Lauren was treating her like an honored guest.

"Why are you being so…"

"Civilized?"

Jenna nodded.

Lauren rose to her feet. For a moment, she stared down at Jenna, then she turned away to pace the room. Finally, she came back to stand in front of her. "The Conclave recruits many new members, but those people tend to know very little of the inner workings of the organization. They are usually content with the benefits membership brings, but the inner circle, those at the top, are usually hereditary. The children of those families are brought up to know their destiny."

"How melodramatic," Jenna drawled.

Lauren smiled at her obvious sarcasm. "Believe me, it was."

"That was the case with you?"

She nodded.

"Why are you telling me this?" Jenna asked.

Lauren held out her hand. Jenna eyed her suspiciously for a moment.

"Come, if you want to understand."

Jenna ignored the hand but stood up and followed Lauren across the room to stand in front of a large gilt-edged mirror. The reflection showed them standing side by side. They were of a similar height, both blond, both blue-eyed. Something stirred deep down in Jenna's mind, but for a minute, she refused to acknowledge it. In the mirror, she saw Lauren smile, and her own eyes widen in horror. She stepped away and shook her head as though she could somehow make the idea go away.

"Earlier you asked who your mother was."

Jenna's mind was screaming a refusal. "No. I don't believe you. You said you and my father had never—"

"Oh, we didn't. You can be sure of that, but then you were hardly a conventional baby."

Nausea churned in her stomach, her mouth flooding with saliva, and she pressed a hand to her lips. Lauren drew her brows together and pointed across to the door. "Bathroom across the hall."

Jenna whirled, stumbled into the bathroom, and only just made it, vomiting into the toilet, retching until her stomach was empty and then some more. Afterward she stood studying her face in the mirror. She could see the resemblance now. It was why Lauren had appeared so familiar.

Like staring into a mirror.

It didn't mean anything. Nobody got to choose their family, but she couldn't help but wonder what other genetic traits she shared with an immoral killer.

She wanted to deny it, but the truth was she remembered her now. One of her earliest childhood memories. She could see an image of a tall woman standing over her. Her father had always cuddled her, held her close on the occasions he came to visit. But this woman held herself aloof, and Jenna was glad—she didn't want to be touched by her. She scared her, and she didn't know why, when the woman was so pretty.

But one time she had reached for her, and Jenna recoiled. The woman's eyes had narrowed on her.

"You know, I don't think the little bitch likes me," she murmured.

Her father had laughed and taken her in his arms so she could hide her face against the curve of his shoulder.

She opened her eyes and banished the memory. Turning on the tap, she splashed her face then patted it dry with the towel, taking her time, putting off the moment when she would need to go back and discover the truth.

Finally, she took a deep breath and returned to the sitting room. Lauren handed her a glass. Jenna raised it to her nose and sniffed—brandy. She sipped it, swirling the liquid in her mouth to take away the sour taste, and sat down.

The laptop was open on the table, still showing the image of Callum dead, and she reached out and slammed down the lid.

Lauren sat opposite and sipped her own drink while studying Jenna. "You know, I've never considered myself the maternal type, but that was hardly a flattering reaction."

"Why the hell would I want to flatter you?" She finished the drink and placed the glass carefully on the table. "Why are you telling me this? Why now?"

"I believed you were dead."

"Why?"

"Because twenty-two years ago, I gave the order for you to be terminated, and until these last couple of days, I never doubted the order had been carried out."

"You wanted me dead?"

"At the time, it seemed like a good idea. I did tell you I wasn't the maternal type, and I never really considered you my child."

"I don't understand."

"Well, ask. Whatever you like, because you

may not get this opportunity again."

Jenna thought for a moment. Back to when it had all started and the letter from her father. "What is Descartes?"

Lauren smiled. "An excellent question." She sat back in her chair, swirling the drink in her hand. "What do you know?"

Jenna forced down the frustration. "It's a place on the moon."

"Yes, it is—the Descartes Highlands. It was the site of the Apollo 16 landing. What isn't generally known is the astronauts found something on the Descartes Highlands, something not made known to the public."

Lauren paused to take a sip of her drink, and Jenna bit back the need to scream at her to hurry up. Her whole body tingled with the knowledge that she was on the edge of learning something huge. Some truth that would change her world forever.

"Tell me."

"They found the wreck of an alien spaceship. It was old, maybe thousands of years old, probably crash-landed. They brought back samples of what was found there. It came into Conclave hands, as many things do, and the discovery was hushed up. As a matter of interest, do you know the name of the astronaut who brought it back? John Young. Trust your father to pick that name."

"What has this got to do with me?"

"Well, part of what was brought back was dust collected from inside the wreckage. The dust appeared to contain something similar to our own DNA. We were carrying out all sorts of experiments, but John decided it would be interesting to try to combine alien DNA with human DNA and see what we could produce. The technology was new and experimental, but your father was at the forefront."

Jenna's mind went blank at the implications of what she was being told.

"We used in vitro fertilization, your father's sperm, my egg—"

"Why?" Jenna interrupted. "Why did you use your eggs? Why not some stranger's?"

Lauren lifted one slim, elegant shoulder. "To be honest, it was John's idea, and I thought it would be amusing."

"Amusing?" Jenna glared at her, allowing the hatred to show in her face.

Lauren ignored the question and the look. "Anyway, once we had a viable embryo, the alien DNA was added into the mix. You were grown in an artificial womb, and at nine months, you were 'born.'

"At first you seemed like a normal baby. Well, not quite normal—you were perfect. Your father had gotten a little creative with the genetic modification. They were still learning how, but he identified any genetic markers that might result in imperfections and altered them." She smiled. "You were his creation. He was so proud of you. I should have known he would never have terminated you, that he would lie to me to save you."

A flash of rage shot through Jenna. "Terminated? Don't you mean murdered?"

Lauren pursed her lips. "That would imply I thought of you as human." Her gaze wandered over Jenna's figure, finally coming to rest on her face. "At that point I didn't. You were an experiment."

"Would it have made any difference? You seem to find killing humans easy, as well. I saw the report of the people you slaughtered in Ivory Coast."

Lauren shrugged. "I don't see them as people, either. They're just numbers. The tests had to be done. We had to know the poison would dissipate."

"And they didn't matter?"

"Now, you can't accuse me of being a racist. I'm not, but the place was convenient and easy to hide…though obviously not easy enough."

Jenna shook her head. It occurred to her she was standing in the presence of pure evil. Pure evil with her blood. What did that make her?

Lauren was still studying her, a small frown furrowing the spot between her eyes. "It never occurred to me John would lie."

"Why was I supposed to be terminated? What happened?"

"For the first few years you appeared quite normal. Maybe a little brighter than average, stronger. Your vision and hearing were actually off the scale, but nothing disturbing. After you reached four, your metabolism altered. At first, we just monitored you. Then people started to die. Your nanny, one of the lab technicians, a member of the Conclave who'd been unfortunate enough to visit." She looked at Jenna and smiled. "So you see, we're alike after all. Or maybe you're worse—I didn't kill my first person until I was at least twenty-one."

Bitterness etched into her mind. "You made me what I am."

"Perhaps, but really your father must take some of the blame. We discovered your system was producing some sort of toxin, highly poisonous to anyone you made contact with. Your father and I became ill, but he'd already been working on a suppressant. He modified that; we took it and recovered. He claimed he could keep you safe, you wouldn't be a problem, but the orders had come from above. It was decided you were too dangerous to keep alive, and we were ordered to terminate immediately."

"Of course you always follow orders."

She raised an eyebrow. "Actually, yes. I didn't always find it easy, but you don't disobey the Conclave and expect to live. These days I tend to give more orders than I receive, so things are considerably easier."

"What happened?"

"John told me he'd terminated you, destroyed your body. Instead, he spirited you away along with a supply of the suppressant he must have been stockpiling. He told me he'd destroyed that, as well. I could see he was distraught, and I believed him. Turns out, he was a good actor. Afterward, he wanted out. He said he'd lost faith, couldn't go through it again, and so I let him go."

"Why did you help him?"

"Why? Because he was my friend. I'm not quite so sentimental these days, but he had to disappear. The Conclave don't allow their employees to just leave, not while they're still valuable. I told him how and where to get a new identity, but I didn't want the details. I believed that was the last I'd ever hear of him."

She stood up and crossed the room, poured herself another brandy, and raised her glass to Jenna. Jenna nodded and Lauren brought the bottle over and placed it on the table in front of her. "You look like you're in shock. But really, what did you think was going on? Your father must have told you something. You must have been taking the suppressant all these years or you'd have been leaving a very obvious trail of dead people."

"He told me I had a strain of Huntington's."

"And you believed him?" Lauren's eyes widened in mock disbelief.

"Why shouldn't I have believed him?" she snapped. "He was a doctor and my father. I had no reason not to believe him." She leaned forward, poured half a glass of brandy, and took a large gulp. The liquid burned her throat and lit a fire in her belly. Swallowing another mouthful, she glared at Lauren. She could see the faint amusement in the other's woman's expression and the ever-present anger uncurled inside her. "What was I supposed to think? That no, I didn't have a perfectly normal human disease, but I was half alien? You know what? That never even occurred to me!"

"Not half, actually. Only about five percent."

"Really? That makes me feel much better." She got to her feet. "I've had enough of the company. I'm going to my room." She turned to go then stepped back and picked up the bottle and glass.

"I'll get Summers to bring you a meal."

Jenna's anger flared again. "Will you stop being so fucking civilized?" She glared at Lauren.

"You're a murderer. You tried to have me killed when I was four. You no doubt gave the order for me to be tortured two days ago. Now you're being all sweet and nice and…" She broke off. "I don't understand why. What is it you want from me?"

"You mean you haven't already guessed?"

No, she hadn't guessed. Or maybe she wasn't ready to know. Hugging the bottle to her chest, she stalked out of the room.

Jenna slammed the door behind her, crashed the bottle and glass down on the table, and flung herself on the bed.

Her head was spinning, and it wasn't from the alcohol.

She lifted her hand and examined it. Could it be true that she wasn't entirely human? She looked human. She felt human. But even as those words went through her mind, she knew they were a lie.

Over the last few days, she'd experienced changes within herself, as though something was awakening, uncoiling sleepily inside her, stretching and peering out through her eyes.

What were they like, these aliens? Where did they come from? As a child she'd often had dreams of a land she'd known wasn't earth, a place of cerise skies and purple haze. Her father had blamed the drugs and adjusted her medication. But had that land been their home, or another planet they had visited?

How much did Lauren know? Did they have any information? Had they done any other research?

Something struck her—she didn't have Huntington's disease. The truth might be much worse, but the specter of the inevitable slide into insanity had hovered over her all her life. There was no cure for Huntington's. Her father had told her that. Now a weight lifted from her mind.

Lauren must have a supply of the medicine her father had been giving to Jenna. Otherwise, she wouldn't have been so willing to spend time with her. Maybe she could keep taking the medicine and have some sort of normal life. A vision flashed before her of Luke. Where was he? Was he even still alive? She wished she had some way of contacting him.

Luke was out there, and he would be infected. The poison they had tested in Africa had taken only hours to kill. Obviously, whatever she was producing was less virulent, but all the same, she needed to get the cure to him, if Lauren could be persuaded to give it to her.

Lauren—her mother.

As a child, Jenna had dreamed of a mother. She'd always presumed whoever she was, she'd had good reasons for abandoning them. But then, she'd also believed her father had loved her mother and was pining away for her, which was why he'd never dated anybody else.

Maybe he'd been pining for Professor Merrick. She gave a shudder. The man had given her the creeps, yet her father had obviously cared for him.

Had she ever really known her father at all?

He'd seen her as his creation, Lauren had said. But had he *loved* her? She believed deep down that he had.

A light tap sounded on the door, and she glanced up. Summers entered the room, carrying the tray, which he put down on the table next to the bottle of brandy. The savory scent of warm chicken filled her nostrils, and her stomach rumbled.

Summer's expression was blank, and Jenna didn't bother trying to question him, because she knew it would be a waste of time.

Once the door had closed behind him, she fell on the food. Afterward she sat back and thought about how to approach Lauren.

She needed to find out exactly what the other woman wanted and decide if she was willing to give it in exchange for the medicine and the information she needed.

CHAPTER FORTY-SIX

"Can you test to see if I'm infected?"

Smith looked up as Luke entered the cell. "You have the things I asked for?"

Luke had sent one of his men to procure the list of chemicals the doctor had given them. As he passed the bag to Smith, it occurred to him he was putting himself in the hands of a man who was far from trustworthy. But what choice did he have?

"What do you need to do?"

"The poison causes the DNA to mutate. Usually, I'd take a sample of your DNA, add a stain, and it would highlight those mutations. But I don't have the equipment here to see that."

Luke clenched his fists and fought the urge to hit the man. "So what *can* you do?"

"The mutated DNA causes changes in the blood, specifically to the hemoglobin. If I add a chemical, they become clearly visible. Those I can check for." Smith opened the bag and laid the equipment out on the table in front of him. He glanced up. "I'll also need a microscope to examine the sample for changes. A simple basic model is enough."

Luke pulled out his cell and called Talbot. "I need you to get something for me." He handed the

phone to Smith. "Tell him exactly what you need."
He listened as the doctor reeled out the details
and then took the phone back.

Smith attached a needle to a small syringe.
"Your arm."

Luke rolled up his sleeve and held out his arm.
Smith inserted the needle into the vein below his
elbow, and the syringe filled with blood. "That's
plenty," he murmured, stepping back.

Leaning against the counter, Luke watched as
he injected a portion of the blood into a glass dish,
added a few drops of various chemicals, and
placed the lid on top.

"How long?" he asked.

"Three hours."

Luke considered his next move. While he
needed rest, he also needed to get things moving.
He planned to threaten to expose them, a solution
he'd never considered before. Always in the past,
he'd told himself it was because he knew they had
people and resources to quash any story, but in
fact, it was because he had wanted to take them
down himself. He had wanted to stand before the
person or people responsible for Leah's death and
pull the trigger.

Now Jenna's life was at stake. If she was still
alive. He pressed a finger to his forehead to clear
the doubts—he had to believe. He would offer
himself and his silence in exchange for her life. If

he was infected, he was a dead man anyway. Maybe they would kill him quickly.

It was the only plan he could come up with, so he had to make it happen. He turned back to the doctor. "I want you to get a message to the Conclave."

"I told you, we don't contact them, they contact us."

"You also said you had a protocol in place to get a message to them in an emergency."

Smith looked as though he would like to deny it, but finally he nodded slowly. "There is a way, but if I go anywhere near the Conclave, I'm a dead man."

Luke allowed a small smile to curl his lips, while keeping his eyes cold. "You're a dead man if you don't." Then he relented. "You don't need to go near them. Just send them something."

"What?"

"Information, and after that you can disappear."

"You'll let me go?"

"If this succeeds I'll let you go."

He'd already passed the doctor's information and photograph to his CIA contact, along with a copy of the film he had made of the Ivory Coast tests the doctor had carried out. No way was the sadistic bastard walking away from this one.

The doctor licked his thick lips. "Okay. I'll need

access to a computer."

"You've got it. But we'll be monitoring your every move."

The alarm woke Luke. He'd had less than two hours sleep, but he felt refreshed, ready to go. It would be over soon.

He showered, dressed, and rode the elevator down to the basement. Smith glanced up as he let himself into the room.

"Well?" Luke felt his muscles tense as he waited for an answer.

"You're positive."

Luke had an instant flashback to the test cases on the film, how they had died. The air left his lungs in a sigh. The results were hardly a surprise. Now he needed to decide what difference it made. Smith had said there was no cure, but obviously Jenna's father had had access to a drug that suppressed the poison. Maybe it could also act as an antidote, which was a tenuous hope, especially in view of the lab report on Jenna's medication. If he had a sample, he could send it for further analysis, but he had nothing, and he was out of time.

He glanced back at the doctor, and a bitter smile flashed across Smith's face. He waved toward the table behind him. Two glass dishes sat beside a microscope. "If it makes you feel any better," Smith said. "So am I."

"Not really, though I suppose there is a kind of justice in there, somewhere."

He took a deep breath; all he asked was enough time to ensure Jenna's safety. So far, he had no symptoms. "I feel fine," he said. "When can I expect that to change?"

"I don't know. If you'd been infected with the real stuff, you'd be dead by now—we both would. This is a much slower progression; presumably the poison is less concentrated. It could be hours, it could be days. You'll know when it starts. The first symptoms are shooting pains in the limbs and cramps in the abdomen."

As soon as he heard the words, Luke's stomach tensed. He forced himself to push aside his fear; he had to get through this.

"I can give you something—" A light flashed on the screen behind him, and Smith turned away and pressed a button. A moment later, he turned back. "The Conclave will see you."

CHAPTER FORTY-SEVEN

Lauren looked up from the desk as Jenna opened the door. A tall, good-looking young man in a dark business suit stood at her shoulder. He glanced at Jenna, his eyes widening as he took in her face.

She stepped into the room, and the door clicked shut behind her. Striding forward, she came to a halt in front of the desk.

"What do you want from me?"

Lauren smiled and turned to the young man. "What do you think, Mark? Is she a chip off the old block?"

His gaze hadn't left her face, but now it slid over her, lingering on her breasts and running down the length of her legs. A shudder of revulsion trickled down Jenna's spine, but she held it straight and kept her face expressionless.

"I can't believe I didn't see it," he replied in a clipped public school accent. "She's beautiful."

"And deadly, so keep your hands off. Now leave us. We have things to talk about."

Jenna waited until the young man had left the room then stepped closer. "Do you have the medicine my father was giving me?"

"We have something better. I've had my best

people working on it. This will suppress the toxin production while allowing you to keep the enhanced powers. You'd like that wouldn't you? I saw the tape of you killing Lynch. It was truly magnificent."

Jenna wasn't sure she wanted to keep the powers, wasn't sure she wanted to be different. But that could wait until later. "And do you have a cure, for anyone who's been infected by me?"

"I wonder who you could be thinking about. Mr. Hockley perhaps? Just how close did you two get?"

"Mind your own business."

Lauren laughed. "Yes, we have a cure, but you must have guessed that."

"Why keep it secret from the doctor who interrogated me?"

"We had a different facility working on the cure. It doesn't do to have your employees know too much. Though we did send Dr. Smith a dose of the antidote—he was a valuable employee. Unfortunately for Smith, your Mr. Hockley stole him away before he received it."

"You'll give me the cure and the medicine?"

"Yes."

What was the catch? "And you'll let me go?"

Lauren relaxed back in her chair as she considered Jenna. "Earlier, you asked what I wanted of you. Have you guessed what that is yet?"

Jenna shook her head but said nothing.

Lauren gestured to the chair opposite her. "Why don't you sit down?"

"Am I going to need to?"

Lauren smiled again. "Perhaps."

The word did nothing to ease her mind. Jenna took the seat opposite and tried to calm her nerves. Was Lauren—she really couldn't think of her as "mother"—about to ask for something she wasn't willing to give?

"What do you know of the Conclave?" Lauren asked.

The question came as a surprise, and Jenna blinked and gathered her thoughts. "Nothing much. Only what Luke told me. Before that, I'd never heard of it."

"Well, perhaps we should start with a little background. There are three types of people involved in the Conclave. At the bottom are the employees like your father; they know nearly nothing of who and what they work for. Then there are the members who are recruited by other members. They know of the existence of the Conclave, they do what they're told, and they gain certain benefits from membership."

"Benefits like...?"

Lauren shrugged. "It could be anything, business advantages, political success. It really depends on what they want and how useful they can be. And finally, there are the founders. The people at the top. Neither the employees nor the members know of the existence of the founders, though I'm sure a lot of them suspect."

"Why are you telling me this?"

Lauren raised an eyebrow. "Obviously, you must realize I am one of the founders. I was brought up to believe in the Conclave, to accept it as my right. To do what was needed for the greater good of the organization."

"How can you justify what was done to those villagers? How can you justify what you were going to do in London? Millions would have died. What could you have possibly gained?"

Lauren ignored the question and continued as though the outburst hadn't happened.

"The Conclave have existed for hundreds of years, and in that time we have been happy to stay in the background, exist in secrecy. Our goals have always been wealth and power, but a number of us believe the time has come to take up a more prominent position."

"Why?"

"The world is falling apart. Acts of terrorism grow more frequent. It can be only a matter of time before something is done that could destroy the Earth and the human race forever. One nuclear weapon in the hands of some religious fanatic, and it could be all over for mankind."

"You plan to fight terrorism with more terrorism?"

"We like to think of it as a demonstration of what we are capable of. Something so definitive we can gain the cooperation of governments and bring them under our control. The Descartes poison will do that. It will cause instant devastation and vanish without a trace."

"What is the poison? Where did it come from? The doctor said it was a by-product of the real experiments."

"In a way he's right—if you think of yourself as the original experiment. After the Descartes project was terminated, we carried on with the work but took it in different directions. We combined the alien DNA with human DNA again, but this time kept it at the cellular level. Eventually we created an organism that manufactures the toxin. It was refined, concentrated, until the product you saw tested in Ivory Coast was produced."

"Is it all destroyed?"

"Of course not. The major stocks, yes, but we can produce more…eventually. The plan has been delayed, not abandoned, and we will become a benign dictatorship. Controlling the world from behind the scenes. Stamping out disaffection before it can turn into something worse. The world will be a better place."

"Yeah, right. And where do I fit into all this?"

"Members are recruited, but founders are born. Only those born to a founder may become a founder."

Jenna had a sudden inkling where this was going and at first, the idea was so alien it refused to take hold.

"I don't have any children," Lauren continued. "Well, at least I always believed I didn't have any children." She looked at Jenna and smiled.

"Did you try?" Jenna asked, suddenly curious.

"Of course, but I had ovarian cancer not long after your eggs were removed, and I was never able to conceive. So you see, my line in the Conclave will die out. Unless you agree to join us."

Jenna had guessed this was coming, but still the words shocked her to the core. "I don't believe this." She rose to her feet and paced the room, paused at the window to stare out. Dawn was coming—the start of a new day. She turned back to where Lauren sat in her leather chair, watching her, her expression blank.

"What happens if I say no? Will you kill me?"

"Probably not. At least not straightaway, because there's a lot we can learn from studying you." She paused then gave a small shrug. "But you won't be allowed to leave here, and Luke Hockley *will* die. You saw the film. It's not a pleasant way to go."

"Bitch," Jenna muttered.

What were her choices?

She could agree, join this organization that went against everything she'd ever believed in. She thought again to the film, all those people dying. Could the end ever justify those sorts of means? She didn't think so.

Then again, she would have access to so much information. Information about where she came from, what she was.

"Just consider," Lauren murmured. "You could be a source of good. Think what you could do with all that money and power. The people you could help."

There was something Jenna wasn't getting here. "Why bring me in now? What do you get out of it?"

"An ally."

Shock hit her hard. That this woman could stand before her and suggest such a thing was beyond belief, and her anger rose as she took in the similarities in the other woman. Her mother. "What makes you think I would be your ally? You're not going to tell me blood is thicker than water, are you? That, coming from the woman who tried to have me put down at the age of four, would take some convincing."

"I was given a direct order, and I was brought

up to follow such orders. I'm never going to have your squeamishness about taking life—it's not the way I was raised. We see a bigger picture."

"Really? How clever of you. Cut the crap. What is it you really want? What will you gain by bringing me into the Conclave?"

"I told you, an ally. There's a side to the Descartes project I want to explore, but there is some opposition to it among the founders."

"What is it?"

Lauren smiled, and Jenna could see the barely suppressed excitement in her eyes, which glittered with blue fire. Her hands flexed against the smooth wood of the desk, and she pushed herself onto her feet as though she could sit still no longer. She came around to stand in front of Jenna and leaned in close so Jenna could smell the expensive perfume. She wanted to back away but didn't want the other woman to know she was uncomfortable, because she had a feeling that to Lauren, appearances were important.

You could feel fear, but never show it.

She forced herself to stare directly into Lauren's eyes without flinching. They were of an identical height, which only made Jenna's anger rise higher.

"What is it people have desired throughout time?" Lauren asked, and her voice was tense with excitement. "What is the one thing all the money and power in the world have been unable to buy?"

Jenna shook her head at the question.

"Immortality."

For a moment, she was speechless. "Immortality? You really think that's a possibility? You're mad."

"Maybe not immortality, but extended life span. There were changes in the cellular organisms we created from the mixed DNA. The cells mutated, but they never aged, and they never died. I bet if we looked at your cells we'd see the same thing."

Jenna turned the information over in her mind. "Are you saying I could be immortal?" She forced a rusty laugh from her throat.

"I told you, maybe not immortal, but far longer-lived than a human."

"I am human," she snapped. "So why are the Conclave against this? It sounds just up their alley."

"Some of them are for it, but we're split. Many want the whole Descartes project shut down, and tonight's fiasco is only going to give them more ammunition. Also, so far the research on prolonged lifespan has been inconclusive, and some of the Conclave believe it to be nothing more than a 'flight of fancy' on my part and a waste of resources. They're old men with no vision."

Jenna blinked in disbelief. Immortality? This was crazy, but again, here was maybe the one person who could help her understand who and what she was. All her life she had felt isolated, different. At least now she knew why. She *was* different.

"How do you know I won't agree, say I'll join you, and then double-cross you?" she asked.

Lauren studied her, head tilted to one side. "It's strange, but I do trust you. Besides, there will be safeguards in place. You'd be carefully monitored."

"And Luke? Will you leave him alone? Will you let him go?"

"That rather depends on Luke, doesn't it? He's become something of a thorn in our side, and I'm sure the rest of the Conclave want him dead. But I gather the two of you have become close."

Jenna had a mental flashback to lying in Luke's arms, to the feel of him on her, in her. It sent a shiver of sensation through her body, tightening the muscles of her belly.

Lauren laughed softly from beside her, and Jenna came back to herself with a start.

"Yes," Lauren murmured. "I see you've become very close. Close enough that he would give up his quest for revenge for you?"

"Never. He holds the Conclave responsible for the death of his family. He won't let that go."

"Hmm, and yet he broke into our facility to

rescue you, and he sounded most put out when he heard I had you in my evil clutches. Did that make you feel all warm and fuzzy?"

Jenna wasn't about to admit to this woman that yes, it had. But she'd accepted she was expendable and been relieved when she'd heard he'd gone ahead and destroyed the toxin; she couldn't have lived with the responsibility. And in a way, it showed he truly cared, that he knew her well enough to understand her.

All the same, it might stretch their relationship a little bit if she became one of the very people he'd been trying to destroy for the last ten years.

The thought brought her up short. God, she couldn't believe she was even considering it.

"Well?" Lauren asked. "What are you thinking?"

"I don't know, and that's the honest truth." She took a deep breath. "Give me the suppressant and the antidote right now, as an expression of good faith, and I'll consider it."

"No."

Jenna's heart sank. She saw no way out of this.

"I'll tell you what," Lauren said. "If you persuade Hockley to give himself up, I'll make sure he gets the antidote. We might kill him later, but at least you won't be guilty of poisoning your lover to death like you did your poor nanny."

"Bitch," Jenna said again, and Lauren laughed.

A knock sounded on the door, and Lauren called out, "Come in."

Mark entered and came to stand in front of them. "We've had a call from Hockley."

Lauren frowned. "How the hell did he find a number?"

"It came through the priority protocol channel."

"Ah, Dr. Smith, I presume. Oh well, I suppose it saves us the trouble of trying to find him. What does he want?"

"Plenty. Proof that Ms. Young is alive and well, and to meet and exchange her."

"Exchange her for what?" Lauren seemed amused by the concept.

"He says he's amassed considerable information on the Conclave over the past ten years, and he's going to go public with it if we don't give him the woman."

Lauren raised an eyebrow. "Really. I wonder what he's got exactly." She turned to Jenna. "I don't suppose you know?"

"Not everything, but he does have the film of the test in Ivory Coast. Surely that's worth a swap."

"Did you not listen to what I told you? We're about to come out into the open. Why the hell would we care if he tells the world what he thinks he knows?" She released her breath on a huge sigh. "On the other hand, your Mr. Hockley is becoming a pain in the ass. We might as well resolve this." She turned to Mark. "Arrange it, but make sure there's backup. I want him covered at all times." She turned back to Jenna. "Looks like your boyfriend wants you back."

"I doubt he'll feel the same once he finds out who and what I am."

Lauren's expression became serious. "Maybe not, but join with me and you have a chance to do something, perhaps change the Conclave."

"You think that's possible?"

"What's the alternative? That your boyfriend dies a particularly horrifying death, caused by you, and you spend the rest of your days as some sort of lab rat? As my daughter, I can protect you. Otherwise, you're on your own."

Jenna studied the floor. What choice did she have?

Either way she would lose him, but at least if she chose the Conclave, he would be alive to hate her.

CHAPTER FORTY-EIGHT

The first cramp hit him as he parked his car. The shock doubled him over, crashing his forehead into the steering wheel. The pain faded quickly, but he sat for a minute, breathing deeply, gathering his strength. He needed to finish this before it was beyond him.

Luke climbed out of the car and slammed the door. There was no sign of life; the warehouse was in darkness.

He'd set up as many safeguards as he could, but the plan was in no way foolproof. At least Jenna was alive. They'd let him talk to her on the phone. She'd sounded strange, their conversation stilted, and he was worried that maybe they had done something to her, given her drugs.

She told him she was fine, just tired and worried. Then she'd asked how he was, and he knew she must know about the infection, had likely had confirmation that she was producing the poison. He was aware there was a good chance they would die here tonight, but better a bullet in the brain than the relatively slow torture of bleeding to death from every orifice. He just wished he could save Jenna.

"I'm sorry about Callum," she'd said at the end,

and he'd felt the familiar lurch of grief.

"So am I."

Why hadn't they killed her? It was unlike them to not carry through on a threat.

She must be valuable to them in some way. Had they done something to her as a child, some sort of genetic modification? That had been her father's and Professor Merrick's field.

They were all dead now; perhaps there was a God after all.

How could a father do that to his own child? What must it have been like for her growing up believing she had an incurable disease? Yet, how much worse was the truth?

He still had no clue as to the significance of Descartes. If he asked nicely, would they tell him before they killed him?

The information for Jenna's life. That had been the deal. They hadn't mentioned his life, but maybe they already knew he was dying. The only question was—how long would it take?

His one regret was he hadn't gotten to the killers of Leah and his baby. No, that wasn't his only regret. He regretted not having the chance of a life with Jenna, to go somewhere new, start over. Somewhere clean. But maybe that was an illusion, and the world was turning to shit. He was sure that's what Callum would have said.

A sharp jolt of pain shot through his left leg,

and he almost stumbled to the ground. He reached out a hand and braced himself on the wall. The pain came again, and cold sweat broke out on his forehead.

"Fuck."

Headlights shone through the open doorway, and a car pulled up. The lights went out, and a door slammed.

Pushing himself upright, he wiped his hand across his forehead and gritted his teeth against the pain. It was fading to a dull throbbing ache that echoed the pounding in his head, and he found he could stand up straight. He needed to appear in control, so he took a deep breath and stepped forward out of the shadows.

Five people entered the warehouse. At the same time, the place flooded with light. Luke spotted Jenna straightaway at the center of the group. She appeared fine—better than fine. There was no sign of any injuries, and she didn't seem to be restrained in any way. She looked at him, her eyes clear, and she smiled. He nodded and moved on to the others. Beside Jenna stood a woman, blond, beautiful, and obviously in control of the situation, the rest of the group forming a semicircle around her.

A young man in a suit stood immediately to her left. Luke couldn't place him, and two others who were obviously muscle, heavily armed and not hiding the fact. Semiautomatic pistols in their hands. He could tell they were pros and knew he'd be lucky to see this through.

But things became a lot easier when you removed yourself from the equation.

He wasn't coming out of this alive, but then he didn't want to come out alive and end up like those poor sods in Ivory Coast. No way. He'd rather go down shooting. As long as he got Jenna out first.

He turned back to study the woman. This must be the one he'd spoken to on the phone last night. The one who had threatened to kill Jenna and who was responsible for Leah's and Maddy's deaths. For his father. And for Callum. A rush of hatred swept over him so strong he swayed. He forced it down and continued to examine her. She appeared to be maybe in her thirties, beautiful, but more than that, something about her appeared familiar, and a ripple of unease shivered across his skin.

His gaze shifted to Jenna. They were both the same height, pale blond hair, blue eyes. He'd never discovered how Jenna tied in to all this or where she had come from.

Now he wondered just who her mother really was.

• • •

Jenna ate him up with her eyes. She wanted to run to him, hold him, but it would be a mistake to let Lauren see how much she cared. Her gaze ran down over his body then back up to his face. He didn't look well. A faint sheen of sweat glazed his forehead, and his skin appeared flushed. Her chest tightened as she realized the poison had already taken hold.

"Your Mr. Hockley doesn't look too good," Lauren murmured from beside her.

A flash of hatred hit her in the gut, and she fought the urge to lash out, very aware of the two men with the guns standing behind her. She had to choose her time. She didn't have a plan, hadn't known what to expect until they got here and she saw Luke.

She realized she'd been living with the hope he would be fine, that he wasn't infected, and she wasn't some form of poison that would kill anybody she got close to.

For a little while, she'd allowed herself to dream there might be a life for her, a future with Luke. Now she knew that would never happen. Perhaps that was why her father had told her she had an incurable disease, so she wouldn't expect much of life and wouldn't allow herself to get close to anyone, to love anyone.

All she could hope for was to save Luke's life, persuade Luke to give up his revenge and go with them to the lab where the drugs were stored.

She forced her expression into blankness and turned to Lauren. "I want to go talk to him. Alone."

Lauren raised an eyebrow. "All right, but don't take too long. We need to get him back to the lab and treated, and I don't know how fast the progression of the infection will be. He might have only hours. Or minutes. Better hurry and persuade him to cooperate."

"I've told you I'll stay," she growled. "Don't push your luck."

Lauren looked mildly amused, but she nodded.

Jenna cast a brief glance at the two men; their pistols were raised and pointed straight at Luke. He stood, his body loose and relaxed, but his eyes were tense as he watched her.

She walked toward him, coming to a halt only inches from where he stood. For a moment, she hesitated, but thought what the hell, if this was the last time she would see him, she needed to touch him.

"Are you okay?" he asked.

She nodded and stepped in closer, wrapped her arms around his middle and laid her head against his chest. She could hear the rapid thud of his heart, feel the unnatural heat of his body beneath her cheek. He held her for a minute, and a shudder ran through him, his breath catching in his throat.

She pulled free and stepped back. "I'm sorry."

A small smile curved his lips, and his face softened. "What for?"

"For Callum. For you—I did this to you." She shook her head. "I didn't know."

"I know." He watched her for a moment. "I'm going to get you out of here."

"You can't."

"I think I have enough information. They won't risk it getting out. I'll give it to them in exchange for releasing you."

"You don't understand. I don't want to go. I've agreed to stay with them."

He blinked as though he couldn't quite understand what she was saying, and she forced herself to go on. "I'm poisonous, Luke. I'll infect anyone I come into contact with."

"You'll find the treatment; you know it exists. You can go back to the lab where it was sent for analysis. They might have kept the sample—tell them it's not contaminated, to look further... They'll be able to copy it somehow."

"No, they won't, because one of the components doesn't exist. Not on earth, anyway."

He frowned. "What are you saying?"

"I was..." She paused, not sure how to word

this. What was she supposed to say? *Hey, I'm not entirely human. I was made in a test tube and part of me is an alien.* Not going to happen. She didn't want to get into that right now; she wasn't sure how she felt about the whole alien thing. "I was infected by some agent they found on the moon."

His eyes widened. "Descartes?"

"Yes, the Descartes Highlands. On one of the lunar landings. The medicine my father gave me contains the same agent. No one will find it here."

Understanding and despair dawned in his eyes. "There must be some way."

"There is. The Conclave have agreed to give me some of the medicine."

"In return for what?" His tone was harsh.

She ignored it and continued, "They've also agreed to treat you if I cooperate with them."

"Cooperate? What the hell does that mean? What do they want from you?" He took a step toward her as though to take hold of her, and she edged back out of reach. She could do this. All she had to do was persuade him to go along with them. She walked away, coming to a halt beside Lauren.

"This is my mother. She wants me to join the Conclave and work beside her."

"I don't understand. How..."

"My father kidnapped me when I was four and pretended I was dead." She decided not to reveal why he had felt the need to do that. "My mother discovered I was alive only a few days ago. She wants me with her." She forced herself to say the words. "And I want to stay."

"I don't believe you."

"You should, but then you don't really know me. All my life, I've felt as though I'm different, as though I didn't belong. Now I've found somewhere, something I can be part of. I thought I had no family left, and now I find that all this time I had a mother, and she wants me with her."

Luke's gaze shifted from her to Lauren, who stood silent beside her. Jenna saw his eyes darken with hatred. "Your mother? Do you know what that woman is responsible for? You saw the film of Ivory Coast. That happened under her orders." The hatred turned to pain, and Jenna thought her heart would crack. "She murdered my wife and my baby. Maddy was three months old."

He glanced away, and Jenna knew he was getting himself under control. When he looked back, he opened his mouth to speak again, but pain flashed across his features. He staggered. She thought he was going to fall, but he managed to pull himself up. A trickle of blood appeared beneath his nose. He wiped it with the back of his hand and stared at it for a moment.

"Time's running out, Jenna," Lauren said. "If you want to save him, I suggest we move."

"Luke, please, you'll die." Fear tugged at her. She had to convince him. "You have to come; they won't touch you, they've promised, they'll just give you the medicine, and you can leave or stay. Whatever you want, but you need to come now."

As he looked at her, something close to understanding flickered in his face, as though he realized at last why she was doing this. His expression softened for a brief moment until resolve hardened his features.

"Don't sell yourself for me," he said. "I'm not worth it, and I won't thank you for it."

She bit down on her lip to stop herself from pleading with him. Deep down she'd known he would never agree. That he would never compromise his morals just for the chance to live. He might have done it to save her, but never to save his own life.

She watched as he turned away and headed for the door.

"So," Lauren said softly. "What do we do now?"

Jenna understood then that they would not let Luke walk away. He knew too much. She glanced sideways to where the two guards were standing. They were focused on Lauren, waiting for her command.

Lauren gave a small shrug. "Kill him."

Jenna could do this. She was fast and strong,

and if she died trying was that such a bad thing?

She spun around, kicking out at the man nearest her. He crashed down, and without looking at him, she launched herself at the second. Things seemed to move in slow motion. His gun pointed at Luke, his finger tightening on the trigger, but as his companion went down, his gaze flicked from his target, and Jenna kicked him in the throat. The force of the blow knocked him out, and he fell to the floor. There was a movement behind her, and Jenna leaped toward the first man as he lifted the pistol, stomping on his arm, the crack of snapping bones loud in her ears. Reaching down, she grabbed the semiautomatic pistol, whirled around in one fluid move, lifted the pistol, and aimed it at the two people left standing.

Lauren was deadpan. Mark's eyes were wide as he looked from Jenna to the men on the floor then back to Jenna and the gun in her hand.

She glanced away briefly to check the men. One was unconscious; the other was awake, his eyes open, but he was in no state to do anything more than watch, his broken forearm cradled on his chest. To be sure, she stepped across and pulled the second pistol from the holster at his waist and threw it across the room, then did the same to the unconscious man. As she made to toss it, she looked up and across the warehouse.

Luke had come to a halt at the door. He was

watching her, a slight smile on his lips that turned to a grimace as a surge of pain hit him. She tossed the pistol toward him, and he caught it.

She turned back to face Lauren, who hadn't moved.

"I take it this means you've decided not to join us after all."

Jenna nodded.

"So you would have joined us to save his life, but you won't do it to save your own. Perhaps we aren't so much alike after all."

"We aren't alike at all."

"You can't go out there, Jenna." Her tone softened, and Jenna almost winced at the pity she could hear in her voice. "You'll infect everyone you come in contact with. Do you want to be responsible for that?"

Jenna looked away and found Luke watching her. She needed him to leave; she wasn't sure she could do this with him there. "Go," she said.

He shook his head, as she'd known he would, and she turned back to Lauren. "I'm not going anywhere."

Lauren studied her for a moment. "So what are you doing?"

Jenna had suspected all along that it might come to this. She didn't want to die, and she wasn't being heroic; she just couldn't see any alternative. However civilized Lauren appeared on the surface, there was something inherently evil in her, and Jenna would not put herself under the woman's control. This was a better alternative.

She stepped back to give herself space in case they tried to stop her. Raising the pistol, she pressed the muzzle under her chin, aiming upward toward her brain. She heard the indrawn breath.

CHAPTER FORTY-NINE

"Stop," Lauren said quietly.

Jenna ignored the word. Her finger tightened on the trigger. She held Luke's gaze for as long as she could, his expression filled with understanding that sent a stab of pain through her. Closing her eyes, she focused her mind. She'd thought this would be easy, but her whole being railed against it. She wanted to live—just not at the price she was expected to pay.

"Jenna, stop!" Lauren spoke again, her voice filled with urgency. Something in her tone made Jenna open her eyes and look at the woman. Lauren reached into her pocket, and Jenna swung the gun to point at her. Lauren withdrew her hand slowly. She held a small case in her finger and thumb. "It's the antidote and suppressant."

"You told me you didn't have them here."

"I lied. You can have them." She waved to where Luke stood in the open doorway. "Save him and yourself."

This had to be a trap. "You'll let us leave here?"

"Why not? There's not much I can do to stop you anyway."

"Of course. You have no backup waiting outside."

Lauren smiled. "I always have backup. It's something you should learn, but you'll be allowed to go freely. As long as your friend there doesn't decide his revenge is worth more than your life after all."

She looked at Luke; he held the pistol she had given him, and it was aimed at Lauren, but his gaze swung to her, and he lowered the gun so it dangled loosely at his side. He nodded.

Jenna turned back to her mother. "Why?"

"Because death is the one sure permanency in this world. Once you are dead, there is no turning back, no other choices." Lauren shrugged. "Up until that point, there is always a chance."

Jenna inched closer, and her hand fastened around the small case. She slipped it in her pocket and crossed the space to stand by Luke. His skin shone with sweat, and his eyes were dull with the pain he was trying to suppress. She reached out and touched him lightly on the cheek, needing the contact. "Let's get out of here," she said.

At the door, she turned back to look at Lauren.

Her mother.

Something shifted in the other woman's eyes. Some sense of recognition.

"Thank you," Jenna said.

Lauren smiled. "There's a month's supply in there. After that, you'll need more. Contact me."

Well, she'd always known there would be a price. "Of course."

Jenna drove for five minutes, peering in the mirror constantly to check they weren't being followed. She could see nothing on the road behind them.

Beside her, Luke coughed, a soft, wet sound, as though he were choking. Glancing behind her one last time, she pulled over to the side of the road and switched off the engine. She turned to study him. In the dim light from the streetlamps, he appeared pale, with dark smudges of crimson at his nostrils and eyes.

"How are you doing?"

"Fine." He spoke through gritted teeth and coughed again.

"Jesus, sorry—stupid question." She pulled the case from her pocket and opened it. Inside lay a syringe filled with a clear liquid and a small bottle of tablets. She opened the bottle and shook out one of the pills. It tasted bitter on her tongue, and she had to force it down her dry throat.

Next, she pulled out the syringe and looked at it uncertainly.

Luke rolled up his left shirtsleeve. He held his arm palm up and clenched his fist. "Give it here."

Jenna handed him the syringe. He pulled off the cap with his teeth and held it up, his hand shaking visibly. He swore softly.

"I can do it." Jenna took it back. "Just tell me

where."

"Straight into the vein, just below my elbow. You need to insert the needle at about forty-five degrees."

Jenna traced the dark blue vein. She bit her lip and gently pushed the needle into his skin.

"Hold it," Luke said. "You need to check you've hit the vein. Pull back the plunger just a little."

She did, and a drop of dark blood stained the clear liquid.

"Good. Do it. Slowly."

She depressed the plunger until the liquid was gone then pulled out the needle.

Luke leaned back against the seat, his arm clutched to his chest, his eyes closed. "Now, get us out of here," he said.

Jenna drove. She wasn't sure where she was going yet, but she wanted to get as far away as possible. The roads were clear, and soon she was heading north out of the city.

They'd been traveling for half an hour when Luke broke the silence between them. Already his voice sounded stronger. "So, you found your mother? That must have been nice."

She gave a short, incredulous laugh. "You should have been there. It was a real warm, fuzzy moment."

She glanced at him sideways. His head still

rested back against the seat, but he was facing her, and his eyes were open. They were clearer, and some of her tension drained away. At the back of her mind, she'd worried Lauren had lied and there was no cure.

"I'll bet. You want to talk about it?"

"I just want to forget it, but I guess that's not going to happen."

"Probably not."

"We'll talk later. There's other stuff I need to tell you, but right now, I need time to get things straight in my head."

"Okay, but I'm here when you want to talk."

"I know."

He fell silent, and soon after his breathing became deep and even as he slept. Jenna gazed out at the road ahead and tried to think of what her options might be, where she could go from here.

Lauren had told her she could be a source of good. Was it possible to change the Conclave from inside? Or should she work with Luke to destroy them?

She had one month to decide.

There was something else to consider. The Conclave had been doing research into Descartes for years. They were the only place she might get information as to what she was, and she wanted to know.

Searching inside herself, she could sense that part of her that didn't belong. She recognized it now, realized it had always been there, sleeping but still present, loitering just beyond the edge of her consciousness.

What had they been like, these aliens? Would she ever find out?

She wanted to know, but not at any price.

In the end, she might conclude that killing herself was really her only option. She glanced again at Luke. She didn't want to die.

Deep in the recesses of her mind, the alien stirred.

It didn't want to die, either.

ACKNOWLEDGMENTS

I want to say a huge thank you to everyone at Sideways Books for all their help with getting *The Descartes Evolution* to where it is now. Especially my fabulous editors, Liz Pelletier and Lydia Sharp. Thank you!

ABOUT THE AUTHOR

After a number of years wandering the world in search of adventure, N.J. Croft finally settled on a farm in the mountains and now lives off-grid, growing almonds, drinking cold beer, taking in stray dogs, and writing stories where the stakes are huge and absolutely anything can happen.